To
will

Gillian is an English woman living in rural Australia with her husband and cattle dog, Jess. She loves writing and also enjoys gardening, cooking, horse-riding and singing, amongst other interests. She has travelled widely in Australia, meeting people and hearing their stories.

She has three children and four grandchildren living in England, France and Australia. She loves to spend time with them as much as distance and time allows.

Dedication

This is for all women who have been physically or mentally abused. May they find happiness in the end.

Gillian Wells

POSSESSION

AUSTIN MACAULEY PUBLISHERS™

LONDON • CAMBRIDGE • NEW YORK • SHARJAH

A CIP catalogue record for this title is available from the British Library.

ISBN 9781788780001 (Paperback)
ISBN 9781788780018 (Hardback)
ISBN 9781788780025 (E-Book)

www.austinmacauley.com

First Published (2018)
Austin Macauley Publishers Ltd™
25 Canada Square
Canary Wharf
London
E14 5LQ

Acknowledgements

To the Austin Macauley team; my husband, Neil, and my children, Christopher, Sharon and Judy.

Chapter 1

Marie groaned. The groan became a scream—"I can't do it, I can't, I can't."

"You have to," said the midwife. "Come on, love, nearly there." As the pain subsided, Marie sobbed. "I'm too old, why did this have to happen?"

"Come on, love, you're doing fine," said the midwife, but she had a worried frown on her face. As the pain gripped Marie again, she suddenly yelled out, "You come out, you miserable child! Do as I want, it's me or you."

The midwife had heard many odd things from women in labour but nothing quite like that, she said, "Breathe some more gas love, it will help," and she put the mask over Marie's nose again. Half an hour later, a small baby girl slithered out and was scooped up by the midwife. She yelled her indignation loudly. "She has a good pair of lungs on her, what are you going to call her?"

"Anna," said Marie tiredly as the little bundle was placed in her arms. She took her automatically and didn't really take any notice of the baby girl at all. Her fifth child, much younger than the others and the only girl. A few minutes later, her husband came in, a home birth as was normal in the late 1950s in rural England.

Tim took the little bundle from his wife and looked down at her, four boys and a girl at last! She wasn't pretty; she had a rough trip out and her little head was rather bruised. "The girl we've been wanting at last," he said, bending over his wife to give her a kiss.

"The worst labour I've had too, the little so and so wouldn't come out," said Marie.

Tim looked at Marie worriedly, she hadn't had an easy pregnancy and she hadn't wanted another child either. Four boys ranging from 14 to 6. The youngest was actually nearly seven. They hadn't planned to have more children especially now that Marie was over forty. It would be OK once she got over the birth though; Marie loved her boys to bits.

But it wasn't OK. Marie was a good mother to Anna physically but she found it hard to love her. Maybe the baby sensed it because she was a very fractious child and would cry and cry for no apparent reason. The only time she seemed happy was when Tim picked her up. She would lie in his arms looking up at him and instead of crying would make small contented noises.

The boys all loved her and played with her when they could, but they all had busy lives: school, friends, sport, helping their father on the farm. Silas, the youngest, spent more time with Anna, though, and spent more and more time with her as she grew. By the time she was three, it was obvious she would be a beautiful girl when she was an adult; she was very pretty now. She had dark auburn hair with a natural curl and huge brown eyes. Her skin was very clear, almost like porcelain, and she was full of fun and it showed; her eyes would sparkle with mischief, and she could twist both Silas and her father around her little finger. She was a complete tomboy too, and everything the boys did, she would try to do too. They had an old pony that had passed from one to another, but no one had taken riding seriously. Anna did. Self-taught, she was soon jumping poles that were suspended between empty oil drums, galloping across the fields after harvest and doing gymkhana races against herself. She fished in the stream, climbed any tree she could and was keener to help on the farm than any of her brothers had been at a young age.

She refused to wear dresses and would raid her brothers' bedrooms for their cast offs; she drove her mother mad. Because her birthday fell in early July and the local school didn't take in children until September, she was well into her fifth year before she started school. She was horrified to find that she had to go to school; that was for other people, not her!

Her general knowledge was good; as was her vocabulary, that was growing up with older siblings. However, school was a huge shock to her; firstly, she had to wear dresses, she had to keep her hair under control, which was hard as with a natural curl, it was rather wayward. She had to sit still for what seemed to her to be hours on end, and there were so many rules. Her mother had rather given up trying to tame her, and her father and brothers either ignored her or indulged her wishes.

She could already write well but reading seemed completely beyond her, as did arithmetic. The trouble was that she was really extremely shy though she covered that up by being brash and loud. So whenever she was asked to read aloud which was normal at that school, or to do sums in front of the class, she just froze inside and couldn't think of anything except that she was going to mess up and then, of course, she did.

She was kept in the infants class another whole year which knocked her confidence, and she became very introverted and unhappy at school. She wasn't that comfortable with the other girls either and much preferred playing football with the boys or joining in whatever rough and tumble they were up to. In her third year, they had a new head teacher who was quite progressive and, having looked at Anna's profile at school, suggested to Anna's parents that maybe some tests should be done to find out what her problem was. She seemed very bright and her maths was now good but she struggled with her reading and spelling. Tests were done and it was found that Anna was dyslexic and needed extra help. So extra help was arranged with a special teacher, and Anna blossomed once she got the hang of reading. She was actually a very bright child and reading opened up a whole new world to her; she couldn't get enough.

When she reached ten, her parents decided to send her to an all-girls boarding school as they thought it would be good for her and maybe iron out some of her continuing boyishness. Marie especially felt she wouldn't be able to cope with a teenage Anna; the school holidays would be enough.

Anna wasn't happy with the idea at all. She had made some good friends during the last three years in junior school and none of them would be going where she was going. She had found making friends quite hard as she was so full of life and away from adults, very gregarious. She was inclined to get into

11

trouble too which some parents didn't like, so they told their children to stay away from her. It was never anything very serious but nonetheless, until the last three years when she had settled in more, she had not had any real friends. Now it was all going to change again. She hoped she wouldn't be as lonely as she was when she first started school. She resolved to get on better with the girls at her new school. The summer holidays flew by and before Anna knew it, she was saying a tearful goodbye to her brothers. Silas, now a strapping seventeen-year-old, gave her a huge bear hug. "Take care, little sis and enjoy. You'll have a ball, I'm sure." She felt overawed as her parents drove her up to the front entrance of the school. She didn't go when they looked round as she was on a school trip. However, the Mistress who met them seemed very kind and escorted Anna and her parents up to her dormitory. She found out she was sharing with four other girls. That was a worry for her as she had never shared a room with anyone before. Her father brought her cases and trunk up, and then her parents said goodbye. They would see her in three weeks' time. Anna had a job to keep the tears at bay as she watched them go but managed it; she didn't want anyone to see her cry.

Her shyness returned in force now and, unfortunately, the other girls all knew each other and had been at the school sometime. They shared the fact that all their parents were in the armed forces too, so that meant they had a common bond. Later, Anna found out that many of the girls at the school had parents in the forces.

Her roommates seemed nice and Anna tried very hard not to be too full of herself and show off as she was wont to do when she was feeling shy. Gabby, Alice, Muriel and Karen were also trying to make her feel at home and showed her where to put things and generally helped her find her feet. Things weren't plain sailing when it was bedtime though as Anna didn't want to get undressed in front of these girls that she had only just met. She fussed around and did everything she could think of until Muriel said, "Anna, it will be lights out in a minute and you will be in trouble if you aren't in bed."

"Oh." Anna turned her back and got undressed and into her pyjamas as discreetly as she could; behind her back, the other girls stifled giggles. There was a wash basin in the corner of the room for teeth cleaning and washing face and hands. The shower room which had a row of showers was down the corridor as were the toilets. Anna hadn't cleaned her teeth so now she went to the basin to do just that when at that moment, Miss Doyle, the housemistress, put her head round the door. "Come on, child, whatever are you doing, you've had plenty of time. Hurry up, everyone else is in bed, why aren't you?"

"Sorry, Miss Doyle." Anna slid into bed feeling very small. After lights out, the girls bombarded Anna with questions about herself and her family. All this was done in stage whispers as they were supposed to be going to sleep. Anna found out that Karen and Muriel's fathers were both officers in the Army and Alice's father was in the Navy and Gabby's was in the Air force. They were all amazed that Anna had four brothers and how old they were. Karen and Alice were both mature enough to be getting interested in the opposite sex and the questions flew fast to Anna about her brothers. However, Anna was bored with questions about her brothers and was feeling homesick too so only gave short answers which disappointed the others. They then started to talk about people and things that excluded Anna as she was new and once more Anna found herself on the outside of things. During that first term, she tried really hard to settle in and to make friends. But the girls in her dormitory had all been together for some time and had a common connection with their father's professions. Many of the other girls were from service families too. Some of Anna's class mates were friendly enough but she soon found out there was a distinction between day pupils and boarders as the school took both. She got on better with the day girls as some of them were from local farming families. One girl called Jane asked Anna to tea one Saturday and on gaining permission from the housemistress, Anna went. It was so good to be out on the farm again. Anna just got so excited that she forgot she was out from school by permission only. There was a big Dutch barn at the farm full of old hay bales. "Come on, let's climb up there," said Anna.

"Oh no, I am not allowed in there," said Jane.

"Why not?" asked Anna.

"Well, Daddy says the bales are not stacked very well and they might slip."

"They look alright to me, come on just this once, won't hurt. I climb the bales all the time at home," Anna replied.

So, they climbed up on the bales. Jane took her time and it was clear she wasn't happy. She wasn't used to disobeying her father and she felt uncomfortable. After that, they explored further and coming round a corner, there was a lovely chestnut horse. A small horse but a horse nonetheless. "Can we ride?" Anna asked.

"No, that is Mummy's horse, and she doesn't like anyone else riding her; her name is Bella by the way." Anna felt really disappointed but she already knew Jane didn't ride at all. 'What a shame.' Anna climbed over the gate and going up to Bella, she started to stroke her and pat her. Anna had a way with animals and they all seemed to love her. Bella put her head on Ann's shoulder and snuffled in her ear. Anna put her arms around Bella's neck and buried her face in Bella's mane. "Come on Anna, let's go inside; I've got some new clothes to show you that Mummy bought me yesterday."

Anna liked clothes well enough but they didn't excite her, and there was so much to see and places to explore. Anna groaned inwardly, it wasn't her thing at all, and grudgingly, she went back to the house with Jane.

When a little later they were having afternoon tea, Jane's father came in and looking hard at Jane said, "I was across by the engine shed but I am pretty sure I saw you two girls coming out of the barn where the bales are. Did you go in there?" Jane went very red.

"Sorry, Daddy, we just had a look."

Jane's mother spoke up then, "Judging by the amount of hay on the two of you when you came in, I think it was more than a look."

"Sorry," mumbled Jane looking down at her plate. Anna felt very guilty and thought she should speak up.

"I am sorry, it was my fault. I wanted to climb up. I always do at home."

"It isn't something we allow to happen here; it's too dangerous and it's silly," said Jane's father.

Anna felt indignant, "My dad doesn't mind," she said quietly.

Jane's father looked angry then but all he said was "Well I do," and turning around, he walked out.

Not long afterwards, Anna was dropped back at school but as she had already guessed, she was never asked back and her friendship with Jane dwindled very quickly. It was soon after this that Anna found herself the butt of the joke going round that she was from a very rough family that allowed her to do as she liked. She knew that it had come from Jane and was hurt by it; however, she didn't let it show. So Anna withdrew into herself and though she still tried to make friends, it seemed harder than ever. Then the girls in her dormitory started to play unkind jokes on Anna. The trouble was, Anna was extremely pretty and clever too, so there was a lot of jealously involved. They made apple pie beds, sewed up her pyjamas, hid her belongings, the worst being when they hid her hockey boots. Anna loved hockey and was a very good player. The sports teacher came looking for Anna.

"Come on," she said. "Why aren't you ready? Everyone is waiting."

"I can't find my boots," said Anna. "They should be here." She indicated her locker.

"Did you put them away there the last time?" said Mrs Barlow.

"Yes, I definitely did." Anna was close to tears.

Mrs Barlow swung on her heel and went outside where the girls were all assembled. "Who has hidden Anna's boots?"

"No one," they all chorused.

"I will look the other way while you get them and give them to Anna," she said. The girls all looked at each other. How did she know? Had Anna accused them or one of them? However, Mrs Barlow had a good idea that Anna was being bullied and was guessing about the boots. Three of the girls went into the changing room and retrieved Anna's boots, which were on one of their lockers, and threw them at Anna.

"You'll pay for this," hissed Jane, one of the trio. Sure enough, things got worse, ink was spilt over her prep, more things were hidden, clothes were sown up; it was horrid. Alice was the only one who stuck up for Anna but she backed off when they started to treat her the same way. The end of the year came and not soon enough for Anna. Her parents were concerned, especially her father who noticed a change in her. She seemed withdrawn and didn't seem to sparkle the same. However, she threw herself into helping out on the farm at harvest time as always. Silas was the only one of her brothers at home now as the others had all gone off elsewhere. One worked for an estate agent; one worked on a stud farm, and Matthew, the nearest in age to Silas, had gone to a job in Canada on a big apple growing farm. John, the eldest, had a lovely girlfriend, Clare, and they announced their engagement while Anna was at home. They intended to get married early the next year, and Clare asked Anna to be a bridesmaid. Anna was thrilled and as she found herself back at school, she hoped that everything would improve for her.

It wasn't to be. They hadn't been back at school long before the bulling started again and matters came to a head when Karen accused Anna of stealing her pocket money. They were allowed so much each week to spend on toiletries and sweets in the small shop in the school grounds which was open every Saturday morning for a few hours. The housemistress kept the money and doled it out accordingly.

Anna was sent to see Mrs Goldsmith, the headmistress, a formidable lady who had long experience of girls and their jealousies. Anna was extremely upset but Mrs Goldsmith was very kind and understanding, and questioned Anna gently about what she was accused of and her general troubles that she seemed to be having. At the end of the interview, she sent Anna back to the classroom and called in some of the other girls who were tormenting Anna and gave them a dressing down. She was scary when aroused and the girls were very subdued after that for a time. However, Mrs Goldsmith went on the telephone and had a long chat, first with Anna's mother then her father, and it was decided that for Anna's sake, she should leave and go to school elsewhere as she didn't really seem able to fit in. Karen felt worse than any of the others as she found her money which had slipped through a small hole in the lining for her pocket. She owned up to this and Anna forgave her, and for the rest of the term, things were quite calm and Anna felt happier. A shock was in store for Anna at the end of term, though, when her father told her she wouldn't be returning to that school.

So, Anna found herself at yet another school and as it was already two thirds of the way through the school year, Anna had an even greater challenge on her hands to fit in. It was the same as before; being very pretty and brainy was exactly the combination that the other pupils took exception to, and the harassment soon started again. Her mother wasn't very sympathetic but her father was more understanding and chivvied Anna along whenever he could. So time passed; Anna learnt to cope with the teasing and sometimes cruel jokes and tried hard with her studies.

At sixteen, she took her GCSE exams. Her favourite subject she passed with excellent marks, others that didn't interest her, she did miserably at. Her parents didn't know what to advise her to do as she was adamant that she had had enough of school and couldn't wait to leave.

"What do you want to do?" asked her father.

"Stay at home and help out on the farm," said Anna.

"There isn't enough for you to do nor is the farm big enough to support the two of us, your brother Silas and you," said her father.

"But you bought more land recently," said Anna looking pleadingly at Tim.

"I know, love, but believe me, it's still not large enough to be viable, especially if Silas gets married."

Anna had a good relationship with her sister-in-law Clare and had found it fun being a bridesmaid, but she didn't really like June, Silas's girlfriend, and felt rather resentful when her father said this. "I am sorry, sweetheart, but that is how it is," said Tim looking at his beautiful daughter worriedly. She had lovely, wavy dark-red hair, which she wore long. With big brown eyes, clear skin and an hourglass figure, she looked stunning. More so, perhaps, because she was completely unaware of it and wasn't vain in any way. Tim worried that some unscrupulous man would sweep Anna off her feet and that she would be taken advantage of and left broken-hearted. Her confidence wasn't very high; she didn't need any more knocks.

Chapter 2

Anna drifted from dead-end job to dead-end job; she couldn't seem to find anything that suited her though she was never unemployed for long. Tim had suggested that she did a short typing course but she rejected that and so, worked in supermarkets stacking shelves; in a kennels, sweeping up dog poo and helping out. She enjoyed that but found the woman who ran it difficult and didn't stay long. She went and helped out in the local hairdressers and they did offer her more than sweeping up and making tea and coffee for the customers, but she was basically an outdoor girl and didn't want to get involved with hairdressing. Her mother tried to convince her it would be a worthwhile job for her but Anna wasn't interested, and they had a blazing row. So it was back to the supermarket stacking shelves. Rows were becoming very frequent between them. Marie had never really understood her daughter and Anna always felt that her mother didn't really love her, that she was an afterthought and not really wanted. Tim took Anna on one side and spoke to her about the way things were headed, telling her that they couldn't live like this with all the tension and bad feelings that were just under the surface. Anna was hurt that her dad seemed to be taking her mother's side or so she felt. In reality, he was just trying to get Anna to see that she had to calm down and look at everything more rationally. He had said much the same to Marie; in some ways, mother and daughter were very alike. Anna stormed off and went for a long walk across the fields. She missed having the old pony to talk to and all the dogs on the farm were either her father's or Silas's. She felt she needed an animal by her side now; she always had a special relationship with animals. She suddenly wished she had taken her subjects more seriously at school, maybe she could have become a vet! She mentally shrugged, *too late now!* Maybe she should move out of home and find a place of her own. *Not enough money for that!* She felt trapped and suffocated, lonely and miserable. She stayed out until it was dark, then stumped back indoors and went straight up to her room. It wasn't long, however, before her stomach told her she had better go and join the family for the evening meal. June had come over, and so it was the five of them that sat down to eat.

"Now you are here, Anna, I have something to say to you, and you two as well." As her father said this, he looked across at Silas and June. "Your mum has a big birthday coming up shortly and I would like you, Anna," he said turning towards Anna, "to organise a big birthday bash for her." Anna was taken aback. It was not what she expected at all; if anything, she had expected her Dad to tell her off some more but to the contrary, he was involving her in a surprising fashion. She looked at her mum who was smiling at her.

"Mum?"

"We don't always get on as we should, Anna. Maybe we are too alike, but anyway, the thing is, your father and I have had a long talk and we think you are more than capable of doing this for me and it will give you something worthwhile to get your teeth into. How about it? You will have free rein to do whatever you think fit and Dad will, of course, give you a budget to work with." Anna jumped up and gave both her parents a big hug, something she didn't do very often.

"I take it it's a yes then," her father smiled at her.

June then said, "Of course if you want any guidance or help, Silas and I will be on hand." Tim held up his hand before Anna had a chance to speak.

"Thank you, June and Silas, but this is Anna's project, if she wants to include you, by all means, but all the decision making and ideas will be Anna's."

Anna felt very excited and ideas already started to race around in her head, and she hardly noticed what she was eating. The others round the table looked at her in amusement as Anna was quite a chatterbox when with family and for once, she was very quiet. As soon as the meal was over and cleared away, Anna excused herself and, going to her room, started to jot down ideas for this birthday bash. Suddenly, the doubts crept in, was she up for this? Would she really manage to make it a good event? Supposing it all went wrong and was a big flop, she would never be able to hold her head up again. She couldn't do it; it was too difficult, she would have to tell her parents.

Just then, there was a tap at the door and her Mum put her head around the door. "Can I come in?"

"Yes, Mum, please, I was just thinking of coming to see you and Dad, and to say I can't do this. I am not good enough or clever enough and no good at dealing with people," Anna was speaking very quickly trying to get all her doubts in before her mother could stop her.

Her mum came and sat on the edge of the bed that Anna was sitting on. "Dear Anna, please don't think these negative thoughts; Dad and I have complete faith in you. We both think because you have had sometimes a rough time at school, your self-esteem is low and you need something to give you confidence. You are a clever girl and that has made some of your peers jealous, plus you are lovely to look at. I know that we haven't been as close as you are to your father and that is my fault. I was pretty sick a lot of the time while I was expecting you and then you didn't want to be born! Or that is how it seemed, but I have always loved you to death, though I have to admit, I was a bit envious of how you seemed to take to your dad more than me. If this goes well and you enjoy it, then maybe it will lead you on a career path that none of us have considered. I think, with your flare and imagination, you will come up with a great party. I don't want to know what to expect, just run it all by your dad, OK?" It was the most her mother had ever said to her in one breath that Anna could ever remember her mother saying. She put her arms round her mum and hugged her tight.

"Love you too, Mum. Lots and lots." So, for the next few days, Anna spent every minute she could dreaming up ideas, then mostly rejecting them. However, after that time, she had finally made up her mind as to what to do and went in search of her dad to run it by him. "This is what I am thinking, Dad," she said and, holding her breath, she passed a sheet of paper to him to read.

"Guest list, good; caterers, good; live music? OK; venue, good; theme, well, we must talk about that; fireworks, not sure." Anna opened her mouth but Tim stopped her, "If we are talking the theme that you have here, we need the music to match, yes?"

"Yes, you are right, Dad, but I am not sure where I can get a band that will pay music from that era."

"Well, pet, that is one of the things you will have to research and in the meantime, get some quotes from the caterers and if as you have suggested, we have it here, then you need to get a marquee organised." The next few weeks, Anna eat, slept, just lived the party. *Endless phone calls, letters, and lots of worry; though in a way, a nice worry, if there was such a thing,* Anna thought. Once she had the caterers and a marquee sorted, she had invitations printed and sent them out. It was to be in a few weeks' time after harvest in September; hopefully, it would be an early harvest but the weather seemed fairly settled. She had struggled to find a band that would do it but in the end, was put onto one that that wasn't too far away, as some she had approached wanted travelling expenses, which, on the budget her dad had given her, was out of the question. Then her four brothers all said that they would contribute as they had no idea what to give their mother and so the party would be the ideal thing to give her. As an added surprise, Matthew let it known to his dad that he would make a surprise trip home. They were all sworn to secrecy.

Consequently, Anna's budget grew and she was able to hire a very good band. The theme was the forties, which was one thing Marie had to know so she could get her outfit sorted. One thing that wasn't from the war years was the food as, of course, there was rationing then and the fare would have been rather mega to say the least.

The day before the party arrived and Anna found herself directing the erection of the marquee and making sure the tables and chairs were put out in the right order. Then, as she had got her mother's flower club in on the act, she had to make sure everything was ready for them to start very early in the morning. As her parents were very active locally and had a wide circle of friends, there were about a hundred people coming. That included relatives too.

"Anna, isn't it? Where would you like this, love?" Anna turned to see a tall man with a fake stone pedestal in his arms. He was not particularly handsome but he had a sparkle in his blue eyes and an engaging smile. He looked to be in his late twenties or early thirties.

"Oh that is for a big flower display near the top table," said Anna. She smiled back at him. Having grown up with four brothers, men didn't faze her, and she went to Young Farmers sometimes, and had had the odd date and a few stolen kisses, but she had never met anyone who attracted her. This man did. "I'll show exactly where if you like," she said as her heart seemed to go into overdrive. She marched up the marquee and showed him the exact spot she wanted it.

He put it down carefully and straightening up, he said "My name is Paul," and gave her a big grin. "Looking forward to the party then, are you?"

"Yes, yes, I am," Anna didn't normally stutter. What was the matter with her?

"You've gone to a lot of trouble I see. It's for your mum, I gather. Is she around?"

"No, Dad has taken her out; she knows about a lot of it, obviously, but not the detail."

"She is a very lucky woman having you to organise it all and to be so beautiful too, wish I had someone as lovely to organise a party for me." Anna blushed; this was all new to her. If anyone had complimented her before on her looks, she hadn't really noticed but this man was getting under her skin. She found herself completely tongue tied. "Perhaps you could show me where to put some of the other stuff, and by the way, my name is Paul." He held out his hand. Anna automatically took it thinking, *you already told me that*, and it was as if an electric shock ran up her arm; she felt weak and shaky. Blushing madly and being slightly wobbly, Anna managed to show him where she wanted things put. Then she offered him a cup of tea and as she did that, realised she should offer the others who were helping too. In the end, there were six cups of tea made for the workers, but Anna only had eyes for Paul; she kept looking at him. She couldn't help it. It was as if she was drawn by some giant magnet. Before long, everything that they had to do was done and it was all down to the decorations tomorrow. The party was in the evening. Anna didn't want Paul to go; she wanted to talk to him some more and find out more about him, and just to be near him.

Impulsively, she suddenly said, "Why don't you come along tomorrow and join in, it will be fun."

Paul looked thoughtful, then shrugged, "We'll see how we go, but thanks anyway. See you, beautiful," and with that, he climbed into the big vehicle that they had come in and off they all went. Anna watched it go with an empty feeling in the pit of her stomach.

"Well, Paul, you've done it again," said John, one of his workmates. "You always manage to pull the birds wherever we go and she certainly looked hot." Paul grinned.

"Yea, I reckon I'll just have to check out that party tomorrow night."

Chapter 3

The big day dawned. Anna hadn't slept very well as she couldn't get Paul out of her head, but she soon threw herself in to the final stages of the party. As the theme was to be the war years, everyone had either made or hired costumes for the occasion. Tim and his sons were all going as RAF personnel. Matthew had arrived the day before but was staying with friends nearby thus keeping the secret that he was over from Canada.

Anna wore a full skirted dress of emerald green with a scoop neck. Marie was in a similar dress but hers was gold; they both looked lovely, but Anna looked stunning. As the guests started to arrive, Anna kept a lookout for Paul. She was rather regretting her hasty invitation as everyone was to be seated for dinner first and all the chairs were taken. Also, she realised that she didn't really know him or anything about him; he may even be married for all she knew. She dreaded to think what her parents would say. They were by no means narrow-minded but nonetheless, she didn't think they would be that impressed. When everyone was assembled, Tim banged a spoon on the table and asked everyone to take their seats in a few moments. In the hush that followed, a tall, handsome, young man strode into the tent and swept Marie into his arms. "Happy Birthday, Mum!" Marie was completely overwhelmed and burst into happy tears.

"Someone I want you all to meet," said Matthew looking round at everyone, and into the marquee walked a very pretty blonde girl. "This is Sally, everyone, the love of my life," Matthew said rather dramatically. Hastily, another chair was found for the top table and introductions were made. Anna liked what she saw of Sally but also thought it was as well that Paul hadn't turned up. Later, she managed to get to sit next to

Sally and found her very easy to talk to. Sally's father owned the apple orchards where Matthew worked and from what Sally told Anna, Matthew was very much part of the family now and had asked Sally to marry him, much to her parents' joy. She had a brother but he was away teaching in America's south, and they didn't see much of him or have much contact.

"Do Mum and Dad know?" asked Anna.

"Matthew told them about half an hour ago just as the dessert was being served," Sally giggled. "I hope we can be friends. Will you be my bridesmaid?"

"Yes! Does that mean you will be getting married here or in Canada?" asked Anna.

"Well, if I am honest, we have only just got engaged so I simply don't know; all I know is that I can't wait." The meal finished and tables cleared, the band arrived and dancing began. The band was very good and soon everyone was jiving away. Those that had never done it before were causing much laughter but everyone was having a good time and what did it matter how people danced so long as they were enjoying themselves. Anna sat talking to Sally a little longer then Matthew came over and dragged her, giggling, onto the dance floor. Both girls had been drinking champagne and as Anna wasn't used to drinking, although she hadn't had much, it had gone to her head and she was feeling quite woozy. Brother Peter came up and pulled her onto the dance floor and Anna was completely unfazed by the fact she hadn't a clue what she was doing, and in the end, she and Peter collapsed helpless with laughter. "Oh I am so hot," Anna managed to say as she recovered a little. "I am just going outside to get some air."

"OK, sis, watch where you are putting your feet, you seem to have two left ones!" said Peter. Anna stuck her tongue out at him and ducked out of the marquee. It was very still and a beautiful night. The stars glimmered in the sky, it was cooler too and Anna weaved her way a short distance from the hubbub to enjoy the quiet and the evening. Suddenly, a figure appeared in front of her.

"Hello, gorgeous." For a moment, Anna felt confused, then realised it was Paul.

"Hello." She then hiccupped loudly and stifled a giggle.

"Sounds as if you have been having fun, sweetheart." Paul came closer and draped his arm around Anna's shoulders.

Anna's pulse rate went up, and she felt breathless. Paul leant towards her and touched her lips with his. For a second, Anna froze, then without thought, her lips parted and his kiss deepened, his tongue exploring her mouth. Anna had never experienced anything like it and she felt as if she was drowning with many feelings rushing through her body. She was dizzy from the champagne and even more so now with this intense kiss that was so exciting and mind blowing. Still exploring her mouth with his tongue, Paul moved his hand and slipped her dress off her shoulder, then put his hand on her breast. Anna shuddered but felt too weak to protest. Paul slipped his hand inside her bra and gently squeezed her nipple.

"NO!" Anna pulled her head away and pushed his hand at the same time. "What are you doing? I hardly know you." Anna was sobering up fast. She knew the facts of life all too well especially being brought up on the farm.

"Aw come on, sweetheart, nothing to get upset about." Paul stepped back and spread his hands as if to indicate innocence.

"Well, you were going too far." Anna was feeling slightly sick now and just wanted to go back inside the marquee and find her family.

"Sorry, honey. You are so lovely you can't blame a bloke for trying. Tell you what, meet me for a coffee at the little café next to the supermarket in town, my shout, just to show you how harmless I am."

"I'm not sure."

"Tell me Monday when we come to take this lot down then." Anna nodded and with that, Paul grinned at her and walked away. Anna still felt sick and shaky so she went across to the house and going into the downstairs toilet, splashed her face with cold water and leaning against the washbasin, tried to get her thoughts and her body into some sort of order. On the one hand, Paul had awakened her sexually, on the other, she knew instinctually that he was just using her and she was torn between never letting him near her again and finding out just what having sex was really all about. After a bit, she felt better and having nipped upstairs to repair her makeup, she returned to the party.

"There you are," said Silas, "we were about to send out a search party."

"Sorry, I felt a bit sick so I went back to the house for a breather."

"Are you OK now?" Silas looked at her keenly.

"Sure am. Are you going to dance with me or not?" Anna threw out a challenge to her brother.

"Why not? I expect June can spare me for a bit," he said linking his arm in hers. The rest of the evening passed quickly and it didn't seem long before people were saying their goodbyes and heading home. Anna excused herself as soon as she could and went to her room. The clearing up could wait. She sat in front of her mirror in her night clothes brushing her hair and looked at herself hard in the mirror. What was it that made people behave as they did towards her? She seemed to have trouble making lasting female friends, and her parents and brothers told her they were jealous and any men or boys seemed to want to have sex with her even without any encouragement from her. If it was really because she was beautiful, then she sincerely wished she wasn't. Looking in the mirror, she couldn't really see what all the fuss was about! Surely the person beneath the face was what was important, but no-one outside the family seemed to look that far.

She didn't know what to think about Monday either; should she wait to hear what Paul said or just ignore him completely. She would play it by ear, she decided.

The next morning, everyone was late up and there was a distinct morning-after feeling. However, when Anna walked into the kitchen, Marie jumped up and gave her a big hug, much to Anna's surprise. "Thank you so much for organising that, it was amazing, darling; I had the best time ever. That's not all, Auntie Kate is going to be sixty in two months' time and wants you to organise something for her too!"

Anna looked at her mother with her mouth open, "Really; you are joking?" she said. Auntie Kate, as everyone in the family called her, wasn't really a relation but Marie's best friend since school days and was married to a barrister; they had no children and because of this, Marie's children were almost Kate's surrogate family. She loved and spoilt them all.

"But surely they will want the best of everything and I am not sure I would know where to start," Anna felt panicky already.

"Sweetheart, don't sell yourself short," her father joined in the conversation. "You did a great job with your mother's party and we all have faith in your organisational skills, especially it seems Kate."

"What does Uncle Vernon think?"

"He will go along with whatever Kate wants, always has, always will," said Marie.

"Wow!" Anna sat down suddenly. "Do you really think I can do it?" She looked anxiously at both her parents.

"Of course," they said together.

"I said you would meet Kate Tuesday morning and talk about it," said Marie.

Later, Anna went back to her room and started to jot down ideas. She still wasn't convinced that she could organise such a big event; half the country would be there, everybody who was anybody. *Help!* she thought to herself. Monday morning and she had almost forgotten about Paul in the wake of her new role in organising another event. She went out to make sure that all other clearing up had been done before the marquee was taken down and no sooner had she got there than the truck turned up. Paul was driving and leant out of the window as he drove by saying, "Hello, gorgeous."

Anna's stomach flip flopped and she couldn't help but grin back in answer. It took a remarkably short time to get the marquee down and packed up. Anna watched in surprise; she hadn't realised it would be so quick. Paul kept looking at her and passing silly remarks as he worked. Anna didn't say much; she was still trying to decide what she wanted to do. When they had finished, Paul came and stood in front of her. "Well, darlin', what do you say to that coffee then?" His eyes seemed to bore right into her and she melted under his gaze.

"OK, when?" she said.

"Tomorrow just before lunch, say 12:15?"

"OK," Anna said.

"Good, see you then, my lovely," and with that, Paul jumped in the truck and with a cheery wave was gone.

28

"You still hoping to lay her then, are you?" asked one of his mates as they drove away.

"Not hoping, will, my friend, I will," said Paul. "There is nothing like the challenge of the innocent, don't think she has ever had a man and I intend to show her what a man can do for her."

John, one of the others, looked at Paul in disgust. "You are a rotten bastard, just deflower them then leave them and go after the next one, no matter what harm or heartache you cause."

Paul shrugged. He didn't care; once the chase was over, he always lost interest. He didn't want any sort of commitment and was often disappointed with the girls that he went to bed with anyway. The actual chase was the best bit.

Chapter 4

Ten o'clock found Anna outside Aunt Kate's house. It was a grand townhouse that stood in its own private grounds which were quite extensive in spite of the fact it was in the centre of town. Georgian by appearance, it was actually older but had been changed considerably during that period, and Anna always found it quite intimidating. She was, however, quite relaxed coming here. It was the meeting later that had the butterflies in her stomach doing a dance. Kate answered the door herself though they did have a maid.

"Anna darling," Kate swept Anna into a warm embrace. "I am so happy that you are here and have agreed to do this for me. Marie's party was just fab and you organised it all so well." Anna was rather taken aback as she didn't really think she had fully agreed to organise Kate's party but she kept quiet. She had been having second thoughts again. Following Kate into the large and airy sitting room, she took stock more than she ever had before thinking of the party. "Coffee?" asked Kate.

"No, thank you; um yes, please." Anna started to feel nervous; a party here would be a huge undertaking. However, once she had sat on the sofa beside Kate and started swapping ideas, Anna felt better about it; maybe it would be fun and then Kate dropped a bombshell by saying that they were more than happy to pay Anna. Not only that but when she mentioned the sum that they had in mind, Anna was speechless. "Are you sure, Auntie Kate?" said Anna breathlessly.

"Uncle Vernon is very fond of you Anna; you are the daughter we couldn't have. We have watched you grow up and life hasn't always been easy for you, you've had your setbacks. This is something it seems you are good at, so go for it sweetheart." Anna threw her arms around Kate

"Thank you, thank you," she said.

"Right, now let's get serious. I want to know what's planned differently to your mum's. I will be more involved, so are we having a theme or just a party?" So for the rest of the morning, the two of them sat there discussing ideas and Anna scribbled notes and suddenly realised it was gone twelve o'clock.

"Goodness, is that the time!" she exclaimed. "I had better get going, I have a shift at the supermarket starting soon." In truth, her shelf stacking didn't start until 1:15 but she was meeting Paul, wasn't she? She didn't want anyone to know and didn't examine her own feelings about that as she knew the answer.

"Hopefully you will be able to find something better soon, dear," Kate said as she walked Anna to the door. Anna jumped on her bike and with a cheery wave, cycled off. When she was out of sight of the house, the nerves kicked in and she was almost shaking by the time she got to the café. Paul was already there sitting up the corner at the back.

"Hello, gorgeous. I took the liberty of ordering you a coffee, is that OK?"

"Thank you. I work next door so they know me in here," Anna was gabbling rather, she was nervous.

"I know I have seen you in here but didn't realise where you lived or anything," said Paul. "I was so pleased to find out when we came on Friday to put up the marquee."

"Really!" Anna was surprised; she had never noticed Paul but then she mostly kept her head down.

"Yea really, thought a beautiful girl like you would be doing something better than that." Anna was embarrassed; Paul was only a tent handler after all, and yet even he thought she could do better.

Their coffees arrived. Paul sugared his generously, then started to gulp it down. "Hurry up, darlin', I have to get on, work to do and all that."

"Oh yes, sorry," Anna felt disadvantaged and flustered. She gulped her coffee down as best she could. Paul stood up to leave, Anna was even more flustered. Was this it?

She followed him outside and he turned down the little alleyway between the supermarket and coffee shop. Before she

31

had a chance to speak he pulled her into his arms and kissed her long and hard his tongue once again exploring her mouth. Letting her go almost as suddenly as he had taken hold of her he said, "You are so lovely you shouldn't be out on your own. What time do you finish work?"

"About nine, then I cycle home," Anna was breathing very fast after the mind blowing kiss.

"I will be waiting for you and will give you a lift home; you are much safer with me than peddling away alone in the dark."

"No, no. It's fine." But Paul held up his hand and kissing her again on the lips strode around the corner and was gone.

Anna stood there dumbstruck for several minutes. It had all happened so fast but her body had betrayed her and she had felt desire raising through her like a flame. At the same time she didn't feel she could trust Paul, didn't really know him. Didn't even like him, she decided. Pulling herself together she glanced at her watch and getting her bike from the cycle rack in front of the coffee shop wheeled it round the back of the supermarket and put it in its usual place there.

The evening came all too soon for Anna who was trying to decide what she would do if Paul was indeed waiting for her. She almost crept out of the shop fearfully then looking round realised that he wasn't there. Part of her was upset and disappointed but the other part thought it was as well. Two nights later he was there! As she was retrieving her bike, he spoke to her and made her jump.

"Sorry not to be here before sweetheart but we had to go away with the marquees and I couldn't get here in time."

Anna was holding her bike between them like a shield. "It's OK really." She felt breathless.

Paul took her bike from her and leading her across the car park to an old Land Rover opened the back door and popped her bike in. Anna was too confused with her conflicting emotions to protest. "Hop in, I don't bite," he said.

Anna did as she was told and soon they were speeding out of town towards her home. Then Paul swung the vehicle into a lay-by and switched off the engine. "Wha—" Anna didn't get the chance to say more and Paul leant over and started to kiss her passionately. Before she knew what was happening he had her laid across the bench seats and while still kissing her hard his hands were pulling her clothes apart. First her bra was pushed up then his fingers were sliding down into her knickers. Anna tried to protest but her body was responding in ways that completely made her brain freeze and feeling his erection and knowing he was going to take her for the moment it didn't seem to matter. She welcomed it, she wanted to experience it; she was nearly eighteen after all and other girls had boyfriends and sex all the time. At least, she thought they did. So after a small protest she helped him with clothing and opened her legs to welcome him. However what she hadn't expected that though she was thoroughly aroused it hurt a lot! It was also over very quickly and it seemed as if only seconds had passed and Paul having grunted a few times pulled himself off her and started to sort his clothing out.

"Come on, your folks will be worried if you are too late, hurry up," he said and started the engine. Anna automatically got dressed and sat upright as again they set off. She felt dazed, was that it then? Was that all there was to it? She felt unfulfilled and let down her body saying it wasn't satisfied but it was worse than that. Paul seemed very matter of fact suddenly. He had used a condom so maybe that was why it wasn't as good as she thought it would be and, of course, she knew that the first time for a girl was often uncomfortable. That was it, of course it was. Paul stopped short of the farm gate and hopped out getting her bike. "When shall we meet again?" Anna asked. She stood close expecting a kiss.

"I don't think it's worth it, do you? Got what I wanted, didn't I?" Paul was grinning at her in the semidarkness. Anna had red hair and a temper to match.

"You bastard!" Her hand came up and she slapped him hard across the face.

"Silly cow." Paul pushed her hard and together with her bike she fell over. Before she could get to her feet and untangle herself from her bike he had jumped into his car and had gone. Tears of frustration and humiliation ran down Anna's face; what a stupid girl she was and what a rotten bastard he was, how could this have happened to her she had been warned by her mother about men who were predators but she hadn't really listened.

Her coat was muddy and she had grazed her hands when she fell but most of all her pride was much damaged, and she didn't know how she was going to walk into the kitchen in a few minutes and pretend that everything was alright. Somehow she must. A few minutes later she did exactly that. Only her father was there reading the paper, he glanced up then put his paper down. "What happened to you? You look like you've been through a hedge backwards!"

"I fell off my bike, I hit a lump of something in the road way back and fell off, and I think I have hurt my wrist." Anna was trying hard not to cry. Putting down his paper Tim came across to look at her hands but Anna pulled back. "It's OK Dad, I'll just go and have a wash, maybe a shower. I feel grubby."

Tim looked at his beloved daughter searchingly, she looked like a little girl again, he thought. Suddenly rather bewildered and unsure of herself. "Anna," he started to say but she was gone and a few moments later he heard the water running.

Marie came into the kitchen; she had been on the phone to Kate. "Anna made a great impression the other day with Kate, she has some great ideas. Vernon said they will pay her generously too." Marie stopped. "You look a bit bemused, what's up?" Tim shrugged.

"Don't really know just Anna didn't seem herself when she came in, said she fell off her bike."

"Well you wouldn't feel too hot if you fell off yours, not that you ride one. I am sure she is fine just a bit shaken up I expect." Half an hour later Anna walked into the kitchen in her dressing gown with her wet hair plastered to her head. She seemed to be her normal self and nothing more was ever said about that evening.

Chapter 5

Kate kept Anna so busy that in the end she gave her notice in at the supermarket. Not that she minded; it was a pretty dead end job and she was earning anyway. Vernon and Kate were being very generous, she knew, and she appreciated it. There seemed so much to do and Kate was happy to just sit back and let Anna get on with it. It seemed she had even less to say than Marie had when it was her party. All at once it seemed, it was the day before. As it was a very big house and also late in the year, they only needed a small marquee attached to the dining room as a kind of overspill in case it became too over crowded. Anna had approached another firm to do it so she hadn't got to worry about seeing Paul. It still rankled and, she thought, always would but she knew part of the blame lay with her and that she had been pretty silly. She decided she was off men for good and would remain a spinster all her life.

There was to be a quartet playing and later in the evening a harpist was due to play, there wasn't to be any dancing this time. It was a buffet style menu with canapés and all sorts of wonderful delights to try. People could wander over and help themselves from the huge spread that was laid out. There were waiters and waitresses everywhere filling people's glasses and replacing any dishes that were emptied on the buffet table. Anna, of course, was at the party but in her role as organiser not a guest. Her parents, however, were guests but none of her brothers as it was more for the older generation unless they were near relatives and as neither Vernon nor Kate had any very near family, younger people were rather thin on the ground. Not that Anna noticed; she was far too busy making sure everything ran like clockwork. Just before the guests started to arrive, however, she managed to slip away and changed into a bright emerald-green dress; it was a shirt waiter and having seen it in a shop window a few weeks back Anna thought it would be ideal for the evening as wasn't in any way a party frock but was neat and tidy. What she hadn't really realised was that with her hair colouring she looked absolutely stunning in it.

Two hours into the party she looked around and breathed a sigh of relief, so far so good; everyone seemed to be enjoying themselves. "Well, well. This IS a surprise," said a familiar voice behind her. Anna swung round and there stood Karen from boarding school. Anna was so surprised that without thinking she blurted, "What are you doing here?"

Karen looked at her disdainfully, "My father retired from the army and is working with Vernon," she said. "Not that it is any of your business, are you a waitress or something?"

"As you say, none of your business." Anna turned away.

Karen caught her arm, and smiling slightly said "I guess I deserved that, let's talk; there is no-one here our age and I am so bored, Daddy made me come with him as Mummy is unwell." Anna looked at Karen then gave a small smile back.

"Well I guess we can talk for a few minutes but I am working as I put this whole thing together for Auntie Kate and I don't want anything to go wrong."

"You did!" Karen looked at her in amazement. Then she took in Anna's simple but lovely outfit, the way she stood her hairstyle; everything was so perfect. Karen felt jealousy and admiration all at the same time. Karen was wearing a grey dress which was really too old a style for her age and her hair which was really a rather mousy colour was cut and styled with high lights in it but beside Anna she felt pale and insignificant. Anna, meanwhile, was feeling gauche and her confidence seemed to be deserting her when, to her surprise, Karen said "That's amazing Anna, well done you." Anna looked at her sceptically. Karen saw her look,

"No, I really, actually mean it. It must have taken some organising to put on such a great party; I am not very good at organising anything. I got fed up at school and didn't do well in my exams and have tried several things since but nothing seems right."

"Oh," Anna was at a loss as to what to say to this confession, in the end she just said "Well, Auntie Kate and Uncle Vernon have been very kind as I was sort of drifting. They gave me this opportunity." Just then there was a small cough behind Anna and turning she found one of the waitresses standing there waiting to speak to her. Excusing herself she moved away to be told that it was nearly time for the speeches and should they be getting the huge birthday cake—which was to be a surprise to Kate—ready. So for the next hour Anna was kept busy, speeches were made, champagne was poured freely and amid much laughter the cake was cut. Then it had to be taken into the kitchen to be cut into small pieces for distribution. Just as she came out of the kitchen to make sure everyone who wanted cake had some, Vernon banged loudly on the table nearby and as everyone quietened he said, "Please everyone, charge your glasses to drink a toast to Anna without whom this party wouldn't have happened. Her attention to detail has been key to making this such a huge success and Kate and I consider ourselves very lucky to have had her to do it all for us. Not only that but she looks beautiful too, what more could one ask! Anna!"

A chorus of Anna resounded around the throng of people. Anna wanted the ground to open up and swallow her but she managed to keep her cool and nodding her head in acknowledgement she turned back to the kitchen. However the people nearest her started to chant 'speech' and Aunt Kate came over and asked her to say a few words. Stammering, she just said how much she had enjoyed it and thanked Vernon and Kate for letting her do it and on that note fled back to the kitchen. A short while later Karen came and found her in the kitchen. "We are off now, see you soon," she said.

"OK, see you." Anna looked after her feeling puzzled; she didn't think they would be seeing each other very soon.

The next morning Vernon called to Anna to come to his study when she had finished supervising the clean-up. It was after lunch by the time everything was back to normal and Anna was feeling rather tired when she finally knocked on Vernon's study door.

"Come in, Anna love, and sit down. I have a proposition for you," Vernon said.

Anna sat and just then Kate walked in. "This is my idea so I want to hear your answer," she said.

Anna looked from one to another as Vernon said, "Hang on Kate, I haven't asked her yet."

"Sorry." Kate sat herself down next to Anna and smiled.

"Now, Anna, you have done a great job with organising these two parties, it's not the easiest to get everything going to plan without any major hiccups so well done! That has led us to thinking maybe you should consider getting a few business studies under your belt then starting up your own party organising business." Anna went to speak but Vernon held up his hand. "Bear with me a minute Anna, what I am proposing is this: you go to technical college and get a few skills under your belt then I will set you up in your own business and when you can afford it you can repay me and then the business would be entirely yours. What do you say?"

Anna sat there in stunned silence for a minute. It wasn't something she had thought she could do and she had always found taking orders from people difficult. She liked making her own decisions and that was partly what she had found so appealing organising the two parties, but could she do it on a more professional basis? It was one thing doing it for friends and family, but strangers?

Anna realised that Vernon and Kate were both sitting looking at her holding their breaths. They had faith in her even if other people thought she was useless, so why not? "Yes," she said, "sounds an amazing idea."

Chapter 6

So a short time later Anna found herself studying again. Not what she had thought she would be doing but then she hadn't had a clear plan anyway, so she had just drifted along not finding the niche for herself; she wanted or needed.

At first she found it hard but once she got into the routine of college and learning again she settled down and got on with it, and to her amazement she found she was actually enjoying it. She learnt to type, how to be professional answering the phone, how to do accounts and make the books add up and how to sell herself in a professional sense to anyone she may have to deal with. This was pointed out to her near the beginning of the course as she had to come over as completely confident otherwise people would think they couldn't trust her with their event.

Time passed and the summer approached, her course was only three months long so she would be finished by June that year. She would also have a birthday and her brother Matthew was getting married, sadly this was in Canada and though her parents were going there wasn't enough money in the pot for the family to all go, besides, with the farm it was nearly impossible, especially during summer. Anna was disappointed as Sally had asked her to be a bridesmaid but it wasn't to be. The weather turned very hot and it was very, very dry. Coming home at weekends Anna found herself roped in the help on the farm. Hay that was cut one day was ready for turning and baling the next. Something unheard of in England. Tim at his son's wedding in Canada kept fretting but as it was he need not have worried. Peter managed to get a short break from the stud farm, June took holiday from her office job, and Anna managed to help too. Silas was, of course, in charge but what with the weather and conditions being as they were they had nearly finished harvest by the time Tim and Marie arrived back; it was extraordinary.

Anna had to take some exams which she had done but was worried as her attention and focus had been on harvest so she wasn't at all sure how well she had done. However, when the results came through she had done very well indeed and soon a very proud Vernon and Kate were on the phone, with plans to come over and bring the champagne.

When they were all seated comfortably and toasts had been made, Kate said, "One thing we must do is think of a name for the company."

They all sat quietly for a moment. Tim, Marie, Anna, June, Silas and Peter who had managed to get time off to pop over. "What about Anna's Amazing Parties Ltd?" said Silas.

"Sounds good to—"

"We can't have that," said Kate interrupting. "What would Karen think?"

"Karen? What has she got to do with it?" Anna could hear the disbelief and horror in her voice. But deep down she knew what was coming, she remembered her last conversation with Karen.

"But I don't understand, what has Karen to do with it?" Marie looked very puzzled as she repeated what Anna had just said.

"Karen's father works for me and was very keen for Karen to join Anna in this venture, she has good contacts through her father and the girls were at school together. We thought it would be good for the two of them rather than Anna being on her own." Vernon sounded a little defensive.

Tim looked across at Anna who was sitting very still and looking both angry and disappointed; he remembered that Karen had given Anna a hard time at school. She looked towards him and not knowing how else he could offer comfort he gave her a big wink. Anna gave him a ghost of a smile in return.

Anna sat dumbly not knowing what to say. Kate and Vernon were chatting on not realising what a bombshell they had dropped. Only Marie seemed to be listening and finally she

40

said, "I am sure Anna will be happy to have Karen on board with her, won't you dear?"

Anna glared at her mother, why was it Marie never seemed to understand her only Tim and Silas came near to that. Kate had always been good to her and she was grateful for Kate and Vernon's offer but it was spoilt now and she didn't know what to do or say. In the end Silas got up from the group and said, "Oh, by the way Anna, I have something for you. It's a surprise, come and see."

Anna got to her feet and muttering an apology she followed Silas across the lawn. When they got out of earshot, she exploded as Silas had guessed she would. "How could they, how could they do this to me? Surely they knew Karen and I had a history; she was a bitch at school, got me into big trouble and then she worms her way into my life again, I never liked her what am I going to do now?"

Silas put her arms around her and she burst into angry tears. He let her cry for a moment then said "It's a bugger, I know, sis, but unless you want to back out and let Karen have a great chance given to her I think you will have to swallow your pride and anger and go with it. Maybe make sure you have final say in decisions. I am sure Kate and Vernon will go along with that. I am sure they didn't mean to upset you, they just didn't realise."

Anna took a few minutes to calm down and dry her eyes. "You are right, I know. I can see that I am not sure I can do it that's all."

"Anna, you are a strong person, don't let them see you are upset. You can do it, hold your head up high and go with it for now. You never know how Karen will be maybe she will be better than she was or maybe she won't last long, give it a go."

Anna squared her shoulders and giving Silas a wan smile started back across the lawn. Suddenly she stopped "What was the surprise?"

"Sorry sis, there wasn't one really I just knew you wanted some time out."

Now Anna smiled properly "You are something else, you know that? But thanks for everything, I love you."

When they got back to the others, June gave Anna a hard look she didn't appreciate Silas going off with Anna and was curious about the surprise.

"Thank you very much Vernon and Kate. I am sure Karen and I will be fine together, just one thing, if we are to be partners can I please be the one who has the final say, my word goes?"

Vernon visibly breathed a sigh of relief, they had both been worried about Anna's reaction. "Of course, my dear. That was always the intention. It was just that Karen heard what was in the wind and nagged her father into approaching me and letting her be part of this venture."

"Now we need a name," said Marie.

Everyone had ideas, some were awful some were OK, none were wonderful. Finally they all agreed on Anna's idea of Great Parties 76 was the one. Anna had actually suggested Hot Parties 76 but Vernon clamped down on that straight away saying it sounded as if they were erotic or steamy 'not very nice' was how he put it.

Vernon had already organised a spare office in his building and had installed telephones and desks everything they would need. He was keen to get advertising going too.

The following week Anna found herself at her office waiting for Karen to arrive. She felt nervous though she didn't know why. As she had arrived first, she had chosen the desk that was nearest to the window and was looking out of it when Karen came bursting in.

"Gosh hello, sorry I am late. You look fab, oh is that my desk?" Karen said all this in a rush and Anna suddenly realised that Karen was nervous too. It gave her the confidence to take charge.

"It's fine this is the first day after all. We already have a client, a friend of a friend of my mother's so we need to go and see her straight away, I think."

"Oh really, that is quick. What do I need to bring?"

"A notebook might be good, I have mine," Anna replied, getting her jacket from the back of the door where she had hung it, "We'll go in my car as I know where we are going."

So off they set both feeling full of hope and trepidation.

Chapter 7

As they started their venture, as summer was drawing to a close and people's thoughts were turning towards Halloween, Christmas Parties, New Year's Eve, Hunt Balls, though the latter was usually organised by the respective hunts, Anna was optimistic that they would have a good start.

She wasn't wrong; the word had spread and soon they had nearly as much as they could cope with and even better they were earning enough to take home a modest amount of money each month. Anna didn't always see eye to eye with Karen but she managed to keep her cool and the girls rubbed along OK.

Anna was still living at home but Karen found herself a flat with two other girls and started to live life at full speed, they asked Anna over several times but away from work she was like a fish out of water. She was happy to dress smartly for work but at home she was far more comfortable in jeans and a tea shirt or baggy jumper. Also, she hadn't really anything in common on a personal level with Karen and her friends. She wasn't a big drinker, she didn't much like parties, she liked music but not what they liked. Being very much an outside girl made it hard too as it was the only thing she didn't like about her job. So at weekends she just stayed at home on the farm helping out if she could. She was off men too after her experience with Paul. He had made a fool of her and she vowed to herself she wouldn't let that happen again. Sometimes she felt lonely, she and her mother got on better than they did but they weren't really that close. It was when she was with Silas or her dad that she felt completely relaxed and at home. In time, however, this led to problems as June got quite jealous of the time that Silas and Anna spent together and finally had a row with Silas about it.

Anna was mortified when she heard they had fallen out over her and although she didn't have a great deal of time for June she went to find her and tried to make amends for Silas's sake. Then the two girls had a blazing row and Silas got cross with Anna. "Why don't you mind your own business? It's no concern of yours what goes on between June and I. Don't poke you nose into my affairs again, do you hear me?"

They were standing in the middle of the farmyard at this point and Tim coming out of the barn said "I should think the whole village if not the town heard you now stop it the pair of you, you are both old enough to know better."

Silas looked sheepish at that but Anna stormed off across the yard and climbing the gate she marched off across the paddock.

Silas watched her go then turning to his Dad said "Women!" and took off in the other direction.

In his turn Tim shrugged and went back to work on a piece of the cultivator that had broken off. He thought it would be OK when they had all calmed down.

It was up to a point, Anna tried not to spend quite so much time with Silas but it meant she was lonelier than ever. June was cool towards her and her mother had taken June's side when she heard what had happened.

"You are grown up now, Anna, you need to make your own friends and stop hanging around here so much; Silas and June will be getting married before long, you mustn't be so needy."

"Why can't I enjoy being at home why do you have to treat me as if I don't fit in, this was my home before June came along, I pay my way now, why do you want to get rid of me?"

Marie sighed, Anna was being difficult again in her eyes. She had never really understood her daughter and probably never would. "Look, dear," she held out a conciliatory hand, "I am only thinking of you, you are young, you should be out having fun at weekends, not mooching around here."

The arguments went back and forth for another couple of weeks and finally Tim had had enough and told both his wife and his daughter to put up or shut up. They were both completely shocked by this and for a few more weeks an uneasy truce reigned. However, the writing was on the wall and later that spring Anna moved out into a little bedsit in town on her own. She was very unhappy as she felt like a square peg in a round hole but her pride wouldn't let anyone know and although she dreaded weekends, she was determined to make the best of it. Work was fine, Karen and her got on OK so long as they kept it strictly work as on a personal level they were still poles apart, but they were doing well with their fledgling company and the jobs kept flowing in. Of course from time to time things would go wrong and sometimes they had really difficult clients to deal with. Strangely Anna was much better at dealing with them than Karen who was basically arrogant and had a short fuse. Anna had the ability to put herself in other people's shoes so was good at seeing things from another perspective.

The girls did disagree from time to time, of course, but as Anna had the final say it was usually resolved fairly quickly and Karen seemed reluctant to go to Vernon for arbitration.

So their first full year was drawing to a close and it had been a good year. Their reputation had spread which was good. Also, both Vernon and Karen's fathers had friends in high places and as they started their second year they found themselves being asked to organise parties in London. Some with no expense spared.

Not long after this Karen met a young man and started to be unreliable. She was often late and sometimes hung over. Anna kept her mouth shut for a while but finally could take no more especially as Karen had more than once forgotten to organise something important.

Finally, after taking a phone call from a woman that had asked Karen for white roses only at her party the previous weekend and had ended up with yellow ones instead, Anna flipped.

"What the hell has got into you? I have had to give her a large amount of her money back because of you, what were you thinking?"

"You give me a lot more to do than you do yourself I was overworked and made a mistake OK." Karen glared at Anna.

"It's not OK. And I do as much as you; you are the one getting here late in the mornings and letting everything slip. I suppose this is because of this Jason bloke you have been on about, this started out as going to be my business and I am not going to let you spoil it."

"What makes you think it is just yours, Daddy put money into it as well as Vernon, and that gives me as much right as you and I am not going to take this from you, you were a pain in the butt at school and you still are Miss High and Mighty." Karen was looking very angry now as was Anna.

However, Karen's words had brought Anna up short. Had Karen's father put money in to get them started? They had paid Vernon back though they still had their office in the same building. "Well not as high and mighty as you are, swanning in here at all times and I haven't forgotten how you accused me of stealing at school when I had done no such thing, you were nasty then, and you haven't changed!"

Karen had always felt guilty about that and Anna's words calmed her a bit.

"Yes, well, we all make mistakes, but I am doing my best, if that isn't good enough maybe we should call it quits now."

"Maybe we should." Anna felt suddenly tired and dispirited. Her anger had disappeared as quickly as it had come. "Do we owe your father anything then?" she said. They had agreed at the beginning that Anna would do the book keeping but as she didn't know about this money and nothing had been said; she was completely in the dark.

Karen shrugged and looked uncomfortable, "Well, actually it was just a personal loan to me."

Anna's anger was back at this, "So you are being less than honest about this too, it wasn't that he put money into the business after all."

Karen was squirming now "You make me say things I don't mean, you are always so perfect. I wanted to bring you down a peg or two."

At this point Anna felt she would explode with anger, but she just bit her lip and walked out of the room. Leaving the building she marched down the street to a small park and sat on a park bench near the children's play area. Tears threatened but she fought to control them, no good crying over spilt milk she told herself. She should go and talk to Vernon and Kate. Maybe Kate first as talking to Vernon might be difficult for him given that he and Karen's father worked together.

So she set off to their house only to find that Kate wasn't home, so she returned to her office, only to find Vernon sitting in her chair apparently waiting for her. She stood in the doorway her heart hammering in her chest, what now? Vernon stood up and held out his arms to her, "Come here, love," he said.

Anna crossed the room and allowed herself to be folded into his arms then tears came. Anna wasn't used to being cuddled since she had grown up as none of her family members were very tactile and the feel of Vernon's arms around her was so comforting that she couldn't help breaking down. After a few minutes though, she pulled herself free and Vernon stepped back and offered her his large handkerchief. "Now tell me word for word what you said to each other this morning and what has led to this."

So Anna related the whole story and told him about school and what had happened there too. Vernon sat frowning. "Karen made out that you were bosom buddies at school when she got wind of what you were going to be doing and persuaded her father that it was something she really wanted to do and it would be great to be working with you."

"The headmistress could back up what happened and so could Mum and Dad, and we have never been friends, not really. We have rubbed along at this and that is partly because we don't socialise. We aren't friends, just working partners, well we were but it isn't going to work especially now." Anna sighed again.

"Well, after what you have told me I am surprised you managed to get this far, Anna you should be proud of yourself; you have handled the situation very well. You are very young in years but very mature emotionally."

"What happens now?" Anna asked. "I don't think we can work together anymore. I don't trust her."

"No, let me sort this out. I am afraid you may have made an enemy but that can't be helped. Why don't you go and visit your parents for a day or so unless there is something pressing you have to see to."

There was nothing that couldn't wait. Anna went to her flat and packing a few clothes and her toothbrush set off for the farm.

Chapter 8

After spending a few days at the farm and relaxing more than she ever did in town, Anna resolved to go back more frequently. Her mother seemed more relaxed too which helped. Anna found doing everything on her own hard though, Vernon seemed to have sorted Karen and her problems out. He didn't tell Anna any details and she didn't ask, preferring to trust his judgement. Karen was given a lump sum which wasn't too huge and that seemed to be that.

A few weeks later a young girl knocked on her office door and then slid into the room nervously. "I hear you might be wanting an assistant and I am looking for a job, just something to keep me going as I am off to uni in a while all being well."

Anna smiled; she guessed Vernon had sent her. "What is your name and what can you do?"

"Mary, and I can type and answer the telephone for you, and maybe make the tea." She gave a nervous giggle.

Anna liked her immediately and so Mary became part of Anna's life.

Mary lived at home with her parents and her elder brother and one weekend after she had been with Anna a little while she asked Anna if she would like to go for Sunday lunch. Anna jumped at the chance; if she stayed in town at weekends she was always lonely but she didn't go out to the farm every weekend as she didn't want to get back to being a source of irritation to June or her mother.

Mary gave instructions to Anna where she lived which was on the outskirts of town in the opposite direction to the way out to the farm. Anna didn't know that area too well but found her way easily enough. It was a fairly normal semi-detached house with a big front garden which was very neat and well cared for. There was a small driveway up to the garage at the side but

Anna decided to park on the street so as not to be in anyone's way.

As she approached the front door, it burst open and a young man came rushing out and nearly collided with her. "Ooops sorry, I was—" He stopped speaking abruptly and stared at Anna. He was of average height with fair unruly hair. He was not at all good looking but had kind grey eyes and when he smiled his whole face seemed to take on such a happy expression that it was hard to resist not smiling back. That happened now as he broke into a huge smile instead of finishing what he was about to say. "Hi, you must be Anna, Mary's boss." Anna didn't consider herself Mary's boss but she smiled back and said she was.

She then started to feel uncomfortable as Mary's brother, as she guessed he was, continued to stare at her, "Have I got egg on my face or something?" she asked, starting to feel vaguely annoyed.

"Sorry, sorry. I'm Drew." He held out his hand and Anna took it automatically, he held her hand so tightly she felt compelled to pull it back hard. "Sorry," he said again.

Just at that moment Mary appeared "Oh, I'm glad you've met. Come in, Anna, and meet my Mum and Dad," she said. Smiling uncertainly at Drew, Anna followed Mary into the house and was introduced to Mary's parents. Anna liked them immediately, because she felt comfortable with them she was more natural than she was when feeling shy. When doing her job, she never felt shy or uncertain it was only on a personal level that she had a problem. However, they made her so welcome and when Drew arrived back indoors having been on some errand she was relaxed enough to chat to him too. The lunch was very good and the afternoon flew by and by the time Anna left she found herself accepting an offer to go shopping with Mary and her Mum.

That also turned out to be a success and was also something Anna hadn't experienced before as her and her mother didn't get on very well shopping as their tastes in clothes were very different. Also, Marie didn't have much time when Anna was free or so it seemed. So Anna had a ball and then stayed on and had supper with the family again at the end of the day.

When she was leaving, Drew followed herself and Mary to the door. "I wondered if you would care to come to the local football match on Sunday," he said. "Just the local team."

Mary grinned at her brother "What he really wants you to do is go and cheer him on, he plays for them."

Drew looked very pink around his ears suddenly. "Well, it was just a thought." He was obviously embarrassed.

Anna laid a hand on his arm, "I would love to come," she said.

"Really? That's great."

"What time and where? Just let me know and I will be there," she said, rather to her own surprise.

Later, driving back to her little flat, she reviewed the day which had been great fun with the icing on the cake being Drew's invitation and her response to it. She hadn't intended to get involved with any man. She was still off them but somehow her mouth had answered before her mind had caught up. However she resolved to go just this once and she could change her mind tomorrow if she wanted to.

In the end though, the week flew by and suddenly it was Sunday morning when Drew was playing for his local club. Anna had agreed to wait for him after the match then they would do something together though what hadn't been discussed let alone decided. Anna arrived when the match was in full swing as she was still unsure whether to go or not. However in the end she thought she had nothing to lose and he seemed a nice guy and Mary and Anna got on well. This was good Anna thought as she had always found the opposite sex easier to get on with, partly because of growing up in a house full of men and the fact her relationship with her mother wasn't that close.

Drew didn't notice her to start with though he did glance her way once and she thought he had, come half time he came across and looking very pink around his face thanked her for coming and would see her after the match. Anna was rather miffed by his casual manner and would have walked off but Mary appeared at that moment. "Hello, thought I would just pop along and see how you are faring. Drew can be rather vague when he is playing; he is so busy concentrating."

Anna laughed, "Well actually to be honest I was wondering what I was doing here!"

"Oh good thing I came then, poor old Drew is shy and not very good with girls. I didn't say anything all week in case he chickened out of it today!"

"That makes two of us," muttered Anna to herself; to Mary, she just said, "That's OK. We will see how we go after the match."

When finally Drew appeared, looking freshly washed and brushed up from the changing room, he suggested they went to the pub nearby for lunch to which Anna agreed. Once they had ordered and got drinks they sat down and looked at each other. Drew went all pink again and Anna hid a smile at his embarrassed expression. "Thank you for coming, it's very kind of you," he said. "Well maybe kind isn't quite the right word." He looked even more embarrassed.

Anna couldn't help it; she burst out laughing. "I like being told I am kind, it makes a change from being annoying or silly or some of the other things my family tell me I am. Kind isn't one I really heard before so kind is OK with me!"

Drew grinned back at her. "That's OK then, I guess you understand what I am trying to say."

From then on they both relaxed and started to enjoy themselves. Drew was a motor mechanic and had some amusing stories to tell about customers. He also had a talent for impersonations and before long had Anna nearly in tears with laughter. The time passed quickly and before long it was time to part company. Drew walked her back to her car. "Will you come again next week? It was fun today, please say yes." It all came out in a rush.

"Yes, it was fun today and yes, I will come again, though not next weekend as it is my Dad's birthday during the week, and I have a big do to organise for Friday night so not next week but certainly the week after." Anna smiled at him. If Drew was disappointed, he hid it well and, rather to her surprise, took her hand and shook it hard then walked off saying

"In a fortnight then."

Anna didn't know whether to be disappointed or pleased with his old fashioned manner but decided she didn't want to rush into anything so being pleased was the best option.

The following weekend went according to plan even the party which had been a worry as the clients were very fussy and kept changing their minds as to what they wanted. Tim was in a good mood and even her mum seemed very upbeat and happy to see her so Anna was very pleased she had made the effort to go as she had been in two minds.

When the next weekend came, it was almost a replay of their first time together except that there weren't really any awkward moments, not until they parted that is when blushing like mad Drew stammered that would Anna mind if he kissed her! Anna shut her eyes and pursed her lips but all she felt was a quick peck in the cheek and once more Drew was off.

So they fell into a kind of routine depending on what commitments Anna had but when she could they met and had lunch then Drew would give her a quick peck on the lips and scuttle off. Finally Anna decided to take matters into her own hands and when Drew got close enough for the cheek peck Anna threw her arms around him and crushed her lips to his. For a moment, Drew stood stiffly within her embrace then yielded to her and opening his mouth kissed her thoroughly back. When a few moments later they pulled apart, they stood looking at each other neither knowing what to say. Anna recovered first; she hadn't expected Drew's reaction to be that enthusiastic but was pleased and so she said "That was some kiss Drew, thank you."

Drew went pink around his ears as usual, "I—I—I—h—h—have been wanting to kiss you properly all along but wasn't sure if it would be alright."

Anna laughed, "I was beginning to think I was very ugly and unkissable," she said.

Drew shook his head "You are the most beautiful woman I have ever seen, that is why I stood staring at you when you came to lunch that day. I keep pinching myself that you actually come out with me."

Anna was quite frequently told she was beautiful by her clients but she never believed them because she didn't think she was but somehow Drew saying it made her feel ten feet tall.

"Thank you," she said again, then stepped close again and they once more kissed.

A few days later Drew asked her to go to the movies with him. It was the first time she had gone out with him midweek and not after football. Anna was pleased to go and so a new routine started and they would go out somewhere mid-week too.

Mary told Anna that both herself and her parents were pleased that Drew had found himself a girlfriend at last and Anna though not feeling very serious about their friendship was happy too. Eventually she took Drew home to meet her family and they all got on well.

Chapter 9

When they had been going out about seven months though, Anna began to feel their relationship was stalling. Drew would kiss her passionately but never more than that and they always did exactly the same things. It was summer now and Drew played cricket so he wouldn't be finished early as he was when playing football but other than that everything stayed the same. So one evening Anna decided once more to take things into her own hands and when the cricket match was over she would invite Drew back to her little flat and she would cook him a meal. She wasn't a bad cook as it happened and put a lot of thought and effort into it.

She got the feeling Drew was a little reluctant to come but said yes he would and Anna said she wouldn't come to the match as she wanted to cook up a storm. Really she found cricket pretty boring but went for Drew's sake and usually hid a book in her bag. In truth she didn't really know what she wanted but just knew if things stayed the same she would get bored. She was in her twentieth year but was immature emotionally. She had her own business as she had long since paid Vincent back and was very good at what she did but in her personal life she was very different and lacked confidence and to hide her insecurities would come over as being brash and loud.

Drew was late arriving but when he came in the door he held a rather wilted bunch of flowers in his hand and thrust them at Anna. She pecked him on the cheek. "Thank you, come and sit. Are you hungry?"

She had prepared a totally cold meal because of the uncertainty of the time Drew would arrive. However, with forethought, it was delicious, and Drew seemed to thoroughly enjoy himself. He was in good form as his team had won and regaled Anna with stories of the players and their lives that he knew. Anna had heard much of it before but listened patiently.

Finally, Drew ran out of steam and said he had to be going. "Don't go yet. In fact, you don't need to go at all," said Anna boldly; with that, she put her arms round Drew's neck and began to kiss him fiercely. Drew responded kissing her back with passion, his hands were rubbing her back but then his right hand found its way under her shirt and Anna shivered with delight as she felt his hand on her bare flesh. For her part, she pulled his shirt out from his jeans and started to explore his body gently. Drew was rubbing his hand gently over the top of her bra when Anna, breaking away for a moment, said, "I will undo my bra."

Drew immediately moved away from her and, rubbing his hand over his face, said, "I am sorry, Anna, I don't know what came over me."

"What do you mean 'sorry' you needn't be sorry I want this, I—"

"Anna, I want you too, but I am not quite ready to make a commitment to you, quite apart from anything else I haven't enough money saved to rent a place let alone buy anywhere."

Anna stared at him, she was didn't know what to think or say! Was he saying he loved her and wanted to marry her or what, and what about her feelings? She wasn't sure what she actually felt, she knew that she enjoyed his company but also knew that they had somehow got into a rut in their relationship. It was the same week in and week out and she was bored, getting into bed with Drew was her way of changing things but it seemed he didn't want that. She said the first thing that came into her head, "You could move in here with me if you want."

Drew rubbed his hand over his face then looked at Anna with a slight frown on his face. "No, Anna, I want to do this right, I love you but I won't live with you until I can make you my wife nor will I take advantage of you physically. I am sure you understand."

Trouble was Anna didn't really understand she was bored with the way things were with them and felt they were stagnating. She was trying to move their relationship along and anyway she didn't want to get married. She knew she didn't want to spend the rest of her life with Drew he was just a very good friend, fun to be with and maybe he would have been a fun lover now she had decided to trust a man again. That wasn't going to happen now.

Anna felt suddenly angry both with herself and with Drew, why did it have to be like this? "Just go, Drew, just go before I say something I shouldn't."

"Anna," Drew opened his arms and stepped towards her "Anna, it doesn't have to be like this. Please don't be hurt or angry. I just don't want to rush into anything and regret it afterwards or upset you."

"Bit late for that now, just go." Anna stepped back away from him.

Drew stood looking at her for a few moments then shrugging, opened the door. He stood in the doorway a few more minutes looking longingly at Anna but he could see she was angry and finally left. Anna got hold of the door and slammed it shut. Then she went into her bedroom and threw herself on the bed and burst into tears of anger and frustration.

As it was Monday the next day, she knew she would have to see Mary and worried what they would say to each other. Mary was very upfront and immediately said to Anna, "I gather you and Drew had a bit of an argument last night. He is such a nut, my brother, and very old fashioned in his ideas. Are you OK?" Anna nodded, not trusting herself to speak. She was, after all, very fond of Drew and hated the fact they had had a disagreement.

"Trouble is Drew spent a lot of time with my dad's dad and he was a very serious and straight laced man, and I suspect some of those ideas rubbed off. Please cut him a bit of slack I am sure he thinks the world of you."

Anna nodded then changed the subject, not feeling like going any further with the conversation just now. In time they would settle their differences but it was never the same and they gradually drifted apart. On Anna's part she felt rejected and it was a familiar feeling for her that she couldn't quite seem to shake off.

Chapter 10

On a business level, though, Anna found that she was very good at what she did and as time went on her business grew, so she was actually employing people, and after a while she started her own catering section to compliment her party format. Although she was a good cook she wasn't a professional but knew what was needed and managed to find a good team to work for her. As mostly parties were held at the end of the week or weekends, her chef and his team were able to do other work too, so everyone was happy. Many of her consignments were now in London and in 1981 Anna moved her whole operation to the capitol. Her family told her they would miss her, though in truth she didn't see much of them. She hadn't the same relationship with Silas as he and June, having got married, now had two small children and the farm kept Silas busy. The same went for her father and as they had bought more land, life was hectic. Marie and Anna still weren't that close, maybe Anna sometime thought they were too alike. In her private life Anna was very lonely and the fear of rejection made it difficult for her to form a close relationship with anyone, male or female. She had a few lovers but nothing serious, as she was so beautiful she wasn't short on offers but always held people at arm's length.

She found life very busy in London not just from a business point of view but on every level, and a part of her longed to return to her roots and the countryside, she always seemed to be turning down invitations to this and that and found the whole place exhausting.

She had been in London six months when she was asked to put on and host a huge corporate drinks party at a big new venue that had just opened in the west end. She explained very patiently to the client that she didn't actually 'host' parties; that was the client's job. What she did was to organise everything else they may need; decorations, usually flowers, waiters, caterers, drinks, microphones, chairs tables in their place the whole thing so all people had to was turn up. "Well," said the client, a Mr Thoughgood, "I need you there greeting people as they enter."

Anna sighed. "I did explain to your secretary that I will be there but behind the scenes, I am always around just in case of mishaps."

Mr Thoughgood huffed and puffed, and in the end Anna agreed to stand just inside the door to direct anyone that needed help though she couldn't for the life of her see why.

The evening was warm as it was mid-summer so Anna had on one of her favourite dresses which was lime green, a wonderful colour on her. Apart from green earrings she had no other decoration nor did she need it as she looked stunning as always.

It was mostly men at this party which Anna knew would be the case, a few had brought their wives, most of whom ignored Anna with studied indifference as they weren't really too sure they wanted their husbands fraternising with such a beautiful girl. At last the queue of people died down. Anna had greeted quite a few people who had stopped to speak to her, one or two that she had met before at various functions. She had on new shoes which were very high and her toes were beginning to hurt. Just as she thought the last person had come through the door another man arrived. He was tall, with very blonde hair almost white and piercing blue eyes. He looked like a Norse God, Anna found herself thinking; he was very arresting to look at and Anna found herself just staring at him as he held out his hand, she took it automatically. There seemed a frisson pass through her as he held her hand firmly in his. "Pleased to meet you, Anna," he said in a deep cultured voice.

Anna was immediately on the back foot, he seemed as if he knew her but she knew she had never met him before, he was unforgettable. "Likewise," she managed to say.

"My name is Karl and I have been looking forward to meeting you, I have heard great things about you." He was still holding her hand.

Anna pulled her hand away, her heart was jumping around all over the place, he was so good looking and the way he was looking at her made her feel weak at the knees. "Oh, from whom?" she managed to say. She felt breathless.

"Oh, many people, come let me get you a drink, what would you like?"

"I don't normally drink when I am working but a small glass of white wine would be nice, thank you." Anna had recovered from her initial flustered feeling and decided to go with whatever this man wanted to talk about as it seemed he wanted to talk about something, why else would he be offering to get her a drink. It was normal for clients to approach her at events she had put on to book something that they wanted to her to do for them. However, that was usually at the end of the evening or day not at the beginning.

As they made their way through the throng of people, Anna felt his hand in the small of her back guiding her along, it sent tingles up her spine. She was greeted by several people she knew as was Karl but he didn't stop or let her stop until he had found a waiter with a drinks tray. There was a choice of juice, wine or champagne, without asking her for her preference Karl handed her a glass of champagne. He raised his glass. "Here's to you Anna, so pleased to meet you." Somewhat startled by his toast Anna clinked glasses with him and sipped her drink.

Karl then started to ask her questions about her business and Anna relaxed; this was familiar ground and she lost her reservations that had surfaced earlier. She had felt strangely out of control and that was something she hadn't felt for a long time. The evening passed in a flash, Anna had really enjoyed herself and for a while had almost forgotten she was on duty. Suddenly she realised that people were leaving and she had a lot to supervise on the clearing up front to do.

"Sorry Karl, it's been great talking to you but I must get back to my staff and make sure everything is done properly," she said.

"Of course, I will see you tomorrow." He bent his head and gave her a quick peck on the cheek and before she had a chance to say anything or react he was gone striding though the door and away.

Anna, her heart back in flutters and her stomach full of butterflies, stared after him, she didn't know what to make of that.

"Ah, there you are." Mr Thoughgood was at her side. "A very successful evening my dear, thank you, here's a little extra for you and your staff." He thrust a bulky envelope into her hand. "I see you caught up with Karl too, very good, very good." Anna was by this time completely flummoxed and didn't recover enough to ask him what he meant by that before he too disappeared.

Later that night as she lay in bed memories of Paul came back, it was more to do with the way her stomach did strange flip flops and the feeling of being out of control. I won't let that happen again she told herself as she drifted off to sleep.

The next morning, Anna was woken by the front door bell ringing loudly. She groaned and rolled over. It was only eight thirty for goodness sake, who on earth was that. Stumbling out of bed and into her dressing gown she opened the door and was about to tell off whoever it was to be greeted by a young girl with an enormous bunch of red roses in her hands. "Anna Simpson?" Anna nodded, not trusting herself to speak, she guessed what was coming, "These are for you, then." The girl passed them over.

Anna, clutching the roses to her, shut the door and leant against it, never before had she had such a bouquet it was enormous and tied up with ribbon and lovely coloured paper. She went into her tiny kitchen and with slightly shaky hands undid the bow. Attached was a tiny envelope with a card inside. Anna took it out and read "To the woman of my dreams, I have waited all my life for you -Karl."

With her mind and heart racing Anna found several different containers to put the flowers in, there were so many she didn't have anywhere enough vases. Then she had a shower and tried to eat some breakfast but was too wound up and unsettled. She went back to the bathroom and cleaned her teeth. She had pulled on an old t-shirt and jeans, now she wondered if she should change in case Karl followed his roses and maybe put on makeup. She took off her jeans and was still debating what to wear when the doorbell rang, in a panic she pulled her jeans on again and rushed to the door. There stood Karl immaculate and suave as he had been the night before, "Anna," was all he said before he stepped through the door and swept her into his arms, his mouth came down on hers and he kissed her with such passion, she thought she would never breathe again. She found herself responding, it was lust and animal instinct, she knew that but she had never wanted anything so much in her life but to feel him inside her, to have him hold her, kiss her all over and to kiss him back to give him all the physical love she could.

Arms around each other and kissing almost frantically they somehow ended up in the bedroom. Anna wasn't sure when she made the decision to let him make love to her it wasn't a conscious thought, she just knew she wanted to feel his naked body against hers to feel his hands caressing her to be made love to completely without reservation. At one point he stopped and looking down at her with those blue dazzling eyes, he said, "Anna, I have wanted you all my life, be mine forever and love me always as I will love you."

Anna had an orgasm for the first time in her life soon after that and it amazed her and delighted her, she had no idea that love making could be so wonderful.

Karl rolled off her and then lay beside her looking at her. "I didn't plan for that to happen like that but you make me behave in strange ways you are so beautiful. I have been looking for you all my life, you are everything I have ever dreamt of. I seem to lose control of my body and my thoughts when I am with you."

Anna lay there beside him looking at his strong body and very blonde hair and his incredible blue eyes. "You have exactly the same effect on me," she whispered and with that, she started to caress his belly gently working her way downwards. This time they took it more slowly savouring every caress, every kiss. Anna sat astride him and found new heights of pleasure in love making, that she didn't know were possible

When finally they were both spent, Anna sat up suddenly; this was where Karl said goodbye and walked out she was sure, she felt her heart would break if he did. Was this to mean she loved him, they had only just met how could that be?

She sat on the edge of the bed with her back to him and tears started to roll silently down her cheeks, the next minute she felt Karl's arms around her. "Whatever is the matter, was it so bad?"

Anna shook her head. "Of course not, I just think you will walk out the door saying thanks for that and be gone for ever."

Karl scrambled off the bed and knelt in front of her. "My silly beautiful girl, I will be by your side for ever, didn't you hear me say I have been looking for you all my life. I will never let you go, you are mine now and for always."

With that he edged nearer and gently started to caress her breast and all thoughts again fled from Anna's mind.

Later they got dressed, Karl insisting they went out for lunch although Anna had said she would cook something. Because Karl looked so smart Anna dressed up more than she perhaps would have done, she assumed they would go to one of the restaurants not too far away that were decent enough but not that up market. However, Karl borrowed her phone and called a cab telling her that was how he had come as he wasn't sure what the parking was like in this part of London. She didn't hear where he told the driver to go when she was getting into the back, so was again completely thrown when they drove up to the Dorchester. It soon became clear the concierge knew Karl and so did the head waiter taking them to Karl's "usual" table.

After they had sat down and ordered their food and drinks, Anna said what had been on her mind from the minute they had arrived.

"I see you make a habit of coming here with your conquests, turns out I am one of many." She felt betrayed but was trying to hide it. After all, she hardly knew him, the fact they had just had amazing sex didn't give her any rights but she still felt jealous and hurt.

"Anna, my beautiful Anna," said Karl looking deep into her eyes, "How many times will I have to tell you that you are mine and I am yours and always will be from last night onwards? Yes, when I was seeking my ideal woman, I bought a few here but nothing serious. I mostly bring clients here hoping if I spoil them a little, they will buy from me."

"But what is it that you do?"

"I buy and sell antiques, all over the world."

"Oh really?" Anna leant forward, she was genuinely interested; much of the furniture and things she had grown up with had been passed down through the family and while her brothers had always taken them for granted, Anna had always loved them and used to make up stories that she thought they could have told when she was a little girl. She was an outdoors lover but hadn't minded polishing and dusting the antiques that everyone in the family took for granted. "What sort of antiques furniture, ornaments, paintings, what?"

Karl looked at her in surprise "Do you really want to know or are you being polite?"

"I really want to know; I grew up surrounded with old things, I love them so tell me all about what you sell, how you get them, do they want restoring, where do you sell them, have you a shop, everything."

"Wow, hold your horses, you are full of surprises. I never would have guessed all this. Well first of all, I don't have a 'shop' I have a showroom just off the Tottenham Court Road and I specialise in furniture but if I see the right thing then I do have some paintings but it's a very different area to furniture. Ornaments, not really, and clothes, not at all, they are very few and far and don't survive, and anyway again not really my field. We could go to the showroom after if you really are interested if you would like to."

"Oh, yes please, I can't wait; it would be fab thanks, ooh how exciting."

Their food arrived and as they were eating Anna bombarded Karl with questions about his business. To start with he was brief with his answers still not quite believing her interest but when she started to really probe into the running of the business how it worked, and all about the furniture itself then he became more open with his answers.

Their lunch finished. Karl, again, called a cab and took Anna to his Showroom. It was in a large imposing Georgian building which had at some point been someone's house. Anna sucked in her breath as they walked through the entrance. The whole of the ground floor had been opened out to make one huge space which in turn was set out in sections for different rooms in a house. Sitting room, dining room, hallway, bedroom; it was very cleverly done. "I have a good assistant who has a good eye for colour and design." Karl said. "She is also my secretary and general organiser."

Again Anna felt a stab of jealousy but mentally stamped down on it, however, Karl must have read her mind because he then said, "She is in her fifties so no competition to you. Come, I will take you upstairs. I have something to show you."

At the far end of the showroom was a big screen and behind it was a door which led to stairs. There was also a big office, a kitchenette and, later Anna was to discover, a small bathroom. Karl led the way upstairs and opened a door with a spy hole in it at the top. Anna gasped; she was stunned by the luxurious apartment they had just walked into. "Welcome to my home." Karl gave a mock bow.

Anna didn't know what to say she just stared and stared at her surroundings and also at Karl; it was the most sumptuous place she had ever seen. He smiled at her stunned expression, then led the way through the lounge to a beautiful kitchen then on to a small hallway and into a large bedroom with an enormous bed. All the floors except for the kitchen were covered in deep-gold coloured carpets, although the carpet in the bedroom was paler and the general decoration throughout the flat was subtle rather than too bright and garish. Next to the bedroom was a huge en-suite.

"I think you need a little rest now," said Karl, steering her towards the bed and moments later Anna found herself being made love to again very thoroughly.

It was the early evening before they finally surfaced. "Hungry?" said Karl.

Anna was surprised to find she was, in spite of the big lunch she had eaten. Karl wandered through to the kitchen and rummaged in the huge fridge and came up with a carton of eggs. He hadn't bothered to put any clothes on and Anna followed him but she pulled on the top she had been wearing. Karl looked round at her

"Take that off, no-one can see you, only me, and you are far too beautiful to cover yourself up, take it off, please."

Anna felt suddenly uncomfortable and somehow vulnerable but she took it off and Karl smiled, "That's my girl now you are in for a treat, scrambled eggs Karl style with smoked salmon."

The scrambled eggs were indeed very good then after they had eaten Anna looked at the time and was shocked to see how late it was getting. "I have to go home," she said. "I have a million and one things to do. Can you call me a cab please?"

"No, I will take you back, don't worry, relax, we will get dressed, and I will have you home in a jiffy."

Shortly afterwards Karl led Anna back down stairs and instead of going through the showroom he led her further down a small passageway and on opening a door Anna found they were in a garage in which there were two cars one a small hatch back and the other was a Porsche.

It was the Porsche Karl went to saying, "I will take you home in style."

Anna sat watching the streets of London flash by and wondering what had happened to her, it was like a dream, an amazing dream but a dream nonetheless.

Chapter 11

The next morning, Anna awoke feeling somehow stiff but languid and a bit out of sorts. "Too much sex," she said to herself out loud. Then blushed when she thought about it all. At one point, Karl had made her lay still while he just looked at her, all the time murmuring how beautiful she was. It had made her feel as she had felt later in the kitchen but she had soon been distracted and had almost forgotten that until now. Then there was his obvious wealth; what could he possibly see in her. They were streets apart socially. He came from a wealthy family and had had a public school education; was she just one of his conquests and he would dump her when he was tired of her? She remembered Paul and the way he had treated her. In some ways, it had been the same, Karl had stormed into her life and taken her and she had let him! Was she some kind of trollop that just gave in to any handsome man that came along? But she admitted to herself she was lonely and it had been satisfying and fun. She decided there and then that she would just make the most of it all while it lasted after all she had never enjoyed such a wonderful partner in bed and Karl had taken her to heights she didn't know existed. She didn't love him, did she? She wouldn't be hurt if he did throw her over, would she? How could she love him when they had only just met? There was a tiny voice in her head though that said she would be very hurt when he did tire of her.

She was just dressing when the phone rang and Karl's deep cultured voice was ringing in her ears. She was so pleased to hear him after her misgivings that she hardly took in what he was saying. "Dinner. I will pick you up and then you can stay here tonight. Bring anything you need; make-up, whatever," he was saying.

"Yes, yes, OK," Anna hardly took it in; she was still glowing from yesterday and the fact he had rung her so early and couldn't wait to see her.

So it was that Anna stayed the night and the next night, and it wasn't long before it was every night and more and more of her belongings found their way into Karl's flat. Anna still kept her days free even though Karl wanted her to spend more time with him during the day too, but she still had a business to run and pointed out to him that he had to too. "Easier for me. I just delegate," he said.

However, that wasn't quite true and after a few weeks when Anna had come into his life Karl had to knuckle down again and start to entertain clients as that was how he made many of his sales, especially to Americans. Many rich Americans would come over particularly to see Karl as his reputation had spread far and wide. He had done extremely well as he was still in his late twenties. Being from a family with a distant royal in the past certainly helped though as yet Anna didn't know this. What's more the family had fled from Prussia just before the First World War, more to preserve their wealth than any other reason.

Karl was delighted and thrilled though to find Anna had a real interest in his business and took great enjoyment in showing her his stock and instructing her with all the insights of the different periods and types of furniture. She was a very quick learner and very bright, so she continually surprised Karl with the things she remembered and knew from their conversations.

"I'll have to take you into partnership," he joked. "You will soon know as much as me! By the way, keep the weekend after next free. I have a surprise for you."

"Sorry Karl, but I am going home to see my family that weekend, you could come too if you would like to," Anna added shyly. She had been trying to pluck up courage to ask him as she was aware that they were socially poles apart and she was afraid it would end their relationship once he realised that her father was an ordinary farmer. Also, it was her birthday that weekend. It hadn't been at the weekend for a long time and she had booked to go home in her mind months ago.

"But it is very important to me that you come with me. I have it all planned. Please, my darling Anna, don't let me down."

Anna didn't know what to think or do. She didn't want to hurt Karl's feelings, and she was intrigued to know what the surprise was. Maybe she could go home another time? But then why not see her family; she hadn't seen them in ages and June had twins a couple of months ago, and Anna wanted to see them again; they were so sweet.

"Come with me and meet my family," she tried again.

"Anna, dear Anna." Karl wrapped his arms around her and nuzzled her neck then started to nibble her ear lobe, after that her thoughts became very jumbled as her body responded. "Please my darling girl, just for me, please. I beg you come with me instead." Then his hands slid under her top and found their way inside her bra. At this point all coherent thoughts flew out of Anna's head and she whispered, "Yes."

Later that evening she rang home and told her mother she would be home in a few weeks' time and was bringing someone with her as Karl had agreed to visit with her the next time she went. Time flew by as Karl in particular was very busy with clients and Anna had a series of parties to organise. Although it was still July many people were thinking ahead to Christmas and some offices seemed to have a competitive thing going where they were all trying to outdo each other.

Friday night, Anna's birthday was the next day. Anna arrived at Karl's flat only to be told they would have to go back to her flat as there would be things she would need as they were going away for the weekend. Anna still hadn't mentioned it was her birthday but it was hard to hide it when they got back there as there were the cards around her family had sent her.

Karl didn't seem at all surprised by this and finally admitted he knew and that was why they were going away and she would need her passport.

"Please tell me where."

"I suppose you will know in a few hours anyway so yes, I will tell you; Paris."

"Ooh how romantic, thank you." Anna kissed him fiercely.

Anna thought they would be going by road and ferry maybe but no they flew by a private jet which it turned out belong to a friend of Karl's family and who had loaned it and the pilot for the flight to and from Paris.

Anna was so excited she was nearly beside herself. They were staying in a small private hotel near Montmarte and Karl had arranged for dinner to be served in their room. Anna was a little disappointed by this as Paris was just outside waiting to be explored! However she said nothing and the dinner was excellent, so was what followed afterwards and Anna fell asleep in Karl's arms with a contented expression on her face. The next morning Anna was woken to a champagne breakfast in their room along with a huge bunch of red roses. Sometime later they went exploring, though, of course Karl knew Paris well so it was more showing Anna round. They did several touristy things, Arc de Triomphe, Eiffel Tower, Notre Dame then they had a leisurely lunch before Karl announced they were going shopping.

"Shopping, what shopping?" said Anna, who, though knew how to dress smartly for her job, clothes weren't really top of her list.

The next thing she knew she was in a huge department store and Karl seemed to have taken charge of everything. He had the assistants running hither and thither finding dresses, shoes, handbags, coats, trouser suits, tops, lingerie, and Anna was expected to try on this and that and he was very sure what he liked and didn't like. Anna started to object and was horrified by the amount of money that Karl seemed to want to spend on her but he wouldn't listen and over rode her objections. He had good taste as did Anna and at least they agreed what suited her and what didn't.

"I can't accept all this Karl, I can't. It's far beyond a birthday present, it's a whole new wardrobe!" Anna said in a low voice not wanting to cause him or herself embarrassment.

"My sweet girl, of course you can, just to please me. I am so happy buying these things for you. Please don't make me unhappy, please just accept them. I can afford it, I promise."

Anna shifted uncomfortably from foot to foot, now clad in designer shoes. "Put it like that, I suppose I will," she said but still felt very uncomfortable and somehow slightly scared of the implications of it all.

Finally, they set off back to the hotel surrounded by parcels and packages. They, of course, had a cab but it was still a squeeze to fit both themselves and the parcels in the car which was quite roomy.

When they got back, Anna showed her appreciation the only way she could think of which ended up making them late for the restaurant that Karl had booked. They then went on to a night club but by this time were both so tired that they didn't stay long.

The next morning, again dressed in her new clothes, they went to the Louvre and spent a very happy few hours there looking at all that was on offer, including the Mona Lisa. Then it was time to get to the plane and fly home. Afterwards, Anna felt as if they had been on a different planet; it all seemed like an amazing dream. But, of course, she had a whole new wardrobe now to prove it wasn't a dream.

The following weekend Anna had a free day on the Sunday but a late night on the Saturday. It was another of Mr Thoughgood's drinks affairs when she asked Karl if he was going. He said no, which surprised her as everyone else was the same as before and she did think when the invitations went out she hadn't seen one to him. He had an unusual surname which was Von Herbert. She didn't really know the family history and though had asked Karl, he hadn't said much.

It was very late when she got to Karl's flat, and he was not happy. "Where have you been? I thought you would be home long before this. What kept you?"

Anna was very tired Mr Thoughgood could be difficult at the best of times. To make matters worse, a guest had knocked a waitress's arm and drink had been spilt on Mrs Thoughgood's dress. Anna had spent a long time soothing them both down and she was in no mood for Karl's questions.

"You know where I have been don't be silly," she snapped. "I am not in the mood for an inquest on my movements. I am going to have a shower and going to bed."

Karl leapt to his feet, his eyes a steely blue like shards of ice. "You will not until you explain yourself. What kept you?"

Anna felt a small shiver run up her spine, he looked so angry and it was all out of proportion but she held her ground. "You don't own me Karl, so please don't speak to me like that." Holding her head up high she marched into the bedroom and, getting undressed, got into the shower.

Moments later Karl appeared and got into the shower with her saying, "I am sorry my beautiful girl I was just so worried something awful had happened to you, please forgive me." While he was saying this he started to soap Anna's body and massage her shoulders. Anna immediately melted as he knew she would and soon afterwards she was lying beside him sound asleep, all anger gone.

Chapter 12

The next day Karl took her to meet his family. Anna was a pack of nerves. She knew they were very wealthy and couldn't for the life of her imagine that they would accept her. The house was indeed huge and built like a French chateau. A butler answered the door and called Karl 'Sir' and Anna 'Miss'. He showed them into an enormous drawing room.

A man and woman both rose from their seats to greet Karl and Anna. They were both tall and looking at his mother Anna could see the likeness, though not so much with his father. She had been shocked earlier when Karl had told her to call his mother Lady Charlotte and his father was Sir William. Anna wasn't sure whether or not to curtsy but Karl had laughed and said, "No, not to do that."

However, they were kind enough and did their best to make her feel welcome and at home asking her about her business and what sort of things she liked doing and what her interests were. They both seemed delighted to hear of Anna's enthusiasm for Karl's business and it wasn't too long before Anna relaxed a little. However, just as the butler announced that lunch was served a brown haired plain girl marched into the room. She stared at Anna then looking at Karl said in a waspish voice. "You didn't tell me you were bringing anyone with you, who is she?"

"Clare, don't be so rude in front of our guest, this is Karl's friend, Anna." Sir William was obviously embarrassed.

Anna, who had got to her feet, held out her hand. Clare ignored it and said, "Oh really," and turned away.

Now it was Karl's turn to be angry and those blue eyes turned to ice as Anna had once seen. "How dare you, you miserable creature. You will NOT snub my intended this way, apologise at once!"

For a few moments, Clare stared back angrily at her brother then shrugging muttered "Sorry," and swept out of the room again. The tension in the room was making it hard for Anna not to cry, she felt awful, had she caused all this, it was bad enough Karl's parents being upper crust but Clare's hostility was even worse, what was her problem if Karl's parents were nice and kind why wasn't Clare. What had Anna done to her?

The family gathered themselves together and taking Anna's arm Sir William said, "Don't worry my dear; poor Clare has many issues and some we can't help her with. She doesn't mean it."

Later when the dust had settled a bit and they were eating an excellent lunch Anna remembered what Karl had said to his sister; 'intended'. Did that mean he was going to propose? Surly not; she wasn't in his league, she would have to wait and see. Clare had disappeared and was not seen again. Anna didn't mind but did wonder what had happened to her after the confrontation. Later she asked Karl about his sister when they were driving home but he was very noncommittal and Anna eventually dropped the subject reasoning if he wanted to talk he would.

A short time later Anna took Karl to meet her family. She didn't really have to ask him; he invited himself, though she had to admit to herself she was very worried about it as again she realised they were in some respect poles apart.

Karl drove as he always seemed to when they went out in spite of the fact Anna said they could go in her car. She hardly drove these days as driving in London wasn't really necessary and she only had the car for going out into the country as she had to sometimes or to visit her family. She felt slightly embarrassed driving up to the farmhouse in the Porsche but couldn't do much about it. It was a big house and as everyone had left home except Silas, Marie and Tim had divided the house into two so the two families lived side by side. June seemed to get on well with Marie which was as well and of course now she had twins she was very pleased of Marie's help.

Anna was rather self-conscious as she opened the front door and led the way down the hallway towards the kitchen where she knew the family would be. It was late in the summer now but they hadn't quite finished harvest; however, both Tim and Silas had made an effort to be there to meet Karl though Silas would be going straight back to work as soon as he had eaten. Because of this he was still in his work jeans and shirt as Anna and Karl walked in. June and the twins were nowhere to be seen but Marie was busy cooking lunch, and Tim was hovering wanting to get back to work but under orders to meet Anna's 'new man' as the family had called him to themselves.

"Mum, Dad, Silas, this is Karl." Anna's voice sounded shrill in her ears, she was so nervous. Karl stepped forward and taking Marie's out stretched hand bent over it and kissed it, Anna stared at him in shock as did the two men and Marie who was overcome with embarrassment. Without missing a beat, Karl held out his hand to first Tim and then Silas who was by this time scowling slightly. "How absolutely thrilled I am to meet you at last, all of you," Karl said. "Anna has been hiding you from me for so long but here you all are at last." There was a moment of embarrassed silence then everyone spoke at once then June appeared with the twins, one on each arm. *At least he can't kiss June's hand,* Anna thought to herself, *whatever has got into him?* But Karl just nodded to June on Anna's introduction and then asked Marie if he could help her in any way, which flustered her even more than having her hand kissed.

Eventually they were all seated round the dining room table after more offers of help from Karl who insisted on carrying things through from the kitchen and even pulled Marie's chair out for her, something that he didn't always do for Anna nowadays though mostly he did. No sooner than they were seated than Karl cleared his throat and said that he would like to propose a toast to Marie for a delicious lunch and also to the family for making him so welcome. Again, after they had duly drunk a toast most of them in water, there was an awkward silence until Karl started to ask questions about the farm. Tim was on safe ground here and so, relaxed and started to talk at length about current wheat prices and the weather and harvest and for a while the two men carried the conversation.

It wasn't long before Silas said he must be getting back to the harvest field; he got up and kissed June, looked at his babies, who were both sound asleep in a big Moses basket nearby and winked at Anna while saying, "See you Karl." Anna jumped up and followed him out of the room. "Don't I get a hug from my big brother anymore?" she said, putting her arms around his neck. Silas looked down at her upturned face and bit back the words he wanted to say. He just gave her the biggest bear hug he could and said,

"Take care, little sis, and stay safe." With that, he was gone. Anna watched him stride across the farm yard with a frown. What was that supposed to mean? She shrugged and went back into the dining room. Tim was sitting looking bemused and Karl was talking to Marie about Anna; how great she was with the clients and also how good she was in all other areas. Anna felt alarmed, what was he saying? Surely he wasn't alluding to their sex life?

June saw Anna's face and said, "Shall we clear and get the dessert in, Marie? Poor old Silas will have to wait until tonight to have his."

"Yes, of course, let's do that." Marie looked relieved too, so the three women got up and cleared the plates and dishes from the main course. Just then one of the twins, a little boy called Harry, woke and June picked him up in a hurry before he woke his brother Phil. Anna helped her mother in the kitchen stack dishes in the dishwasher and get the dessert assembled together. Marie was even quieter than ever, Anna thought, but couldn't bring herself to say anything either. When they re-entered the dining room, they could sense tension; both men were looking angry but neither said anything and pudding was served. Karl again talking almost exclusively to Marie.

Anna was relieved when Karl had finished eating and standing said, "I think we will have to go as we both have papers to sort out ready for tomorrow and Karl has an important client during the morning to see."

Just then the second baby Phil woke up and started to cry. June had been nursing Harry all this while, "I'll take him." Anna came round the table and took Harry from June. Karl got to his feet,

"I thought we were making a move?" he said.

"Yes, but I must have a cuddle with at least one of my nephews, aren't they just adorable?" Anna moved towards Karl who took an involuntary step backwards.

"No doubt they are but I know nothing of babies and we really do have to be going," he said.

Reluctantly, Anna handed Harry to her mother, and bending down gave both a kiss. "Thanks Mum, lovely lunch." She turned to her father and gave him a huge hug. "Thanks Dad, see you two soon and you June."

"Yes, sure," replied June. Tim said nothing but sat there, looking sad. "You OK, Dad?"

"Fine, take care," Tim sounded gruff, and Anna saw a strange expression on his face as he turned away.

A few minutes later, they were driving away and Anna, who had been looking forward to seeing the dogs and walking around the old haunts, said to Karl, "Well, that was a brief visit. I don't think you liked my family much but then we aren't quite in your league, are we?"

Karl was gripping the steering wheel tightly and Anna realised he was trying to hold his temper in. "Don't be stupid, it's you who is important to me, not your family. You are mine and I am yours forever, how many times to I have to say it? Families don't matter, it's you and me that is important, no-one else." He sounded very angry.

"Well, what was this thing with kissing Mum's hand? It was overdone, and she was embarrassed, it was silly." Anna was on a roll now and couldn't stop.

Karl laughed suddenly, a funny mirthless sound. "You are jealous of your own mother! I don't believe it!"

"Jealous my foot. Of course I'm not jealous of my own mother. How stupid you are being. I didn't realise just how silly you are until now."

Karl clenched his jaw and said nothing more just drove faster until Anna started to feel scared and said, "Please slow down you will get a speeding fine or wrap this thing around a tree and kill us both."

"I thought you said I was silly and silly people do silly things like driving too fast." Karl's foot went down even further on the accelerator.

Anna was really scared now, "Please slow down, I'm sorry, I didn't mean it. Please slow down, please."

Karl glanced across at her and took his foot off the gas and immediately the car slowed, there was an exit coming up and as

Anna started to speak, he turned off the motorway and into a side road where finding a gateway, he stopped and turned off the engine. Anna again opened her mouth to speak but Karl put his mouth to hers and kissed her passionately. Drawing back, he said, "You are so beautiful when you are angry; I want to make love to you here and now." Then his hands started to find their way inside her clothing and it was some time before they resumed their journey, all thoughts of the quarrel forgotten.

Chapter 13

Anna was by now accompanying Karl on some of his trips around the country and abroad and when he met clients. She was certainly an asset, he found, as she could engage people in conversation about other things as well as the antiques and sometimes especially with overseas clients it was a huge help. Then Karl could get them back on track and they seemed more relaxed to the high prices that he liked to get for his stock. He didn't exactly overcharge people but he always wanted top price and often didn't take to kindly if people wanted to haggle. Anna was just so beautiful that the men would be eating out of her hand, the woman were more suspicious but they didn't come across women on their own buying or selling furniture very frequently. She was also becoming very knowledgeable herself and as art was more her thing they extended the number of art works that Karl had in stock. Anna took to studying her subject too.

The months flew by and it was almost Christmas. Anna was gradually coming to terms with the fact she couldn't run her business and play such a big part in Karl's. Karl was always on at her to give it up too. Finally she bit the bullet and told her employees that she was closing the firm. The assets weren't as good as they might have been because she had to an extent taken her eye off the ball. Then out of the blue she had a phone call from Karen.

"I hear you are selling up," she said without preamble. "I hear you have a rich boyfriend and don't need to work anymore."

Anna held her temper in check. "Well, whoever told you all that didn't get it quite straight as I am now working for said boyfriend and yes, the business is closing unless I find someone to buy me out, not that any of that is your business."

"Well, actually it might be." Karen suddenly sounded more conciliatory. "I split up with John and I am looking for something that I would enjoy doing. It was fun when we ran the business together, wasn't it? Dad says he will help me out if this is really what I want."

Anna allowed herself a wry smile. Good thing she was talking on the phone, she thought, Karen couldn't see her. "Well, shall we meet and discuss it then?" she said, instead of the thousand other things that sprang to mind. Actually, it would help her enormously as she could get rid of the business quicker this way as Karen could take on the bookings that were on the books even from a couple of weeks or so hence.

The two girls met at a coffee shop and tea room near the office as Anna insisted they did. If this didn't come off, she didn't want Karen poking around her office. Or making snide remarks within earshot of staff; she didn't trust her.

Karen had put on weight since Anna had last seen her and her hairstyle didn't do much for her either. As for Karen, she took in Anna's Louis Vuitton Handbag and shoes and Hermes scarf and designer coat and was green with envy. She had always been jealous of Anna's beauty and it surfaced again with a vengeance when she saw her. She curled her lip and almost said what a social climber Anna was but something stopped her and anyway she was here to buy Anna out if she could. Maybe it would lead to better things for her. So she smiled as sweetly as she felt able and told Anna she looked amazing and once they had ordered coffee they got down to the nitty gritty of organising the business and Karen buying it.

She was very surprised by the calibre of many of Anna's clients and soon came to realise that the business had grown considerably since she was part of it. She suddenly felt unsure; was she up to it? She ended up saying she would have to go back to her father and talk to him some more, she also was aware Anna wasn't asking as much for the business as she could get for it.

Having gone into the details she was just leaving when Karl, who knew Anna was there, walked in. Without a word he bent down and gave Anna a long kiss. Karen looked on in part embarrassment and in part curiosity. Anna was embarrassed but also used to Karl doing similar things. "Karl, this is Karen who may be buying the entertainment business. They shook hands and Karen said,

"Anna and I went to school together and we started this business together." She was gushing and she knew it. He was so wonderfully handsome and striking looking with his almost white hair and blue eyes, tall too; she liked tall men.

"Really? Yes, I think Anna mentioned it, please excuse us now, we have to go." With that he took Anna's arm and steered her towards the door. Anna looked back over her shoulder and mouthed sorry and the next minute they had disappeared outside. *I suppose I was leaving anyway*, thought Karen, *but what a strange man, maybe I don't envy Anna as much as I thought I did.*

For her part, Anna too was embarrassed at Karl's abrupt manner.

"That was a little bit rude, darling," she said as they walked away.

"Was it? I have been away from you three whole hours today and I needed you, you gorgeous creature. Anyway from what you have told me of her I don't rate her very highly."

"Maybe not, but hopefully she will buy the business and spare me some hassle."

"You realise this is our first Christmas together and I have plans. I hope you will like them," said Karl.

Anna stopped walking and looked at him. "I was planning on going home for Christmas. After all I want to see the children, you haven't met them yet but John has two lovely little girls then there are the twins, and Mum said that Peter has found himself a nice girlfriend at last. In any case what about you; won't you be seeing your family?"

Karl bent his head and kissed her. Anna had realised it yet but Karl's way of controlling Anna and getting his own way was by confusing her senses with desire. She had a big physical appetite and enjoyed love making enormously so she was easy to distract and afterwards very agreeable to his demands. "Let's go home and talk then," he whispered knowing full well he was going to take her to bed and subsequently get his own way.

This time his lovemaking was more intense than usual as he knew she really wanted to go home. Trouble was he was completely obsessed with Anna by now and the longer they were together, the deeper he sank.

Later he got what he wanted, and Anna agreed to go away with him though he wouldn't tell her where he was taking her. She rang her parents to tell them and Tim answered the phone. When she said she was going away with Karl and would pop down in the New Year, he made it plain he wasn't happy. "Oh Anna can't you come home? All the kids are looking forward to you being here, well not Silas's two they are too young but Mum and I and your brothers. Peter is bringing his girlfriend to meet us too."

Anna felt guilty but said, "Sorry Dad, it's all arranged. Karl says it a surprise."

"I bet he does, more money than sense, I reckon."

Anna hadn't heard her father criticise Karl outright before but knew he didn't like him. She decided to change the subject and told him that Karen's father had come up with the money to buy Anna out.

Tim was silent for a few minutes then he said, "Promise me one thing sweetheart; that you will invest that money carefully and keep it for a rainy day. Don't let anyone else touch it please."

"OK, Dad."

"Promise?" Tim sounded upset.

"I promise Dad. Dad, are you OK?"

"Yes. Sure." But to Anna's ears, he didn't sound it, and later she worried about it. When the money came through a few days before they went away, Anna immediately put it in a bond with her bank as she had promised her father. She had picked up that he didn't want Karl to be involved with the money though he hadn't exactly said so. The bond was for five years and the interest would just keep rolling over not be paid into her account. Karl by this time was paying her a wage and also buying her anything she wanted; she didn't need the money.

The day before Christmas Eve and Anna told Karl she needed to know what to pack, was it going to be a cold Christmas or a hot one. Hot was the answer, Anna was slightly disappointed as she liked the idea of snuggling up in a log cabin or some such. In any event she was very excited to find they were going to Thailand. It was a very exclusive resort and Anna sucked her breath in with wonder when she saw their apartment which was actually built like a log cabin in some ways though built for the heat not the cold and it was right on the beach. It was a very romantic setting.

Christmas Day Anna woke to Karl kissing her neck and stroking her tummy. "Happy Christmas sweetheart."

'"Happy Christmas." Anna couldn't quite wake up. Their flight had been delayed leaving Heathrow because of bad weather and she had been in a deep sleep. However, Karl seemed full of energy and soon had Anna awake and after early morning love making and a shower they went down to breakfast hand in hand. "When do you want your present?" asked Anna as they descended in the lift.

"Soon." Karl seemed rather tense. Anna was delighted when they stepped out of the lift into the reception area of the hotel; it was enormous and decorated beautifully with huge Christmas tree lights and even a small tableau with a stable scene. She had been too tired last night to take it all in. A member of staff who seemed to have been waiting for them came up and said, "Sir, this way please." Anna looked at Karl curiously but he still looking tense took her arm and they followed the young man through a large door into a small room again decorated with a Christmas theme. In the centre of the room was a table set for breakfast for two people and there was a small beautifully wrapped gift by one place setting. The young man indicated a buffet table to the side and then withdrew. There was a large curtain across the far end of the room and Anna realised there was gentle music coming from there, it sounded like live music, she didn't know the tune but it was gentle and romantic.

Karl held the chair by the gift out for her to sit down then instead of sitting himself went down on one knee and said "My darling beautiful Anna, will you be my wife?"

He had, of course, dropped the hint months back but Anna had put it at the back of her mind and certainly wasn't expecting it just now, she gasped with surprise and leaning forward breathed a quiet yes before putting her lips to Karl's.

They kissed for a moment then Karl drawing back said, "Open your gift please." Anna turned and took the gold paper of the little box, by now guessing what it was. Inside was a beautiful ruby and diamond ring, the ruby looked huge and was circled by the diamonds, Karl taking the ring from her placed it on her finger, it fitted! "Not a bad guess at size, was it?" he said, smiling at her!

"Now, I'm starving, let's eat. You will find lots to choose from, I arranged to have a buffet breakfast just the two of us but I think they may have over catered."

Sure enough they had and Anna was so excited that she found eating hard; however, she managed quite a big breakfast which was mostly Asian food. They both really enjoyed trying things that were new to them and lingered over their private breakfast for a long time. Anna kept looking and looking at her beautiful ring, she was so thrilled.

The day passed in a whirl, Anna rang her parents and spoke to just about everyone that was there. They had agreed not to say anything about their engagement until they got back, though Anna found it really hard to do.

Their holiday passed by in a blur of eating, swimming, lazing by the beautiful pool, walking on the beach nearby, making love, sleeping, eating; they were peaceful happy days and all too soon it was time to return home.

When they got back, they got straight into working again and arranged to go and see Anna's family the first full weekend they were back. Anna had bought lovely silk scarves for all the women in both families and also for Muriel the lady who ran the showroom downstairs. In fact she seemed on occasion to run the entire business but all decision making was Karl's. Anna had been wary of her to start with but the two had struck up a bond and Anna liked her more and more as she got to know her. After her friendship with Mary had fizzled, she hadn't really got close to any other woman outside her own family and she delighted in their friendship even though Muriel was a lot older.

So it was Muriel who first got the engagement news, she had immediately spotted the ring on Anna's finger. "Well, congratulations seem to be in order," she said and gave Anna a hug, then turning to Karl and hugging him, briefly said, "You have made a fine choice. Make sure you look after her."

Anna was rather surprised by her choice of words but Karl, grinning from ear to ear, said of course he would, what did she think and that was that.

When they got to the farm to tell Anna's family and catch up with Christmas presents and Christmas in general, Marie was over the moon and unlike her, gushed out her approval. June just said her congratulations, as did Silas. Tim looked very serious and merely shook Karl's hand and told Anna if that was what she wanted, then he was pleased for her. Anna was very disappointed but hid it as she didn't want anything to spoil the day. Later, after they had lunch, Tim got up from the table saying there was a cow not well and he wanted to check on her. As he left the room, Anna got to her feet saying she needed the toilet but in truth, she wanted to speak to her father alone. She caught up with him as he was putting his boots on.

"I get the feeling you aren't very pleased about my engagement," she said straight out.

Tim turned and looked at her several moments before replying, he was choosing his words carefully. "Anna, my dear, if it's what you want and you are sure, then I am pleased for you. You are old enough to know your own mind even though you haven't known him long. He just isn't what I want for you, but it's your choice."

Anna felt defensive. "What do you mean by that? What's wrong with Karl?"

Tim shrugged, not wanting to get into this argument any further but also wanting Anna to know his concerns. "I think he is very arrogant and probably very selfish too. I just hope he treats you well always, that's all." With that, he turned and walked away. Anna stood watching him go with a small frown, it wasn't like Tim at all to speak like that, he was mild mannered and very popular, and hardly ever said a bad word about anyone.

When she re-joined the others, Silas raised his eyebrows at her as he did when she was small and needed an ally for some scrape she had got into. She smiled at him to show him she was OK then turning to June offered to help with the twins who were being a bit fractious. Just then, voices sounded in the hallway and Peter came in with his girlfriend and introductions were made as Karl hadn't met Peter and of course, Anna hadn't met his girlfriend. She was small and very pretty with blonde hair and sparkling eyes. "I'm Jess," she said, holding out her hand.

Anna took to her at once but was rather surprised by Karl who hardly touched her hand and was quite curt with both Jess and Peter.

Tim came back and soon, everyone seemed to be talking at once and with the twins making their presence felt, it was very noisy for a time. Anna's ring was admired all over again and Anna wanted to know all about what stallions they had at the stud farm and what Jess did there, and how was Peter whom she hadn't seen for a very long time.

"ANNA," Karl's voice was very loud and suddenly there was silence. Everyone looked at him and he had the grace to look embarrassed. "Sorry, but I couldn't get your attention. We have to leave. I am expecting an important phone call from America and have to get back in time."

Anna was very surprised; this was the first she had heard of it but she wasn't about to say so in front of everybody. She stood up, "Sorry folks, we have to run. It was lovely meeting you, Jess, we will have to have a catch-up soon." She made her way round the room hugging and kissing everybody maybe more than she normally did.

Soon they were in the car speeding back to London. Karl suddenly let out a bark of laughter, "What's funny?" Anna asked.

"Well, if your brother marries this Jess girl, I will have a stable girl for a sister-in-law, I mean I ask you!"

A small worm of doubt curled itself around Anna's heart. "I didn't think you were a snob, Karl," she said quietly.

Karl glanced across at her briefly. "I was only joking, take no notice," he said.

Anna closed her eyes. She felt tired suddenly and an argument was the last thing she wanted so she let it go and it wasn't mentioned again.

Chapter 14

Karl was in a hurry to get married. He didn't see the point of a long engagement and so he pushed for a spring wedding. It was agreed in the end to have a registry office wedding as Karl's family were Catholic and Anna's Church of England, and it was obvious from the start there would be some friction which ever they chose so registry office seemed the way to go. So, Karl approached Westminster which was very near but also catered for celebrities only to be told they would have to wait months as it was all booked up. He got angry but to no avail, then his father stepped in and somehow got a slot on a Friday morning in early April. It was to be a very small affair. Karl, to Anna's surprise, hadn't really any friends, only business associates and then she realised she didn't have any real friends either. They were both loners. *Maybe,* she thought, *that is why we get on as well as we do, and maybe why we got together so quickly; we were both lonely.* When she said as much to Karl, he laughed it off, saying he was always too busy before but found he could make friends if he needed them easily enough.

Matthew and Sally who had a tribe of children were not able to come across from Canada but Anna's other siblings and her parents were coming, so were Kate and Vernon. Karl's parents who had been non-committal about their son's engagement were also coming. Karl had explained to Anna in the end that his sister had mental health problems and had been diagnosed with schizophrenia. She was on medication and was fine when she took it but sometimes didn't and then could be very difficult to deal with. She was invited but hadn't said whether or not she would be there. The only non-family member to be coming was Muriel, and Anna was very pleased she would be there.

Karl and Anna agreed to have a formal cocktail party for Karl's business associates in a few weeks after the wedding. As the business was very busy now that spring had come, they were only going away for a long weekend to a castle retreat in Ireland.

Anna was disappointed not to have bridesmaids but it was so last-minute and also, though she had a choice of nieces, she didn't want to upset anyone so none at all seemed a good option. Karl wasn't having a best man either as there wasn't anyone he wanted to ask. Although there were aunts, uncles and cousins, he didn't want to ask anyone else from his family. Anna was surprised but made no comment.

Anna had a problem getting a dress too; she flatly refused Karl's offer to get her a designer dress as she wanted to do this on her own or at least with her mum. However, they soon found that many dresses had to be ordered months ahead and buying one off the peg was difficult too. Anna, having had a miserable morning trying to sort something out, came back mid-afternoon and met Muriel in the showroom who said Anna looked like she needed a cup of tea.

"I do, thank you, it would be great. I just don't know what I am going to do. I can't find anything I like or if I do, either it will take months to organise or it doesn't fit or there is some issue or another." Muriel gave a little cough.

"I could make you one, if you like."

Anna looked at her in surprise. "You do dressmaking?"

"Yes, I love it but I don't get a chance to do much these days."

Anna knew that Muriel's husband had died young and she had a daughter who lived in the States but didn't really know about her life outside the Antique business.

A few minutes later, Anna and Muriel were deep in discussion about wedding dresses when Karl came back from a meeting with an American client who wanted a certain sort of sideboard and had exact ideas on what he wanted. Karl would have to go on a sideboard hunt. "What are you two plotting?"

Anna turned and smiled. "Wedding dress sorted, Muriel will make me one."

Karl frowned. "I don't want you wearing a homemade dress; that won't do at all."

Anna was shocked that he could be so rude to Muriel and so snobbish and hurtful too, her temper got the better of her.

"How can you be so rude to Muriel and myself without even knowing what you are talking about? All the smart suits Muriel wears to work are things she has made. You owe both of us an apology and you better make it quick or the wedding is off."

Karl reddened; he wasn't used to being put in his place like that and it was only the second time Anna had really stood up to him. He stood clenching and unclenching his fists for a moment. His hands were by his sides but Muriel noticed the movement and was about to step into the standoff when Karl said, "Very well. Sorry Muriel. Anna, do as you will." With that, he went upstairs and left the two women staring after him.

"I don't want to cause a rift between the two of you Anna, forget it, dear," said Muriel, looking very disappointed.

"I will not, you will make my dress or I am not marrying Karl," said Anna robustly.

Later, when she went upstairs, Karl seemed his usual self and Anna decided not to push it so no more was said.

For the next couple of weeks, Anna and Muriel had great fun; Muriel brought her sewing machine over to the office and turned a corner into a dressmaking corner. It was decided to do it this way as she could sew when things were quiet in the showroom. Karl wasn't happy about the arrangement but kept his peace. It was lucky there was room in the office and after a few days he became fascinated with the emerging dress. Then he was told it was bad luck to see the dress and had to stop peeking in on what was happening.

When the wedding day came, he was completely amazed by how lovely the dress was and how stunning his bride looked. Anna and her family stayed in a small hotel nearby the night before as of course it was bad luck otherwise for Karl and Anna to be together the night before their wedding. Neither of them really believed it but went along with tradition.

Everyone gasped when Anna walked into the wedding room on her father's arm. The dress clung to her body almost like a second skin but the skirt flowed out from her hips in soft folds and trailed along the floor behind her. It was all the softest silk and creamy rather than snow white which complimented

Anna's skin; she still had a slight tan from their holiday, her lovely auburn hair was curled loosely on top of her head with a single cream rose at the side of her head. She carried a bouquet of pale yellow roses.

Anna felt quite emotional when she made her vows. She loved Karl, of course she did, and they made a lovely couple, everybody said so. Why then was this strange feeling that sometimes she didn't really know him, but then again it was less than a year and she was a normal nervous bride and it was a big day so it was normal to feel like this, of course it was.

When the registrar told Karl he could now kiss his wife, he did so, then whispered, "You are truly mine now, mine—now and forever." He sounded so serious and passionate about it that Anna gave an involuntary shiver.

The rest of the day passed in a blur for Anna. The wedding breakfast was held at the Grovenor House Hotel. Photographs were taken, wedding cake cut, and the speeches were made. Afterwards, she felt it had all been a dream—a lovely dream but a dream nonetheless. Some memories would stand out like Marie crying because she said Anna looked so beautiful. Anna couldn't really remember her crying like that before; Silas wrapping his arms around her saying, "Please look after yourself, little sis," and Sir William's speech welcoming her into their family. Clare had come to the wedding, she was very reserved but held out her hand and, giving Anna a hard look, said, "I suppose we should be friends but Karl wouldn't like that so we won't be. I wish you luck, you are a brave woman." With that, she turned away and went to sit beside her mother. Anna shrugged thinking Clare was one very odd person and not one she was likely to see very much.

They were flying straight out to Ireland that evening and so went upstairs to a room that had been reserved for Karl's parents for two nights to change. No sooner than the door was closed Karl picked up Anna and almost threw her onto the bed. He started to pull at her dress. "Karl, stop, you'll tear it and we haven't time for this now," Anna exclaimed.

Karl by this time had given up trying to undo her dress instead pushed up the skirt and Anna realised he was serious. "I want to make you my wife now," was all he said.

Anna didn't enjoy it at all; it was so rushed and Karl wasn't at all the kind lover. She knew he was only interested in claiming her as his, and it was over very quickly.

He hadn't spoken and nor did Anna until shortly afterwards when they were both dressed in their going away clothes. Karl said, "Sorry if I took you by surprise, sweetheart, but I just wanted to make you mine so much, I couldn't wait any longer."

Anna mustered a smile though she didn't feel much like it just then; she felt used for the first time since they had been together. "Yes, it was rather a surprise, please give me more warning next time!"

Everybody gathered round to see them off. Anna threw her bouquet to Clare but she didn't catch it or attempt to so it landed on the floor. June picked it up and smiled at Anna encouragingly. When her father hugged her goodbye, she was shocked to see tears in his eyes. "Good luck, darling girl," he said.

Goodbyes over, they sped away in a chauffeur-driven car that belonged to Sir William. Three hours later, they were met at Cork airport by another car and driven to the castle which was very beautiful and secluded. It was a castle that had been a family home but was now a small exclusive hotel. They had an entire floor to themselves. Anna wondered how much it cost but didn't say anything as she had already learnt not to say too much about money and the cost of things. Karl thought it was bad manners on her part if she questioned him and sometimes she felt shocked how much he made on his furniture, so money talk was out of bounds pretty much.

They had a good time though Karl seemed to Anna to be more possessive of her attention than before they were married but then again she thought it was perhaps her imagination. The short honeymoon was over in a flash and they returned to their busy life in London.

Chapter 15

They settled into the swing of their life again very quickly meeting clients and Anna got busy organising the list for the party they were to give to clients and business people that they had planned. Karl gave Anna a list of everyone he wanted or thought they should invite. A day or so later Anna said, "Karl, Mr Thoughgood is not on the list if he hadn't invited you to that reception we wouldn't have met don't you think he should get an invite?"

Karl looked up from the paper he was reading with a scowl on his face. "God no, I can't stand the man," he said.

"But we met because of him," Anna protested.

"No, no. I had seen you at something else weeks before and enquired all about you and your business and got old Thoughgood to ask me along so we could meet." Karl returned to his reading.

Anna stood staring at his bowed head, she felt the rug had been taken from under her feet, it was all contrived, and Karl had been watching her?

"You mean you were watching me?"

"Not exactly, I just kept tabs on what was what so we could get introduced." Karl was still slightly distracted by the invoice he had in his hand. "What's the matter?" He suddenly realised Anna was looking angry.

"How devious of you and underhand, why not just come up to me and say hello, not check me out like some, some piece of furniture."

Karl got to his feet and coming round the table leant down so he was staring straight into her eyes. "You are being ridiculous now. I wanted to make sure you were a free woman, I didn't want to rush in and make a fool of you or myself, that's all. Nothing sinister in that, is there?"

Anna felt slightly mollified but was still unhappy with the thought that Karl checked her out like a prize horse or cow making sure her credentials were good.

Looking into his eyes though he seemed genuinely surprised that she was upset and she thought maybe she was overreacting so she decided to say no more and the subject was dropped.

Anna was soon too busy to worry about it all; the party came and went, it was a great success mostly thanks to Anna's previous business it was the first time she had had a personal stake in a party and she found it more stressful than she expected. She was glad when it was over and felt really tired when finally she got into bed. Karl was already there and to Anna's surprise he was already asleep which was also a first. She felt relived as she was very tired too.

Anna now threw herself into Karl's business as much as he would allow but she soon found that he had already let her go as far as he was prepared to. He was happy for her to accompany him when he took trips away and meet clients though she often felt that she was required as decoration more than for anything else and he sometimes didn't take too kindly if she expressed an opinion. She had thought they might continue to explore the art side of the business like she had started to before they were married but Karl said one day that he didn't want to get too involved with that either. The rest of the time he was happy for her to hang around the showroom with Muriel but she wanted something positive to do. When she said as much to him, Karl told her to go shopping which, of course, wasn't Anna at all.

For a time, she put up with it but one day she told Karl she was going home to see her folks. Karl wasn't happy. "Why do you want to go, just now if you wait I will come with you."

"Karl, I haven't enough to do. I am bored. Besides, I haven't seen my family since the wedding."

"I want you to wait until I can come too." Karl started to look annoyed.

"But why? You don't even like my family that much I can tell."

"Of course I do. I don't like you going on your own that's all supposing you have an accident or something."

"That's silly, Karl, I don't want you to wrap me up in cotton wool. I am a grown woman. I am going and that is that."

Karl got to his feet tipping the chair over in his haste. "I said no you wait till I can come too." His eyes were like shards of ice he was angry now she could see. It was all so ridiculous what was the big deal Anna didn't know and she wasn't going to bow down to something as silly as this.

"Karl, this is very silly. I am going and that is that." With that she moved towards the door but Karl stepped in front of her and grasped her wrist. "You will do as I say, you are mine now, and I don't want you wandering around the countryside on your own. God knows you might like some fellow you see and act like the slut you really are!"

"What, what do you mean? How can you say such a thing, how can you?"

"Well, you took me to bed pretty quickly, slut, didn't you?"

Anna, her tears by now streaming down her face, looked at Karl in horror; where did all this come from? "I thought we wanted each other and you took me by surprise," she said lamely and turning round, she went to their bedroom and threw herself onto the bed and cried like she hadn't for a very long time. She was hurt, confused and had seen a side to Karl she didn't really know existed. Was this the man who had swept her off her feet and been so loving and romantic?

In the end, she fell asleep and when she woke, it was getting dark. Looking around the room, the memories of the quarrel came back and tears threatened again. Just then the door opened and Karl came in, crossed quickly to the bed, bent down and, wrapping his arms around her, said, "My darling beautiful Anna, please, please forgive me. I was out of order. Please, please forgive me." He then started to kiss her face down her neck and was soon undressing her; all the time, she lay unresisting in his arms, not knowing what she felt or how to deal with him at all.

He made love to her, all the time pleading with her to forgive him. He was so ashamed of himself...it would never happen again...he would make sure it didn't...he loved her more than life itself...he would die for her if necessary. In the end, Anna responded to him and they drew a line under their quarrel, making love as thoroughly as they usually did.

93

For some time after this, everything went smoothly though part of the reason for this was that Anna didn't push Karl and agreed with his wishes and tried to be everything he expected of her. But, of course, it didn't last. Anna was full of energy and sparkle and needed an outlet for all her youthfulness.

One evening after they had eaten, Anna snuggled up to Karl who was looking through an antique magazine and said, "Karl, isn't it time we started a family; if I had a baby to look after, I wouldn't have so much time on my hands."

Karl straightened up in his seat frowning. "We are not having any children," he said very firmly.

"Pardon, I didn't hear you correctly, did I?" Anna couldn't believe what he had just said.

"Anna, you are all I want and need. I don't want some squalling baby round me and I don't want to share you with one or have your beautiful body spoilt by having a child."

"But you never said you didn't want any, and I do." Anna was feeling very disappointed; she wanted children. "Please, Karl."

"No, and we are not going to discuss it; it's final: no children. I just want you as you are my own beautiful girl." With that, Karl started to kiss her and smothered anything else she may have said. It seemed the end of the matter.

Anna began to feel she was walking on eggshells, Karl was very controlling and there seemed to be several subjects they could not discuss as they only caused a row. Karl had set her on some sort of pedestal and there it seemed he wanted her to stay no matter what she thought or wanted. Christmas came and they visited his parents as Karl said he didn't want to be caught up with snivelling brats, meaning of course Anna's nieces and nephews. They rowed about it and Karl again said some horrid things but then of course was very contrite afterwards. Anna began to feel she was on a rollercoaster of emotion. It was a very dull Christmas lunch served by the butler, no fun, no laughter, no silly hats or crackers; all very serious. On the drive back to London Karl surprised Anna by saying she could go and visit her family the next day if she wanted. He would come with her of course, but she was delighted.

So the next day they set off to Anna's family farm. John and Clare weren't there; however, much to Anna's disappointment as she loved their children, neither were Peter and his girlfriend who by now were living together. Marie was delighted to see them and fussed over Karl like a mother hen while the rest of them were much more circumspect. Anna had bought presents galore for the twins when she had been shopping earlier in December and she had a great time with the twins playing with them and watching them undo their presents.

"You'll be having some of your own soon, I expect," said Silas who had come into the play room. Anna looked round fearfully not wanting Karl to hear. She shrugged and said soon maybe but was very vague and changed the subject. Silas and June exchanged a look.

Tim was quiet and watched his daughter through narrowed eyes. He noticed how quieter she was and how her sparkle seemed diminished also how she seemed to defer to Karl a lot of the time. She had always had a strong independent streak and he was disappointed to see how under Karl's thumb she seemed to be; she had changed and not for the better he thought. He missed his old Anna.

Chapter 16

Life went on in much the same vein. Anna had been firm friends with Muriel ever since she had made Anna's wedding dress, in fact she was the only real friend Anna had got.

Karl seemed to tolerate this without a problem and so Anna spent as much time in Muriel's company as she could. If Muriel noticed, she didn't say anything for which Anna was grateful as she wouldn't have known how to respond.

Of course, Karl and herself were still very busy as Karl still took her with him to meet clients and when he went on a furniture hunting expedition sometimes in Briton, sometimes abroad. Anna enjoyed all that. She enjoyed the fact that she had a generous allowance, a beautiful home, a handsome husband who seemingly adored her, everything she could wish for but deep down she was very unhappy. She didn't entirely trust Karl not to get angry and berate her which he did sometimes, very often for something quite trivial. She also wanted children and she knew that need wasn't likely to diminish but couldn't see what could be done. She had tried a few more times but was scared of him when he got angry and mention of children seemed to set him off.

It was once again leading up to Christmas and Anna and Karl were invited to a very grand reception at the house of a prominent business man whom Karl had supplied quite a few expensive pieces of furniture to. During the evening Anna who had had quite a few canapés started to feel sick. She thought maybe it was something to do with the fishy ones they were serving. Karl wasn't a fish lover but Anna was. As soon as she could, she whispered in his ear that she didn't feel well and could they go home. Karl who had had enough of the gathering too was only too pleased. Neither of them were very good at parties.

They made it home but Anna spent the rest of the night and all the next day either being sick or having diarrhoea. She was hot then cold and in between bouts in the bathroom lay in the bed shivering and dozing. Another day came and Muriel made Karl call the doctor. The doctor said he thought it was a virus and Anna would feel better in a day or so and sure enough she gradually came through it.

Christmas came and went. They went to Thailand again to a different resort and though they had a good time, Anna was aware that somehow things were different. Karl was still loving and attentive but for Anna the sparkle had gone. She was aware of Karl's moods and tried very hard as she always did now not to upset him. It wasn't a good way to be.

The third week in January she woke one morning and had to rush to the bathroom and was very sick. When she got back to the bedroom, Karl was sitting up in bed. "You OK? I hope the virus hasn't come back."

"So do I," Anna sat down back on the bed. "I feel alright not like before but oops," and off to the bathroom she went. A few minutes later when she was again feeling better she was sitting on the floor when it hit her. She knew what was wrong, she was pregnant!

Karl called through the door, "Shall I call the doctor?"

"NO, NO, I am fine. Please don't worry, I will be out in a minute."

She heard Karl go off downstairs to the bathroom behind the showroom and she breathed a sigh of relief she had a few minutes grace, what to tell him? How to tell him, he was going to be angry. She searched her mind to work out how it had happened and concluded that her tummy upset had meant that the pill hadn't worked or she had thrown it up or something. She had been on the pill since her late teens as she had very bad PMT in fact she had been on the pill since the episode with Paul, God she hadn't thought of him in years! What to do, she didn't know.

The nausea seemed to have passed. She ran her hands over her body and found that her breasts were very tender and slightly enlarged, that confirmed it. Getting up she got in the shower and stood there letting the warm water cascade over her still trying to work out how and when to tell Karl. She was sure

97

of one thing; she wanted this baby so much so very much. Karl would just have to get used to the idea and maybe in time he would come to love him or her. She knew his parents would be happy as Sir William had said that he wanted the family line to carry on.

Anna wasn't sure how she got through that early morning she was very distracted and Karl worried that she was indeed going down with the virus again.

They had a lunch date with an American with whom Karl had known a long time as they had done many deals together. His name was Jerry and he imported items of furniture that Karl found for him back to the States.

They met at small exclusive restaurant in Chelsea, and Karl knowing what Anna usually had when they had lunch out ordered her a mineral water. She hated having an alcoholic drink at lunch time as it made her very sleepy. She wasn't really a big drinker anyway. She was worried about eating though, she felt fine now and had assured Karl she was but was she? I will have something light she said to him in a low voice.

Karl looked at her worriedly. "Are you OK, darling?"

"Yes, thanks, fine."

"Anna was sick this morning," Karl said to Jerry.

Jerry who apparently had a whole tribe of children in the States said, "When are you due?"

Anna looked at him appalled and Karl said, "What are you talking about?"

Jerry having seen the stricken look on Anna's face backtracked quickly. "Sorry, got the wrong end of the stick. I do it all the time, my wife Patsy is always telling me off."

Karl looked at Anna grimly but only said, "Anna has had some rotten bug lately that is hard to throw off." Then he changed the subject.

It was a rather tense lunch after that Karl and Anna were both busy with their own thoughts and Jerry was thinking about the can of worms he seemed to have opened. Lunch over and the men got down to the business side of their meeting, Anna only half listened and when Karl spoke to her, she jumped. She had been going over and over the situation in her mind. "Sorry, what did you say?"

Karl pursed his lips in a sign of disapproval. "I said we are going to the antique fair in Edinburgh tonight so had better be going."

"Yes, yes, of course. Sorry." Anna was flustered now and so they said their goodbyes and left. Jerry watched them go, all isn't so great there he said to himself.

Silence reigned between them until they got back home. Karl stopped and said something in a low voice to Muriel as they passed through the showroom which Anna couldn't hear.

Once the door had closed Karl swung round and said in a voice dripping with malice and anger. "Well, are you pregnant?"

Anna nodded dumbly. She had remembered she hadn't had a period since before her illness but had been too busy to notice especially with Thailand and catching up with family since they returned. "I think so," she whispered.

"You ugly, miserable creature. You have gone against my wishes, I told you no babies and I meant it, no babies squalling and dribbling all over the place. I won't have your body taken over by some brat. You are mine, your body is mine, do you hear me?"

"But Karl, it will be ours." Anna started to cry.

"You can stay here and get rid of it and you will get rid of it I insist. If you don't make arrangements, then I will when I return."

Anna was feeling desperate now and stood her ground "No, I want this baby. I won't have it terminated for you or anyone."

In two strides, Karl had crossed the room and he struck her on the side of her head then punched her hard in the lower stomach. Anna let out a cry of pain and fear as she fell to the ground clutching her stomach.

Karl stood over her breathing hard then going into the bedroom started to pack for the journey north. Anna stayed where she was in too much pain to move her senses were reeling and she could think at all only feel pain and horror at what had happened.

There was a knock at the door and stepping over her Karl went and answered it. There was only one person it could be Muriel. Anna huddled on the floor vaguely wondered what would happen next but Karl must have satisfied her because a moment later he again stepped over her and resumed his packing. Anna stayed where she was and shortly afterwards Karl again stepping over her said, "Remember, little dimwit that thing inside you had got to go." With that, he left locking the door behind him, effectively locking her in.

Anna didn't know how long she laid there, it was late when at last she got first to her knees then staggered to her feet. Her head swam and she felt sick so she stumbled through to the bathroom where she was violently sick. She then lay on the bathroom floor for most of the night, too sore and battered and unhappy to drag herself even as far as the bed. She dozed and was sick dozed again, sick again the night seemed to go on and on. As dawn was breaking, she managed to scramble into bed and finally got into a deep sleep.

She woke to a loud knocking on the entrance door. She could hear Muriel's muffled voice too but not what she was saying. She looked at the bedside clock it was mid-day. She staggered out of bed and standing by the door she croaked "Yes?"

"Anna, my dear, are you alright? Karl said you didn't feel well yesterday and said you wouldn't be going with him?"

Tears threatening again Anna said, "Yes, I'm OK. I was asleep. I will go back to bed now, thanks for asking."

"Are you sure, dear, you don't need anything? You don't sound yourself at all."

Stifling the sobs that rose in her throat Anna assured Muriel she was fine then turned to go back to bed. "I will come back later." Muriel called.

Anna didn't reply. She went and got a drink of water, she was very thirsty then she had another glass and felt hungry so she made herself a slice of toast. She was trying not to think it was the only way she could cope just now, not thinking just see to her body's needs and then sleep again. She crept back to bed. Sleep. Beautiful, healing sleep.

She woke to a searing pain in her abdomen. Tottering out of bed towards the bathroom once more but the pain was so great she ended up crawling and finally collapsed by the bathroom door. Then she felt moisture between her legs and let out a moan. Partly despair and partly pain. She bit her lip, she felt frightened she knew she was miscarrying but didn't know what to do. She dragged herself to the toilet. Then she heard Muriel's voice from outside the flat again but couldn't form the words to answer. However, Muriel had a key and she had heard strange noises coming from upstairs she decided to use it. She was horrified when she found Anna slumped on the bathroom floor bleeding heavily. She was still partially dressed in the clothes she had been wearing when they had gone to lunch yesterday. The side of her face sported a bruise and her eyes were swollen but worst of all was the heavy bleeding.

"Anna, Anna, love, you poor thing, I am going to call an ambulance, lie still, don't worry."

"NO," Anna's voice was made strong in desperation, the last thing she wanted was anyone to know what had happened to her. Muriel was taken aback at Anna's reaction. Anna sat up with a huge effort. "I don't want a doctor or an ambulance it will be fine," she said. "Please, can you help me? I don't want anyone else to know."

So reluctantly Muriel helped Anna undress and get into the shower where she leant against the wall and let the warm water wash away some of the distress as well as the physical evidence of her abuse by Karl.

Muriel was very grim faced as she of course had seen the bruise on Ann's face but also could see a livid mark on her lower abdomen. Eventually with Anna cleaned up a little and feeling a little better she helped her into a loose gown and made her some strong tea. Then sat her down at the kitchen table.

"Do you want to talk about it, dear?" she said. Anna fought to hold back the threatening tears and reminded herself Muriel was Karl's employee.

"Well I—well I—" she stammered. "I have miscarried, but Karl didn't know I was expecting, he will be so upset when he knows." As the words came out of her mouth, Anna was amazed at herself for lying like she was. It was alien to her.

"What happened here, though?" Muriel gently touched Anna's face.

"I felt faint and fell against the doorpost." The lie came more easily that time. Why was she protecting him, Anna didn't know, but deep down she felt Muriel and Karl went back a long way, she wasn't sure how Muriel would feel with the truth anyway would it be fair to tell her?

For her part, Muriel was fairly sure what had happened and was appalled but recognising Anna's loyalty to Karl didn't push it. She got up and coming round Anna's side of the table put her arms around her. "If you ever need anything or need to talk, I am here, my dear, just remember that."

Anna really broke down then and cried as if her heart would break, to her it felt as if it was. She had lost the baby she so wanted and it seemed as if she had lost her husband too. Not only that but he had hit her! Men didn't hit women, not in her world anyway; it was so awful she couldn't believe it. Where did they go from here, what sort of relationship would they, could they have now? All these things were buzzing around in her head.

In spite of Muriel's attempts to get her to see a doctor, Anna refused saying she would be fine with some rest. After a time, she allowed Muriel to change the sheets on the bed and crawled back between the clean ones and fell asleep. Muriel left her after watching her for a while. The thoughts were tumbling around in her head as to what to do but in the end she did nothing as she felt it wasn't really her job to interfere.

Anna was still very stiff and sore the next day but on waking early she thought she would go and see her parents maybe they could help her decide what she should do if anything. Walking was an effort but she made it down to the car which was parked in the basement and gingerly drove out from London to the country. She drove slowly as she was still feeling woozy. She hadn't put any makeup on she had just had a strong coffee, a shower and left, before she had a chance to change her mind.

When she drove into the farm she could see that the car June and Silas drove wasn't there and nor was her father's Land Rover. She made her way slowly to the back door and opening it, called out, "Hello?"

Her mother came through from the hallway. "Hello dear, what a surprise. What are you doing here?"

"Where's Dad?" croaked Anna.

"Oh he's gone with Silas to look at a bull they are thinking of buying, and Jean and the twins have gone to stay with her parents for a few days. Dad and Silas will be back by lunch time. What have you done to your face?" Marie had walked closer and was staring at the livid mark on Anna's cheek.

The tears started then Anna couldn't hold them in. "Karl hit me, he found out I was pregnant and was very angry."

Before she could say more Marie interrupted her. "Karl hit you? Whatever had you done to make him do that? I don't believe it he is such a kind gentle man what made him do that?" Marie repeated herself in agitation.

Anna stood still staring at her mother, she didn't believe her, all she could think was that Marie didn't really believe her. The old animosity she had always felt towards her mother boiled over and suddenly she was screaming at her. "I came here hoping you would help me and understand, Karl hit me, I am pregnant or at least I was but I miscarried. I hate him and I don't know what to do, and you aren't helping."

Marie put her hand out. "If you have miscarried, of course your hormones are all over the place and it's easy to imagine Karl is unkind and hit you, but I am sure—"

Anna wheeled on her heels before Marie said anymore and almost ran back to her car. Getting in she did a u turn and roared out of the farmyard in a spray of gravel. Marie ran to the door but was too late; Anna was gone. Much later when Tim and Silas returned home Marie repeated what Anna had said. Tim in turn was angry then. "What got into you woman, of course Anna is telling the truth. I didn't like him from the start I was afraid something like this would happen. He buttered you up and you fell for it like a silly school girl, my poor Anna I am going to ring her now I just hope she got home alright." He marched off to the phone leaving Marie looking very crestfallen and worried.

The phone rang for a long time then Muriel answered, "No, she isn't back yet. What time did she leave?" she said to Tim's enquiry.

"I'm not sure but at least two and a half hours ago, she should be back by now. To be honest, Muriel, Anna had a bit of a row with her mother and we are worried—" Tim trailed off not quite knowing what to say.

Muriel tutted. "Look," she said. "It's none of my business and I don't really know what has gone on but Anna needs all the love and support she can get at the moment she is in a bad place."

"I know, I know but where do you think she might be?" said Tim, "Where is Karl, anyway?"

"Karl is in Scotland at a big Antique Fair and won't be back for another three days. As for Anna, I have no more idea than you."

"We will give it a little longer then I am going to call the police," said Tim desperately.

Meanwhile Anna had driven to Kate and Vernon's house only to find they weren't there, they were actually away on holiday. She sat outside their house for some time hoping they would return but after an hour or so she realised they weren't coming back very soon she drove slowly back towards London. While she had been sitting outside their house she had time to think and felt a little more rational now.

When she got back to the showroom, she was surprised to find Muriel wasn't there and a young girl that helped out sometimes was floating around the showroom. When she saw Anna, she let out a little squeak and said, "Muriel is upstairs." She looked as if she wanted to say more but then turned away so Anna continued on to the flat. Muriel was sitting on the sofa staring at the phone as if willing it to ring and didn't hear Anna until she closed the door. She leapt out of her chair. "Anna, thank goodness, we have been so worried." She hugged Anna to her. Anna laid her head on Muriel's shoulder, why was it this woman could comfort her while her mother couldn't, she fought the ever present tears.

Gently withdrawing she swallowed hard and whispered, "I am OK. Don't worry."

"Your Dad has been on the phone about half an hour ago. He was saying he would come up he is beside himself with worry. I have to ring him and let him know you are home safely."

Muriel crossed the room to the phone and picking it up rapidly phoned Tim. "Tim, she's back, she is OK." She listened a moment then turning to Anna said, "Your dad wants a word."

"Anna, Anna love are you OK?"

Anna's throat closed up at the sound of her father's voice. She found she couldn't speak for a moment then she managed

"I am OK, Dad, it's all a big mistake, just a misunderstanding. Everything will be fine."

"Mum said you said Karl hit you and that you are pregnant but you have miscarried, did Karl hit you?"

Anna stood still staring at her reflection in the big mirror that was along one wall. She saw a frightened dishevelled girl with a livid mark on her otherwise pale cheek. She had swollen eyes and wild hair, she looked a mess.

"No he didn't, Dad. Mum said my miscarriage made me imagine things something to do with hormones. She said it's OK. I will be fine."

Tim didn't believe her but having pushed her a bit more and getting the same answer he gave up, she didn't need any more stress. "Well why don't you come back for a few days and get over all this, and maybe see a doctor? We would all love you to come."

"Even Mum?"

"Of course Mum, she loves you to bits, please Anna."

"Sorry Dad, Karl will be back soon and I have lots to do but yes I will see a doctor."

Tim sighed, he knew if Anna had made up her mind that was that.

Chapter 17

The next morning Anna woke with a splitting headache. Muriel had insisted on staying and cooking Anna some supper for which Anna was grateful she hadn't eaten anything to speak of since the lunch with Jerry. The two women hadn't spoken much there was so much between them that neither of them felt they could say. For both of them, it was misplaced loyalty though neither of them acknowledged this even to themselves. What Anna didn't know was that Muriel had telephoned Karl when they had been worried as to Anna's whereabouts and told him she had miscarried. She didn't go into details but let it be known that Anna was being very tight lipped about the whole thing but that she Muriel held Karl in part responsible. It had shaken Karl as he had lost control and was aware he hadn't acted very well and when he heard she was missing he was scared. He was packing his bag when Muriel phoned back to say Anna had turned up though and he had been very relived.

Anna was just getting out of bed when she heard the door of the flat open and a few seconds later Karl appeared in the doorway. He came across the room and threw himself down at her feet. "Anna, my Anna, what have I done? PLEASE, PLEASE, PLEASE FORGIVE ME. I am so sorry, so very sorry. Please, please let's be friends." As he knelt there, tears started to run down his cheeks. Anna had never imagined she would see Karl cry and it completely undid her and sliding off the bed she encircled him in her arms and they both cried together. *It was strange,* Anna thought later as a small part of her brain was telling her not to listen Karl wasn't to be trusted, walk away but she heard herself saying, "It's alright, it will be alright don't be upset. I love you."

They stayed like that for a time then Anna had a shower with Karl who was very tender and though he said nothing

106

Anna saw the look on his face of shame when he saw the marks on her lower abdomen. Her face, meanwhile, looked much better than it had. He insisted on washing her all over very gently and massaged her head while shampooing her hair; she felt quite restored afterwards.

Karl got her breakfast and was very attentive all day and also was adamant that it didn't matter the fact he missed some of the Antique Fair. Later that night lying in bed Anna wondered if somehow all that had happened might be a blessing in disguise, she hoped things would look up.

About ten days after his return Karl came into the showroom where both Muriel and Anna were setting out a new display and said he had found the perfect house for himself and Anna. Anna was surprised, she didn't know he was house hunting. "A house, what house? Can I have a say in it. Where is it? Can I see it?"

"Whoa hang on. Yes we can go and see it again tomorrow but I have put a deposit down and agreed everything so it's all done and dusted."

Anna was disappointed but hid it as well as she could. She wished Karl had included her in the house hunting and decisions all of it but typically he just went ahead excluding her. She just hoped she would like it.

As it happened, she loved it. It was in Chelsea and was a beautifully appointed Georgian house with a small garden at the back. Large airy rooms, a very modern kitchen, a huge master bedroom with en-suite as were the other two bedrooms. The garden at the back was walled all around and had some lovely plants in it. It had been very well cared for. "Karl, it's beautiful, but it must cost a fortune. Can we afford it?"

"That is for me to worry about, you can have the fun of the furniture and décor. I take it you approve then?" Karl took her in his arms and kissed her. "A new start, darling, and one without Muriel downstairs interfering."

Anna felt a slight shiver pass over her. "Muriel doesn't interfere; she is a good friend, but yes this is lovely," she finished quickly before Karl took offence. She would miss Muriel and somehow had felt safer with Muriel nearby. *Safer* she thought, where did that come from? Karl was her husband, what was she thinking? But the truth was that she still felt uneasy if she thought Karl was unhappy about something. Basically she was a bit scared of him now, she didn't like the things he said when he got angry but since the miscarriage she was even more insecure.

For the next few months, Anna was very busy organising her new home, she had the drawing room redecorated before she furnished it. It was a very dark almost deep-red colour but she had it redone in a very, very pale green. It made the room seem even larger. Pale-gold carpet and curtains and large sofas that almost hid their occupants. It was a very beautiful room. Anna had trouble sourcing readymade curtains but found the right material and got Muriel to run them up for her. That gave her an idea which she ran by Karl one evening when he was in a particularly good mood.

"Karl, how about we extend our—or rather your—business into interior design?"

Karl threw back his head and laughed. "Anna, my Anna, whatever for? You are my wife, you don't need to work."

"I know that, but it would give me a sort of hobby and I need more to do. I used to help you more in the showroom and in the business but you don't seem to need me so much now and I have time on my hands." At this point she nearly said if she had a baby she would be more fulfilled but thought that wasn't a good idea.

Karl sighed. "I will think about it," he said.

"Karl."

"Enough Anna, I said I will think about it." Karl was starting to look annoyed and Anna didn't dare provoke him any further so she let it drop hoping he would indeed think about it.

Weeks passed, Anna was so bored she had started to run in the park in the mornings to fill in time and most afternoons she would go to the showroom and talk to Muriel. Apart from wanting her accompany him on sales trips and when he was entertaining clients Karl seemed to want to distance her from the business. He hadn't mentioned her idea at all and a few weeks later she brought it up and he just said "No" and walked away. She didn't understand why and talked it over with Muriel the next time she had a chance. Muriel said she thought maybe Karl was worried that Anna would make too much of a success of it and it would take her away from him in the long term and he also didn't like any sort of competition. A few minutes after this conversation Karl walked into the office, his face betraying he was angry. All he said, however, was that he needed to go home and Anna should go with him. Anna looked worriedly at Muriel as she got to her feet. Muriel said, "I was hoping Anna could stay and help me with these paintings that have just arrived, after all she knows more than either of us."

Karl ignored her. "Come Anna, we have to go."

Anna didn't dare argue and getting to her feet followed Karl out of the showroom and into a taxi he flagged down. They didn't always drive as it was easy enough to get a taxi and the expense wasn't an issue.

They were silent on the drive home, Anna was worried and Karl was fuming.

When the front door closed behind them, Karl took hold of Anna's wrist and swung her round to face him. His face was a mask of anger and his eyes were like flint. "Talking about me behind my back you good for nothing, to an employee too. How dare you? You piece of shit, you worm, you will pay for that," and he hit her hard in her ribs. Anna let out a cry of pain. Karl put his hand over her mouth. "Shut the fuck up, you cow," he hissed. Truth was he didn't want anyone to hear what was going on. He violently pushed her so she fell backwards and hit her head on the bottom step of the stairs. As they had thick carpet over them, it softened her fall but she fell awkwardly and lay there feeling winded and in pain.

"Stay there, bitch." Karl gathered his car keys and stormed out, slamming the front door.

Anna didn't know how long she lay there whimpering and crying but in the end she got to her feet and staggered through to the kitchen where she was sick, very sick in the sink.

Her ribs were very, very sore and it hurt to move. She thought it was likely that one at least was broken. Eventually she made it slowly and painfully upstairs to the bedroom and peeling of her clothes slowly she looked at herself on the mirror. Sure enough she had a huge bruise spreading across her ribcage just below her breasts. Her wrist was also throbbing and her head hurt.

She ran herself a bath and climbed in laying back the water soothed her body but not her mind. Why was Karl so violent when on the one hand he said she was his life, his love everything he wanted in a wife then could be so cruel and thuggish? She thought about his sister, maybe there was a mental illness in the family but she knew nothing of such things so couldn't hazard a guess. She realised one thing for sure he was a complete control freak. He always told her what he wanted her to wear when they went out, in fact, there wasn't really any part of her life that he didn't have a say in. To start with she had liked it but it had become harder to bear especially since their marriage and it was getting worse. What should she do? But I am afraid to leave him anyway where would I go? Since she had rushed to her family and Marie had been so dismissive of her she had only been back a couple of times and Karl had been with her. Her father had said nothing but was decidedly frosty. She did speak to Tim and Silas quite frequently but not her mother. She knew from Tim that her mother was very remorseful but she just couldn't bring herself to play the loving daughter anymore. She stayed there a long time trying to figure out what to do but came up with nothing. Eventually the bathwater got cold and as she had repeatedly topped it up she ran out of hot water.

Clambering out of the bath she towelled herself gingerly then putting on a towelling robe padded downstairs and making herself a hot drink took it back to the bedroom and climbed into bed. After a few sips, her eyes closed and she slid down in the bed and fell into an exhausted sleep.

When she woke, it was 2 o'clock in the morning. She wondered vaguely where Karl was but realised she wasn't in a hurry to see him and after a trip to the bathroom, she again fell asleep.

She woke again with a start, it was day light. She struggled out of bed, very sore and stiff. She pulled on some clothes and went downstairs into the kitchen. She pulled up short when she got to the doorway as Karl was sitting at the table looking directly at her as she entered the room. He looked terrible; he was dishevelled and unshaven and his eyes were red as though he had been crying. He dropped down off the chair and shuffled on his knees to Anna where he bent down and kissed her bare feet. "Darling, darling, Anna. Please, please forgive me if you can. I am so sorry, I just felt so hurt when you were talking

110

about me behind my back and I am so sorry. I didn't mean to hurt you. I love you so much more than life itself, please forgive me. By this time he was in tears and Anna found herself saying,

"It's OK. I am sorry too for provoking you, please get up. Come on, I will make you a hot drink, it will be OK."

Anna pulled at Karl's sleeve and he got to his feet, then wrapped his arms around her. "Whatever you want Anna you can have, I promise. Just say you forgive me and let me try to make you happy. I love you so much, I always will."

So Anna forgave him, and the only thing she said that she would like was to go and see her family as soon as she could. The way she felt now she wasn't ready for interior design so shelved the idea. She had this need to see her family.

Chapter 18

A week later Anna rang her parents and told them she was coming alone to stay for a few days. Her father seemed pleased and her mother also said she was looking forward to seeing her though Anna didn't actually speak to her.

The visit went well, Marie went out of her way to make up with Anna though in truth they didn't speak about Karl. Tim didn't mention him either only Silas asked Anna how things were between the two of them. Anna just shrugged and said fine. Silas looked long and hard at her but as she said nothing else he let it pass. She spent a lot of time playing with the twins Harry and Phil.

"Do you think you might make another start to having a family?" asked June. Anna looked at her, realising that she couldn't know what had actually happened before. But then none of her family did only her parents knew that Karl had hit her but no details. Which was good really she thought.

"We will see," was all she said and June, not wanting to pry, left it at that.

Just before she left, Marie tapped on her bedroom door. "I am glad we are friends again, Anna," she said. "I am glad too that you and Karl are good again. I think he is a wonderful man and if he had a little blip, well we all do the wrong thing sometimes."

Anna stood looking at her mother for a long time; she couldn't believe her. "Anna?" said Marie.

Anna shook her head, "Don't worry about it, mum, I must go," she said deciding it wasn't worth trying to explain Karl. Her mother had on rose tinted glasses.

When she had been home a few days and having had a rapturous welcome from Karl, she took herself off to the showroom to see Muriel. She was going to phone first but thought she would surprise her. When she walked in, a very bossy, middle-aged woman came up to her saying, "Can I help you, madame?"

"Who are you?" Anna blurted, "And what are you doing here?"

"I am in charge here, now can I help you?" The woman looked annoyed at Anna's question.

Just then, Karl appeared from the office saying smoothly, "Margaret, this is my wife Anna. Anna, Margaret."

Margaret held out her hand. "I am sorry, madame, I didn't realise who you were."

Anna automatically shook her hand but looked quizzically at Karl.

"Where is Muriel?"

"Muriel has retired, my dear," he said. "She had been talking of it for some time then the chance came up for her to go to see her son in America and she took retirement so she could go."

Anna felt her legs go weak. She knew Muriel had no intention of retiring yet and had seen her son not that long ago when he came over with his family. She turned away so neither Karl nor Margaret should see the tears in her eyes. No wonder Karl was so keen for her to go to see her family; he then could get rid of Muriel without Anna knowing until it was too late. *A leopard doesn't change its spots,* she thought sadly. She said nothing what was there to say it was done and dusted and Muriel would be feeling very upset too. Anna knew Muriel wouldn't want her to get into more trouble on her behalf so she let it go. She just knew that she was more isolated than before with no friends. If Karl thought she was getting friendly with someone, he made sure to keep Anna away from them.

Time marched on. Anna learnt to keep her head down; she got into tending her small garden, going to the gym, running to keep fit and of course there were trips with work and also Karl would take her away for long weekends when he had time. She had never liked shopping but it got her out of the house and she bought clothes she would never wear. The allowance Karl gave her was very generous and so she also put much of it away in her own name and kept that to herself. She didn't analyse why she just did it that way.

Two years down the track and Anna was still yearning for children. She was twenty eight, time was passing. She thought of all sorts of ways to convince Karl to have children but got rebuffed each time. Mostly so long as she didn't confront him. He was good to her but she dare not cross him or argue about even trivial things else he would fly into a rage and hit her. Then be very contrite and sorry afterwards. Their love making had changed too because Anna was now afraid of him she found it harder to gain any pleasure from it and Karl seemed to indulge in his own pleasure rather than being the generous lover he had been at the beginning. Sometimes, though, it was like old times and then Anna always hoped that things would improve between them. She didn't love him anymore, though and questioned in her own mind if she ever had. Maybe it was a mixture of lust and loneliness. There was one thing that was very clear; however, and that was Karl was a complete control freak and looked on Anna as his and his alone. She was his possession and he got angry if she was very friendly with other females let alone spoke to any men without him being there.

Then Anna had an inspiration; she would get pregnant and tell Karl's parents first. Sir William wanted a grandson and had mentioned the fact on more than one occasion but Karl always fobbed him off. Lady Carolyn never said much about anything.

A few weeks later Anna was sure that her idea had worked, she had to supress her excitement so Karl wouldn't guess something was up. She was thankful she had fallen pregnant quickly after she stopped taking the pill. Her resolve may have come to nothing otherwise. The next week was nerve racking as Anna wanted to be completely sure. Karl asked her twice if she was OK and she lied. He looked at her suspiciously but said nothing; he was very busy getting a shipment of antiques ready for America.

It was now four weeks since her last period so with a shaking hand Anna rang Karl's parents. She got Sir William, much to her relief as at least he noticed her, she was never sure if Lady Caroline even saw her.

"Anna, what can I do for you?" he asked when she had told him it was her. She had never spoken to him on the telephone before.

"I have some news for you, Sir William," Anna said breathlessly. "I haven't had the chance to tell Karl yet but I am so excited I must tell someone. Karl isn't back until this evening and I just couldn't wait. I am pregnant." Anna paused, she knew she had gabbled all that rather but she was very nervous and was feeling sick.

For a few moments there was silence then Sir William cleared his throat and said heartily "Good news, my dear, good news. When are you telling Karl?"

Anna breathed a sigh of relief; so far, so good. "This evening, well, late, as he won't be back very early."

"Well, I am thrilled, a grandson at last. Give Karl my best and tell him about time too." With that he put the phone down. Anna stood looking at the handset and hoping the baby would indeed be a boy for Sir William's sake.

By the time Karl came home that evening, Anna was sick with nerves, how would he react?

She had cooked his favourite dinner and got him a Scotch as soon as he walked in. He looked at her suspiciously. "What's up, Anna. What have you been up to?"

Now it came to it, Anna was so nervous. She said, "Nothing," and fled into the kitchen.

As she served their dinner, Karl kept looking at her quizzically and then asked her again what was up. Before she could answer the phone rang and muttering Karl went to answer it. He didn't come back and finally Anna went into the hall to look for him. He was sitting on the sofa by the phone looking very angry. As Anna came through the door, he lurched to his feet and shouted at her. "What the hell did you think you were doing telling my father you were expecting, you sly bitch, you think that will protect you?" He jumped to his feet and raised his hand to strike Anna but gathering what little strength she had she said.

"How will you explain to your father that you brought on another miscarriage if you beat me up?"

Karl stopped short of hitting her then. He wasn't game to hit her but his foul language left her feeling humiliated and sad. He called her every bad thing he could think of then eventually when he had run out of steam he threw his plate of food on the floor. "Now, you slimy worm, clear that up."

Anna was by now shaking with fear and also she was angry, which was something she hadn't felt for a time. Rather than provoke him further she got busy clearing up the mess. It was a complicated game dish that he liked and difficult to make, it took some time. When she had finished, Karl, who had stood watching her said, "Now you can make me that again."

"But it takes ages and it will be really late before you have it, I haven't anymore game that goes in the dish anyway." Anna was feeling panicky now.

"I don't care, you had better make it sharpish. Go to the freezer, there is bound to be some game in there."

So Anna found herself spending the next hour and a half busy in the kitchen while Karl lounged in the drawing room, drinking heavily. When finally the dish was ready, along with more vegetables, Anna went to tell Karl, only to find he had fallen into a drunken slumber. She tried to wake him but eventually gave up and leaving the food and the mess she had made in the kitchen went to bed.

She woke with a start, Karl was standing by the bed. It was 5 a.m. by the clock by the bed. He pulled back the covers and got on top of her. She tried to protest but he took what he wanted and it hurt.

When he had finished, he simply rolled off her and went and got in the shower. "Karl?" Anna called to him, he didn't answer. When he came out of the shower, he kicked his clothes that he had taken off just inside the bedroom door out of the way and walked out with just a towel around his waist.

Anna got out of bed and with shaking legs followed him downstairs into the kitchen. "Karl, please speak to me."

"Karl, speak to me," he mimicked her. "Why the hell should I? I told you no children. Well, you have gone against me and you will suffer for it, believe me, you will wish you had never ignored my wishes."

"But Karl, please, your parents are so pleased and why don't you want to have a child? What is so bad about it? We can give the baby all the love and attention and education he or she will need and we can have fun as a family together."

"Anna, when I first saw you, I knew that you were MY woman and no-one else's. I share you with NO-ONE. DO YOU UNDERSTAND?"

116

She could see the anger in his ice blue eyes and knew she had to stop; she was making things worse, so she went to put the coffee machine on. Karl grabbed her arm. "DO YOU UNDERSTAND?"

Anna nodded not daring to speak and Karl let her go, they ate their breakfast in silence and Anna had to rush off as the first wave of morning sickness hit her.

When finally she was feeling better, Karl had long gone and Anna set about clearing up the wasted food and general mayhem in the kitchen. She had a cleaning lady who came in three days a week. Anna felt it was unnecessary but as Karl had insisted she put up with it. Her name was Mrs Ragg and she was a very dour women in her late fifties. Mrs Ragg was due at eight thirty but it was still only seven thirty so Anna had time. She had to rush off a couple of times and threw up again. She felt very unwell. However, not wanting to see Mrs Ragg she changed into her running clothes and set off up the street. She spent most of the time she was out sitting on a park bench trying to control her body which seemed to want to make her feel very debilitated.

Finally it was time, she thought, to return, and as she was walking back down her street a woman came out of the house next door. They had moved in not long ago. They were a couple in their mid to late fifties and he was a consultant at one of the big London hospitals. They had two teenage children. They had knocked at Karl and Anna's front door when they had moved in but typically Karl had been almost rude so they had no further contact. Now the woman gave Anna a friendly smile. "Hello again, neighbour, we haven't really seen much of you since we moved in. I keep thinking we should ask you round for drinks or something, but we never seem to get round to it."

Anna smiled back; it was good to see a friendly face. "Hello." She didn't know what else to say suddenly as all sorts of thoughts were racing through her head. Karl not wanting to socialise being upper most in her mind.

The woman held out her hand. "Shall we start again and pretend we haven't really met before. Well, we didn't really, did we? I'm Ruth, would you like to come in and have a coffee?"

Anna was horrified to find that there were sudden tears in her eyes at this woman's kind words and nodded dumbly, then managed to say, "I'm Anna, thanks."

Before she knew it she was sitting at the breakfast bar in Ruth's kitchen with a cup of coffee in front of her and some fresh scones with jam and cream.

Ruth had noted her distress. She had also seen Anna go off to the park alone on numerous occasions and had guessed having met Karl that Anna was not in the happiest of relationships. She didn't want to pry but she sensed that Anna was very lonely and had seen her set off that morning looking more downcast than normal.

Anna drank her coffee slowly while they chatted about the weather and Ruth filled her in on her children and what they were doing and what her husband did. Anna was very reticent when Ruth asked her questions about herself and Karl though and Ruth didn't push it. She had seen Anna's distress when she had invited her in and didn't want to make her feel worse.

Anna suddenly got to her feet looking very pale. "Can I use your bathroom?"

"Of course, it's much the same layout as your house I would think there is a toilet just down the hall—" But Anna had already fled.

When she came back, Ruth said, "When is your baby due? Your husband must be so pleased about it, it's such an exciting time first baby."

Anna burst into tears then and before she could control herself was confessing to Ruth that Karl didn't want children and he was far from happy.

Ruth consoled her as best as she could saying that Karl would come round and telling Anna she would help her with anything or give advice whatever she needed. What she had seen of Karl she hadn't liked and didn't feel that surprised by what Anna had told her.

During the next few weeks the two of them became good friends. Anna didn't tell Karl that she was now friendly with the people next door. Ruth had told Malcom her husband all about Anna and they agreed to watch out for her but not to let on to Karl should they see him. It wasn't long before they

118

realised that Karl was very controlling and that Anna was afraid of him.

As for Anna, Karl hardly spoke to her and started to leave her behind when he met clients. He took his pleasure from her and it became almost like rape for Anna as it was what he wanted when he wanted it with no love or tenderness involved. Many times afterwards he said, "Maybe that will shift the little bastard," which always made Anna upset though she didn't show it as that made it worse.

Then came the day when Karl saw that Anna was beginning to look pregnant and although her breasts had been larger for some time the rest of her body had looked much the same to him.

Anna heard him thumping about upstairs one day and came up to find him dumping her clothes on the landing "What are you doing?" she asked.

"I am not sleeping with an elephant, you disgusting creature. You can sleep in the spare room from now on."

"But, Karl,"

"Shut the hell up." He raised his hand, and Anna flinched away. She knew better than to argue.

Karl still wanted his martial rights though but took Anna from behind not wanting to see her face or her bump. In the end, Anna could take all the humiliations no longer and one day went round to see Ruth and poured out the whole sorry story. She didn't, however, tell her how Karl used physical violence against her. She hadn't told her parents she was pregnant either. She didn't know why but the distance between her and her mother was something to do with it, she knew.

"What about going home to your parents for a while, Anna?" said Ruth. "They must be thrilled to be grandparents again."

Anna shook her head. "I haven't told them I am expecting, Mum, and I don't get on that well and I just felt—" Anna trailed off. "I don't know what to do." She burst into tears again.

Ruth said, "Tell me your parents' phone number and I will ring them, Anna. This can't go on, love, and we live too close, otherwise you could stay here."

Anna reluctantly told Ruth her parents' number but she said she would ring them herself. She promised she would go home and ring them straight away.

Ruth watched her go shaking her head. She had become very fond of Anna and was perplexed by what Anna had told her. She certainly couldn't understand Karl nor could she understand Anna's mother. Anna was her only daughter, for goodness sake, why was the woman so unkind?

Anna let herself into the house. It wasn't a Mrs Ragg day today and, steeling herself and holding back the tears that were threatening, she picked up the phone to dial her mother. Just then, the door was flung open and Karl burst into the hall. He was deathly pale and Anna could see he was shaking. Without a word he put his arms around her and burying his face in her neck he burst into tears. Anna held him totally taken aback; she couldn't understand what had upset Karl so much.

"Whatever's the matter, Karl, what is it?"

He stood back away from her and taking a deep breath said, "Clare hung herself last night."

Anna clapped her hand to her mouth. "Oh my God, no."

Karl nodded with a 'hicuppy' voice. He told Anna that they couldn't find her that morning, then his father went out to the old stables at the back of the house and there she was.

"I didn't know that you and Clare were very close." Anna said this while stroking Karl's head as he sat in a chair again very distressed.

"We were very close as children, in fact, until she went to uni and got mixed up with the wrong crowd. We did everything together as kids."

"Don't ever leave me, Anna, will you? You are all I have now Clare is gone. Promise you will always be here, please?"

Anna stood rubbing Karl's back. She felt trapped but didn't want to promise in case she couldn't keep it. Thankfully as she hesitated the telephone went and she went to answer it. It was Sir William. He sounded upset but when Anna started to say how sorry she was he cut her short saying he wanted to speak to Karl. Anna handed the phone over and went into the kitchen to make some coffee. When she had, she put some brandy in it for Karl. When he came through, he was composed but very pale.

"Father says there is to be an inquest, and it will possibly be a few weeks before we can bury her."

"Oh, Karl, I am so sorry. What can I do?"

"Just be your own beautiful self, Anna. I know I can be slightly difficult sometimes but I do love you and right now I need you by my side more than I ever imagined."

So Anna supported Karl through the next few weeks. He seemed to have forgotten about her pregnancy and was very much like he had been way back at the start of their relationship. He was gentle, considerate and loving and Anna began to think her husband that she had fallen in love with had returned. Then one morning at breakfast just after the funeral the baby gave such a big kick Anna let out an involuntary gasp. Karl looked up. "What is it?"

"The baby just kicked hard, here give me your hand you can feel it kicking, him or her, I should say." She went to take his hand.

Karl recoiled as if he had been struck. "No way. I am not interested." Scrapping his chair back, he left the kitchen and went upstairs.

From then on things gradually went back to how they were before Clare had died only now it was worse as Karl seemed to want to know where Anna was every second of every day.

Anna had organised a room for the baby herself as Karl was adamant that he wanted nothing to do with the baby or anything that was to do with the child. Anna just hoped he would be different when she had given birth and there was this little person to look after.

Then, another blow struck, which, for Anna, was much worse; her father slipped on the catwalk above one of the big grain silos that they had on the farm and fell in. The silo was empty as they were cleaning them out ready for harvest which would commence in a few weeks' time. His neck was broken and they said he would have died instantly. Normally there was safety rail along the catwalk but it had been removed for easier access. It was Silas who phoned and he actually phoned Ruth first and asked her to go and keep Anna company, as he had some bad news for her and didn't want her to be alone. When she rang the bell, it was Karl who answered the door as he was busy in his study and hadn't gone to the showroom.

"Sorry to trouble you Karl, is Anna in?" Ruth wasn't sure whether to stay or what to do.

Karl stepped back, unsmiling. He didn't like Ruth but he knew how Anna felt about her so at least was polite. Almost on cue the phone rang and calling to Anna that Ruth was there Karl answered it. At the other end, Silas too wasn't sure when Karl answered but ploughed on anyway asking for Anna.

"You seem to be in great demand," he said handing Anna the phone and went back to his study without even speaking to Ruth.

Anna didn't know it was Silas and smiling at Ruth she indicated to her to go into the drawing room. "Hello, who is it?"

Silas was having trouble controlling his emotions. "Anna, it's me. I have some terrible news, is Ruth there?"

"Yes, what are you talking about? Silas, you are frightening me."

"Sorry, but there is no easy way to say this. Anna, it's Dad, he's dead."

Anna stood stock still her face draining of colour. "No, he can't be, not Dad, no he can't be, it's not true,"

"I am sorry, Anna, but he had a terrible fall earlier this morning, he fell into the silo he—" Silas could say no more; he was too choked up.

Ruth put her arm around Anna as she looked like she might fall. "Please tell me it's not true." Anna's voice took on a hysterical note. Karl came through from the study into the hall. "What's going on?" He looked from one to another. Anna was holding the phone in her hand staring at it in disbelief. Ruth took it gently from her and spoke to Silas. "She will be OK. We will look after her and I will ring you back shortly."

Thank goodness, Ruth thought, she had persuaded Anna to tell her parents she was expecting a couple of weeks ago, it meant that Silas was more aware of how she might react.

Karl looked at Ruth with hostility in his eyes. "I will take care of Anna and everything now, thank you Ruth."

Ruth ignored him and said to Anna "What can I do for you love. How can I help?"

Even though Anna was still reeling from Silas's news she was aware of Karl's disapproval of Ruth's involvement and mutely shook her head. Drawing a deep breath she managed to say, "I will be fine. Karl will look after me."

"If you are sure then, I'll see you later." Ruth turned to go but not without saying to Karl in a low voice, "Make sure you do."

"Indeed," Karl said.

For Anna, the next few weeks were the worst of her life. Even worse than when she had a miscarriage. She rang Muriel when Karl was out and talked to her for a good hour. Muriel had moved down to Cornwall and other than talking on the phone they hadn't seen each other since Muriel left. They both knew Karl would disapprove and so had contented themselves with phone calls, now, however, Muriel offered to come up to London and stay nearby. Anna was very tempted to say please but then she thought she would soon be going down to the farm for the funeral, so she would manage. Ruth had been as supportive as Karl would allow.

"How are you in yourself, Anna?" asked Muriel. "Don't forget, you have a little one to think of. Try not to stress too much."

"I will be fine."

"Well, I will come up if you need me, my dear, just let me know."

When Anna put the phone down, tears were running down her cheeks. Just then, Karl came in; he was beginning to get fed up with Anna's grief. "What is the matter now?" He sounded very grumpy, which made Anna feel nervous.

"Nothing, just feeling sad. Silas rang, apparently Dad was waiting for a pace maker as his heart beat was irregular. Dad didn't tell me as he didn't want me to worry. It seems as if he may have had a fainting fit and that is why he fell." Silas had rang Anna before she rang Muriel needing to talk.

Chapter 19

Anna was to travel to the farm on her own as Karl wasn't going down until the day of the funeral as he had a big order to fore fill. Anna had been surprised when Karl had agreed to her going but she suspected some of the reason was to get her away from Ruth and also he was getting fed up trying to placate Anna when she got upset which was nearly all the time. Ruth was worried about Anna driving to the farm alone in her emotional state and decided that she would go with her and then catch a train back; they agreed not to tell Karl as by now Ruth was well aware of Karl's hostility towards her.

Karl then decided at the last minute to wave Anna off, she made an excuse to pop into Ruth's and tell her so they arranged to meet round the corner. When Ruth finally climbed into Anna's car, she said, "I am not made for all this cloak and dagger stuff," which made Anna smile the first time in weeks.

"Malcom thinks I should stay nearby for a few days, that is why I have this big bag with me."

"I did wonder what that was for, but are you sure Ruth? It's so kind of you." Anna's bottom lip started to quiver.

"I could see if there is room at home but with so many brothers and their families I am not sure where we would put you."

"Don't worry, I would feel uncomfortable anyway not knowing your family. After all, I am a stranger to them; we have only spoken on the phone. I may stay until the funeral then come back home. You will have family around you and Karl will be there too."

As they got nearer Anna's old home, she pointed out landmarks and it took her mind off what lay in store when they got there. When they pulled up at the house, Ruth remarked what a beautiful old farmhouse it was. Anna looked at it in surprise; she had always taken it for granted. She had her family too she thought with deep regret. She longed to tell her father how much she loved him and thank him for all the love he had given her. Too late now!

The house was indeed full of people and there were two days to go before the funeral. John and Clare, Peter with another girlfriend that Anna hadn't met, Silas of course, June and the twins and lastly Marie. Anna felt quite tired after all the introductions but June soon had the kettle on and Anna helped her make everyone a cup of tea. Ruth was sitting talking to Marie and the two of them seemed to be getting on well. Marie was explaining that Matthew and Sally wouldn't get there until early morning funeral day. Their children were staying at home with Sally's parents looking after them.

Everyone was looking out for Anna as she was close to her time but she seemed OK. She found that she avoided being left alone with Marie and this hurt Marie who wanted things to be right between Anna and herself especially now but Anna kept her at a distance.

It was a big funeral. Tim was well liked and had been an N.F.U representative for a number of years. He also had a small prize winning herd of British White cattle and as they were on the endangered list he was well known in cattle circles too. Everybody who had had anything to do with Tim it seemed was there, so much so that many couldn't get into the church.

An hour before it started Anna went to her mother and said that she wanted to say a few words. Quite a few people were anyway but Anna wanted this to be her own goodbye to her dad. As they were talking, Karl arrived. On hearing what Anna proposed he was immediately against it. "No, Anna, I will not allow this. It will be too upsetting for you."

Marie looked at him askance, "What is your problem, if Anna wants to do it, then I, for one, would love her too."

"I am going too, so don't worry, Mum." Anna looked at Karl in defiance. He shrugged and said nothing. He didn't want to rock the boat just now.

When Anna got up to speak, she was very composed, she was going to do this for Tim and for her family. Taking a deep breath and speaking up so everybody could hear. "I loved my Dad and I know everybody here liked and loved him too. He was so many things to so many of you. N.F.U. British White Cattle, Parish Councillor, but to us his family he was husband and father and grandfather. Now I am older and look back I realise what a difficult child I was. But Dad always believed in me. He knew when I was being treated unfairly he encouraged me to do things I didn't think I was capable of he was my rock and my soul mate. I am sorry this little person in here," Anna patted her tummy. "Won't ever get the chance to meet him but certainly if it turns out to be a boy I hope he grows in the image of his grandfather. What a lucky daughter I have been, he has always been there for me, it didn't matter if we didn't see each other much or speak that often he was there and I knew that he always understood me and loved me. I will miss him for the rest of my life and he has left an ache in my heart that will never really go away." At this point Anna started to cry and hurriedly left the pulpit. Many that were there were very moved by her words and there was the sound of people weeping as the service resumed.

Later back at the house there was a large gathering. Anna tried to catch up with people she hadn't seen for a long time including Vernon and Kate. It was good to see her brothers too and then she saw two of her cousins she hadn't seen since childhood. They had come out of the city in the school holidays and although older had always included Anna in their games.

Steve, the oldest, wrapped his arms round Anna, "Good to see you coz sad though that we are here." Jim, the other cousin, did the same then said he had better go and find his wife and trooped off. Anna thought she was neglecting Karl, and Ruth was about somewhere but she would talk to Steve for a few moments first. They caught up with each other's news. Steve was still unmarried and as he was very good-looking Anna guessed he was enjoying playing the field though he was a lovely person and wouldn't harm a fly on purpose.

Then Ruth came along and said she was going home. Silas had offered to drive her to the station, so Anna said goodbye she would be back in a couple of days with Karl.

Gradually the crowd of people thinned out and though they had had caterers in there was still a lot of clearing up to do. Marie looked exhausted. Anna patted her mother's arm. "I'll go and make you a cup of tea Mum," she said.

The kitchen was empty when she got there rather to her relief and she filled the kettle and had just set it to boil when Karl strode into the kitchen. One look at his face told Anna he was in a rage. "You dirty, little slut. I saw you hugging that fellow, all over him like a rash, you whore." Before Anna could even answer, Karl hit her with his fist just above her right breast. Anna staggered back and crashed into the kitchen table which broke her fall.

"Karl—" she gasped. Suddenly, Marie appeared as Karl went to hit Anna again.

She stepped in front of Karl and he stopped in his tracks. Anna had never seen her mother so angry. "Don't you dare hit my daughter, you animal, get out of my house now." Marie pointed her hand towards the door.

"Your daughter was behaving like a loose woman and she is MINE, MINE. I won't have it."

Peter appeared, then Mathew and finally John; they had all heard the commotion, "What the hell is going on here?" Peter was the first to speak.

"Karl is leaving now." Marie said in her don't argue voice that the boys knew well.

Karl stood looking round at them all. "Country bumpkins," he spat. "I will be waiting for you," he directed this to Anna, then strode out of the room. Moments later they heard the throaty roar of his Porsche and he was gone.

Anna slumped into the nearest chair and burst into tears, "Sorry, so sorry," she sobbed.

"What the hell are you sorry for?" Peter came and put his arms round her. "What was it all about?"

"He must have seen me talking to Steve," said Anna through her tears. "And got the wrong end of the stick."

"I don't care what he thought, it isn't on to hit you. Whatever would your father have thought about all that?" Marie was twisting her hands in agitation. "Anna, be honest, your miscarriage, was that something to do with Karl. Had he hit you then?"

Before Anna could reply, Peter, who was the hothead of the family after Silas, said, "Hit you! I'll kill the bastard!"

Then everybody started to speak at once, horrified at what seemed to be happening, just then, Silas came in. "What the

127

hell is going on? I met Karl down the lane and he nearly ran me off the road. I think he shook his fist at me, though I couldn't be sure."

Again everybody started to speak at once until Anna jumped to her feet and spoke above the hubbub. "Please just stop, please. We have just buried Dad and I can't bear anymore, it's all so horrid, and I don't feel very well." And she sat back in her chair, looking very, very pale.

Marie went to her side and felt Anna's forehead, she felt hot and clammy. "Come on, love, I think you should be in bed."

Anna allowed herself to be led upstairs and with Marie's help, she got into bed. She felt very shaky and unwell. Marie fussed round and then announced she was going to call the doctor. Anna felt too tired to argue and an hour or so later, Dr Jones turned up. Anna had known him since she was a child, he was very old fashioned but also a much respected man.

"Your blood pressure is very high, young lady, have you been prescribed anything for it?"

"Yes, it's been a little high but the doctor in London didn't seem that worried."

Dr Jones just grunted and carried on examining Anna.

"Well, I am concerned for you, my dear, and I am calling an ambulance to take you to hospital."

Anna pushed herself up in bed "But—"

"No buts, you want to keep yourself and your baby safe and healthy, don't you? Well, hospital is the best place for you right now."

Anna lay down again. She couldn't muster the energy to argue. She felt worn out and drained. She decided to let whatever would happen, happen.

Downstairs, the family were all waiting to hear what the Dr would say and were horrified when he said he wanted Anna in hospital as soon as possible as he was afraid of eclampsia. "This is a safety net, really. She will be in good hands there and then should she develop any more worrying symptoms, they will deal with them immediately."

Dr Jones patted Marie on the shoulder. "I was at Tim's funeral but had to go to a call so didn't manage to see you afterwards. Anna's piece she said in church was lovely, but I think all this has made her condition worse. By the way, she is very tender just above her right breast and there is a mark there, what's the story with that?"

Marie shook her head not ready to say anything to the Dr about Karl. Silas had no such hang-ups. "We think her husband hit her," he said.

Dr Jones looked appalled and shook his head in disbelief. "In that case, he should be reported," he said. "But right now, Anna has enough else to worry about and so do all of us. I will wait for the ambulance, if you don't mind."

June bustled about and made tea. Marie went back upstairs and sat with Anna. Shortly afterwards the ambulance turned up. Marie wanted to go in the ambulance with Anna and so it was agreed that she would and when she had made sure Anna was OK, one of the boys would go and pick her up. The doctor had said they would almost certainly keep Anna in for a few days at least.

When they got to the hospital, Anna went into premature labour and was rushed into theatre for an emergency caesarean. Marie rang home in tears to let them all know. Matthew and Sally were booked on a flight home to Ontario the next day, but Marie told them to go; they couldn't do anything and, as they had left their children with Sally's parents, everybody thought it best if they went. They would properly know how things were by then anyway.

By this time it was very late and having made sure everyone was OK at home Silas went and sat with his mother in the waiting room. They already knew Anna had had the operation and one premature baby boy was in the incubator. They were still concerned about Anna; however, and Marie was beside herself with worry.

"Here, Mum, it's hot and wet, if nothing else." Silas had got his mother a hot drink from a vending machine.

"Oh, thank you, dear. This is just so awful coming on top of your father's death. I feel so guilty now that when Anna came to me two or three years ago I was dismissive and didn't think what I was saying or even listen to her. Dad told me I was wrong and it's certainly come back to haunt me now. I have always loved her just as much as the rest of you but somehow she and I always seemed to rub each other up the wrong way.

Dad always said we were too alike. Whatever will we do if she isn't alright, what are we going to do about that husband of hers? He seemed so nice and charming, how wrong I was. Oh Silas, what a fool I've been."

Silas put his arm round his mother's shoulder; she seemed to have shrunk in the last couple of weeks and he thought with a jolt that he would have to look after her now his Dad wasn't there anymore. It hadn't really hit home until then. "Come on Mum, Anna will be OK. She's made of stern stuff, she will pull through and then we will worry about what's best to do both for Anna and the baby."

Sometime later the doctor came through to speak to them. "Anna is awake now but very sleepy, if you want to come through to see her you can. We will be keeping her in for a few days and the baby will be here for longer until we can be sure he will be OK."

Anna had her eyes closed when they went in to see her, she looked deathly pale and very fragile. She opened her eyes when they stood by her bed though and gave them a small smile.

"They tell me I have a little boy," she whispered. "I haven't seen him yet, have you?"

Marie stifled a sob. "No, sweetheart, it's you we are concerned with just now." Anna smiled again and closed her eyes.

"Don't worry Mum. I will be fine."

A nurse bustled in. "I think Anna needs to rest now and it's very late. Why not go home and get some rest yourself, Mrs Simpson? You look done in."

"We buried my father today," said Silas. "Mum has had a terrible day, we all have."

The nurse looked from one to the other. "Goodness gracious, how terrible is that. What about Anna's husband? I see you put yourselves down as next of kin when she came in."

"He is—" Silas stopped his mother saying more by interrupting.

"He went back to London early, business. We will let him know."

The nurse narrowed her eyes but just said they should go home but if they wanted a quick peek at the baby they could.

They couldn't see much but a tiny little bundle wrapped up in the incubator.

By the time they got home, it was the early hours of the morning, and Silas made sure his mother had gone to bed before he rang Karl's number to let him know that he had a son. He felt he should know, and also, he wanted to tell him what he thought of him as he had missed out before.

Karl had only just got to sleep as he had sat up drinking a bottle of Scotch and feeling very sorry for himself and hard done by. "Hello," he croaked.

"This is Silas. I thought you should know, you bastard, that Anna is in hospital, ill. She had to have a caesarean, you are to blame." He didn't get the chance to say more as Karl hung up and left the phone off the hook. Silas was frustrated but gave up and finally crawled into bed at four in the morning.

Chapter 20

The next day Anna was much better and when June and Marie went to see her she was propped up in bed and although still pale looked more her old self. The nurses had earlier put her in a wheelchair and taken her to see her son.

After greeting her mother and sister-in-law, Anna told them she was going to name the baby Charles, Timothy. "Do you think Dad would approve, Mum? He always said he didn't like his name."

"I don't think he disliked it that much, and he would have been so proud sweetheart. I am sad, though, that he won't see this little grandson." Marie wiped away the tears that seemed ever present for now. Not wanting to stress Anna just now, June and Marie didn't ask her any questions about her marriage, or Karl, or the future and given the circumstances, they had a good visit. Clare, John's wife, also popped in to see Anna and by the end of the day she was tired but felt very cherished. She knew she had difficult decisions to make in the future but for now she shut her mind to it and concentrated on her baby and herself.

Ten days later she found herself back in her old bedroom and realised she had to face up to the future. It would be another couple of weeks at least before Charlie came home. "Charlie is what I want him called," she had announced to everybody, so Charlie he was.

Marie came bustling into her room the next morning after she had got home, with a cup of tea. "What's this Mum?" she said. "It's a first!" Marie looked sheepish.

"I know, I haven't been the best mother in the world but I am trying now."

Anna smiled at her. "You have always done your best and no-one can do more than that. You are my mum, and I love you, though I know that I too am partly to blame for things that haven't been right between us in the past. Dad wouldn't want us to be is disharmony now would he, so let's make a fresh start."

"I miss him so much," Marie's lip trembled. "All I know is he was right about Karl, and I was so taken up with the charm of the man I couldn't see past all that, I'm sorry."

"Mum, you've nothing to be sorry for, really. Karl turned my head, I was taken in too and wouldn't have listened to anyone anyway. He is like two different people. One minute kind, charming, generous, the next vicious and cruel, and when he loses his temper, it's the bad character that surfaces. He told me he didn't want children and has been unhappy about Charlie but now I hope to give him a few weeks and he will come round. He is Charlie's father after all, and I don't want my son growing up not knowing his own father. Besides, Sir William will be so excited with having a grandson, especially after Clare's suicide."

Marie, who was sitting on the side of Anna's bed, looked worriedly at her daughter. "Anna, love, are you thinking of going back to him after he hit you and called you names? The man is dangerous and unstable; I think you should stay here, at least for now."

"I can't stay here and sponge off you and Silas. It wouldn't be right, no, when Charlie is well enough we will go back to London. Karl will be fine, I am sure."

Marie shook her head but said nothing more. She knew how stubborn Anna could be and now they were on a better footing she wanted it to stay that way.

So they all played a waiting game not trying to persuade Anna to stay but making a great fuss of her and hoping it would be enough to make her change her mind. She spent a lot of time playing with June and Silas's children and went over and visited John and Clare, their children were older but Anna still enjoyed time with them which was something that hadn't really happened in the past.

Then the day came when the hospital told her she could take Charlie home. She was so excited; she had, of course, spent many hours at the hospital with him but to have him to herself at home was something she had been longing for. When she got home with her precious bundle, everyone wanted to see him and hold him and it was all very exciting. Charlie had proved to be a very laid back baby and seemed not to cry much and was pretty happy to sleep and feed and not much else.

Two weeks later Anna came into the kitchen at breakfast time and announced she was going back to London. She had told them a week before that she had spoken to Karl and he wanted her back. She hadn't told them he was crying and pleading on the phone as she felt it was part of the ritual of asking her to forgive him. She had also spoken to Ruth many times and told her mother that Ruth would be there should she need help in any way.

"Oh, Anna, no, please stay a little longer. I will be so worried about the two of you. I'm not sure you are doing the right thing." Marie pleaded.

"It will be fine, Mum, don't worry. I will ring you this evening, I promise." Anna wasn't as confident as she sounded but she felt she somehow owed it to Charlie and Karl to try. Now she had a son she wanted them to be a proper family unit and she hoped Karl would embrace this and maybe appreciate all that he had more. After all, he had a son and heir now and she knew Sir William was very pleased about that.

So she reluctantly packed her things and the baby bits and pieces that June had given her as she had nothing at all when she had come and with a tearful goodbye set off back to London.

When she drew up at the house, the front door banged open and Karl rushed down the steps and gathered her into his arms and kissed her passionately before she had a chance to hardly get out of the car. She gently extricated herself and said softly, "Come and meet your son." Karl looked almost scared, as Anna got baby Charlie out of his baby seat, and backed away when Anna held him out to his father. "I don't know anything about babies, I might drop him."

"You won't, here take him, and hold him like this."

Karl fumbled rather but managed in the end to hold his son and carry him indoors. Anna led the way upstairs to the nursery and got the baby out of his travelling clothes. "I think he needs his nappy changed," she said.

Karl backed out of the room. "I'll get the rest of your things out of the car then put it away," he said and fled before Anna had a chance to say anything.

Later, when Charlie was settled, Karl and Anna sat down together in the sitting room. Karl patted the sofa beside him but Anna took a seat across the room. "Karl, please try not to be so volatile, we have a little son now and I want us to be a family unit, be together and have some good times. I know I annoy you sometimes but I will try if you will, let's start again with a clean sheet."

Karl sat looking at her for a moment. She couldn't read his expression, finally he smiled and said, "Why not, anyway I do have a surprise for you but it will have to wait until tomorrow."

Anna opened her mouth to ask what it was but Karl held up his hand to stop her. "Tomorrow," he said then coming over to her started to kiss her fervently. "God how I've missed you," he said. He made love to her there and then with a restrained passion which seemed alien to Anna; it hadn't been quite that before. Afterwards, she wondered if it was because her body was different after giving birth.

Karl made himself scarce, though, when it came to feeding and bathing Charlie; he said he had work to do and shut himself in his study. Anna wasn't so sure about that and decided it was because if anything Karl seemed almost afraid of the baby. He moaned and groaned when Anna got up but that was it. The next morning he seemed to be like a cat on a hot tin roof and Anna sensed that something momentous was in his mind but decided to keep quiet. Then at nine o'clock the next morning on the dot the doorbell rang and Karl leapt to his feet and hurried out. Anna heard a murmur of voices then Karl came in ushering a tall blonde girl dressed in a nurse's uniform. "Anna darling, this is Jenny, she is here to look after Charles."

Anna was so surprised she just sat and stared at the woman until Karl said sharply, "Anna."

Anna got to her feet and taking the nurse's hand that she held out in a swift handshake she said to Karl, "Karl, can we have a few words in private please. Sorry Jenny, excuse us."

She marched into the kitchen with Karl behind her. She swung round and before he had a chance to speak she hissed at him. "What on earth are you thinking? I don't want some stranger looking after my baby, our baby. It won't do Karl!"

Karl's eyes had turned to ice. "This isn't negotiable Anna, she is a fully qualified Nanny from a reputable firm and she is employed to live in and look after Charles. I had Mrs Ragg get a room ready for her and it's all settled. No arguments."

Anna stood staring at Karl for several minutes, clenching and unclenching her hands, there was a war going on inside her. Charles was her son, and she didn't want some stranger looking after him; she had been looking forward to that all through her pregnancy. At the same time she admitted to herself she was afraid to cross Karl even more so when he laid it down like that. It wasn't just the physical violence but the way he could humiliate her which in some ways she found harder to bare. He stared back at her daring her to disagree. She straightened her shoulders and holding her head up high said, "Very well Karl, if that is your wish, but don't expect me to like the idea or the girl because that won't happen. I will also have the last word when it comes to any decisions regarding MY son."

"I think you will find he is OUR son Anna, and for now you can have the last word, in the future, who knows." He shrugged.

With a sudden insight, Anna thought, *I hate you Karl,* but she said nothing. She had built herself a trap, she now realised, but to keep her son, she would have to put up with it.

Minutes later, Charles started to cry, ready for his breakfast. Anna hurried out of the kitchen to get him and there was Jenny standing in the hall unsure what was going on and what she should do. Anna felt suddenly sorry for the girl, none of this was her fault after all, so she said, "Charlie needs feeding. Come with me and meet him."

A look of relief spread across Jenny's face, and she followed Anna upstairs to the nursery. Anna picked Charlie up and prepared to carry him downstairs to make up a bottle. With the distraction of Jenny arriving she hadn't got round to it. "Pardon me for asking, but aren't you breast feeding him?" Jenny asked politely. Anna's hackles rose immediately.

"As it happens, no," was all she said defensively. The trouble was, Anna had wanted to very badly but she had been quite ill after the birth and although her milk had come in she had been unable to produce much and Charlie was a hungry baby. In the end, the hospital staff felt Anna and Charlie were better off with the bottle.

The first few days after Jenny's arrival were very difficult for both of them. Anna was both protective and defensive but Jenny was experienced enough to go softly and after Anna had been next door and poured all her heartache out to Ruth, who made her feel better, things calmed down. Eventually Anna came to realise that there were advantages because it restricted Karl and made him keep his temper under more control. He would make cutting remarks but was never abusive in his language and of course physically he couldn't do anything in front of Jenny. Sometimes Anna wondered why he still wanted her there as his wife but then it dawned on her that she was actually a status symbol. People quite often said what a golden couple they were. Both very good looking and intelligent and though Anna was quite quiet, Karl was very charming in company. Also, of course, she was his possession. He had always made that clear with his petty jealousies and as his possession he was never likely to let her go; she was bound to him for ever.

Charlie was a delightful child and Anna was allowed to take him to see her family quite frequently now so long as Jenny went with her. They also visited Karl's parents then Karl would go too. Sir William was thrilled with his little grandson but Karl's mother didn't seem that interested and having had a cursory hold of her grandchild seemed very pleased to hand him back. Then came the issue of the christening. Karl didn't seem fussed over whether Charlie was christened or not nor was Anna really as she took the view that Charlie could decide that when he was old enough to make an informed choice. Anna's mother, though, and Karl's parents kept broaching the subject and finally Anna asked Karl what he thought they should do?

"I don't know, I suppose we will have to go along with it, just to keep my parents quiet, at least."

"How do we go about it, then?" asked Anna. "We won't please everybody, whatever we do."

In the end, Anna agreed for Charlie to be christened a Catholic, just to appease Sir William and explained to her mother what a dilemma they had. Marie was remarkably laid back about it all much to Anna's surprise. Truth was she didn't want to make things difficult for Anna; she felt she had enough to contend with as it was. Karl announced that they would have a lavish party at his parents' house. Anna was allowed to make the arrangements for this but was not allowed much input into the christening itself. Karl had asked a cousin of his to be a godparent. Anna had never met him but she was happy that Silas was going to be another godparent. He agreed reluctantly for Anna's sake. He loved his little nephew though who was a beautiful little boy. He knew it would be an uncomfortable day given the animosity between Karl and Anna's family. Anna had invited Ruth which Karl wasn't keen on but when she said she wanted to invite Muriel, Karl said no, then Anna asked why not and then Karl changed his mind. However, Muriel wasn't keen to say she would come given the time of year. Anna was sad about it but understood.

As it was in the end, it all went better than Anna hoped. Both Karl and baby Charles were on their best behaviour and although it was winter, it was one of those rare winter days which was almost spring-like with sunshine and blue sky.

Charlie grew fast and before they knew it a whole year had passed. Karl wasn't into taking much more notice of his son than before and when Anna said should they have a birthday party, Karl scoffed. "Whatever for? He doesn't know it's his birthday, don't be silly."

So Anna arranged to go back to the farm for his birthday which of course was the anniversary of Tim's funeral. Having a party for Charlie with as many of his cousins as possible was just what Marie and Anna needed to take some of the pain of the previous year away. Jenny, of course, went too. Anna and Jenny got on quite well, but they weren't close. Anna kept Jenny at a distance even though they were nearly the same age and in any other circumstances they would have been friends. As it was, it was strictly employer–employee relationship.

Charlie who was already crawling at great speed and standing up by chairs and things got so excited during the afternoon he took his first steps and was very pleased with himself. In fact, he had a ball and loved being with his cousins even though they were older.

On the way back Jenny said, "Mrs Von Herbert, excuse me for saying so, but I really think Charlie would benefit from seeing more of children of his own age or indeed children of any age. He is with adults constantly and it's not good for him. Sorry, I don't mean to interfere but it's what I think." She lapsed into an embarrassed silence.

"No, you are right, it would be much better for him, I agree, but getting my husband to agree is something else," said Anna.

Jenny sat quietly for a short while considering what to say. She was well aware that Anna and Karl had to say the least a strained relationship. She didn't know what to make of Karl; he could be very charming but also very brusque and almost rude sometimes. She had noticed how he switched on the charm when he wanted his own way or was trying to impress someone. She was very wary of him. As for Anna, Jenny liked her and felt very sorry for her. It was only small things but she had seen Anna flinch sometimes when Karl spoke to her and Jenny knew Anna was afraid of him. So she kept her head down and got on with her job and of course she adored little Charlie. In the end, she said, "Would you like me to put it to your husband?"

It was Anna's turn to sit quiet for a few moments then she said, "You can try."

A few days later when Karl was home, Jenny knocked on the study door and said she thought Charlie would benefit from mixing with children his own age more. Karl was against it for a start but Jenny pointed out that there was a mother and toddler group a couple of street away. They met in someone's house two mornings a week. Karl said he would consider it. An hour or so later he called Jenny into the study Anna was already there looking hopeful that Jenny had succeeded.

"I have thought about this mother and toddler thing you talked about this morning Jenny, and I think you are right. Very clever of you," he smiled at her. "So I would be more than happy if you take Charles along and introduce him to the other children."

Anna looked stricken, and she and Jenny exchanged looks. "But I didn't mean for me to go, they are for mothers and toddlers. I meant Mrs Von Herbert."

"That may be the case but it would not fit in with Mrs Von Herbert's schedule, so I would appreciate it if you would take him along."

Anna, tears threatening at the back of her throat, said, "I am sure I could rearrange to fit it in Karl." Karl turned and looked at her, his eyes cold and hostile. "My dear, I do not want you to take on anything else; Jenny can take Charlie without any disruption to our lives."

Anna knew that look it was dangerous, so she gave in. It was either giving in now or later after he had blown his top. She knew when she was defeated.

Later when Charlie was having his nap and Karl had gone to the showroom, Jenny sorted Anna out. She was sitting in their little garden at the back of the house and although it was an overcast day she was wearing dark glasses. Jenny had a good idea why; she had seen the tears in Anna eyes earlier.

"Mrs Von Herbert, I am sorry. I didn't mean that to happen at all, it wasn't what I intended."

Anna gave a ghost of a smile. "I know you didn't, Jenny, my husband—" Anna was horrified to find tears running down her cheeks. She got up "Excuse me, I have to—" Jenny put her hand on Anna's arm,

"It's OK," she said softly. "I think I understand a little, maybe we can find a way round this. I know you want to take Charlie yourself and that was my idea, you should take him yourself."

Anna fighting for control sat down again. "Well, it looks as if it will be you after all." She smiled wanly at Jenny.

"Let's put our thinking caps on and hatch a plan, even if I take him sometimes maybe we can think of a way for you to take him mostly."

Anna looked at Jenny and suddenly realised that Jenny knew a lot more than either herself or Karl had thought.

Feeling suddenly humble, she muttered, "How much do you know?"

Jenny didn't prevaricate. "I know you aren't very happy and that Mr Von Herbert is hard on you over most things and that he hired me so he could have your undivided attention most of the time."

140

Anna drew a ragged breath again fighting tears. She longed to pour her heart out but knew it wouldn't help and would also put Jenny in an awkward position. She couldn't give in to the temptation but maybe she and Jenny could think of a way so Anna could go most of the time at any rate.

Finally it was agreed that Jenny would leave the house with Charlie, and then Anna would make an excuse of some sort to leave the house soon afterwards. Of course, if Karl had gone to the showroom, it was OK. It worked well for a few months and Anna found it very relaxing talking to other mothers and comparing notes. She managed to parry invites for coffee that sometimes came her way and sometimes Jenny took Charlie if Karl was expecting Anna to accompany him to some function or Antique fair or sale. One or two of the other mothers had nannies as well but not live-in ones. When Anna took Charlie, Jenny had time off to go shopping or meet friends.

Then, in November, Anna had a fright that made her question herself and her feelings towards Karl. He was late home that evening and hadn't let her know which wasn't that unusual; it depended on his mood. However, Anna had got dinner ready for 7:30 and Karl hadn't arrived. He was usually there by 7:00 at the latest. Anna then heard sirens going off all over the place. Was it an I.R.A. bomb, some disaster, what? Supposing Karl never came home again, how would she feel? Relief, sad, happy, what did she feel for him now? She knew she didn't love him anymore and sometimes she wondered if she ever did. But what if she never saw him again, and what about Charlie he would never remember his father. All this was going round and round in her head when Karl came in "Sorry, I am late," he said. "But there has been a fire at King's Cross underground station and everything is in chaos out there. Don't know how it started or if it was a bomb or what." Later, of course, they would know it was a fire. Anna was pleased that he was home but not euphoric. Christmas was looming. There was to be a small party the mother and toddlers organiser decided. Anna was very undecided as to what to do. Finally she told Karl about it and said that parents were expected to go along. Karl shuddered at the very idea. "Well, it is expected and it may be good for business as there are some wealthy people going, Jenny said, and they may be interested in what you do."

Anna didn't want to push it too much as she was already in a small dispute with Karl over their plans for Christmas. Karl and herself had been invited to a Villa on the Amalfi Coast in Italy by a wealthy customer of Karl's. In fact, they had done quite a lot of business together over recent years. Anna didn't like him much and certainly didn't want to spend Christmas there. Karl suddenly grinned at her. "Well, if I come with you to this thing, I will be accepting our invitation to Italy. Jenny and Charlie are invited too. Well, Charlie is, so Jenny will have to come too."

Anna felt she had backed herself into a corner so reluctantly she agreed. Charlie and Jenny had been with them recently to Paris much to Karl's disgust. It was a business trip but Anna had insisted Charlie to come too. It was a small victory but Charlie had been made much off by many of the people there that had seen him and Karl was beginning to realise he was an added asset. He was an engaging little boy with a round chubby face, an infectious smile, and a mop of dark blonde curly hair. When he smiled, which was a lot, his dark-blue eyes seemed to sparkle with joy and mischief.

As it turned out, Karl quite enjoyed the mother and toddler function because he got talking to another father who was refurbishing a house nearby and was looking for furniture and paintings to go with the period of the house. It seemed money was no object, so Karl was feeling very generous when they got home and told Jenny she could have three weeks in January off. Anna and Jenny looked at each other in surprise. Still looking at Anna, Jenny said, "Will that be okay, are you sure, Mrs Von Herbert?"

"Of course it is." Anna nearly said I shall have my little boy to myself!

Christmas wasn't so good; Charlie was teething and unusually for him rather fractious, Anna found their host and hostess a trial and difficult to get on a wavelength with and Karl got some virus and spent Boxing Day, and the day after, in bed feeling very sorry for himself.

When they finally got home, Karl yelled at Charlie who had been miserable the whole flight and car journey home. This frightened him and he yelled even louder. Karl raised his hand and Anna shot forward "Don't you dare hit him. He is only a baby." Karl swung round and Anna flinched expecting him to strike her but Jenny had just come into the room having taken Charlie's things upstairs to his room. She said nothing but stood in the doorway for a moment before stepping forward and scooping Charlie up and glancing at Anna but ignoring Karl she left the room rapidly.

"That bloody girl is a nuisance too, always in the way. She'll have to go, and don't YOU dare to tell me I can't discipline my son if I want to."

"Karl, he is only a baby, he doesn't know he was upsetting you. He is in pain from his teeth that are coming through." Anna pleaded for Karl to understand.

"Oh shut up, you pathetic creature, you make me sick." Karl went out slamming the door behind him.

Anna ran upstairs to see Charlie. Jenny was undressing him ready for a bath. She looked up as Anna came in. "I am sorry if I did wrong to take Charlie just then but—" She trailed off not knowing what to say.

"It's alright, Jenny. Karl is rather miserable not feeling well and it got to him, that's all. He isn't usually like that."

Anna had never confided in Jenny, though they had hatched the Mother and Toddler plan. She felt it would put Jenny in a very difficult position if she said too much, so again she tried to play it cool.

Karl and Anna were going to a New Year Party as it was 1988. Anna was dreading it as Karl had hardly spoken to her since they returned from Italy two days earlier.

They caught a cab as it was at one of Karl's customer's premises not very far away. Anna had been hoping to see her family before now but hadn't had the chance. She made up her mind she could go when Jenny was on her holiday. Anna as always looked stunning and part of her appeal was she always seemed oblivious of the fact she was so beautiful. Karl too of course was very handsome which made them the focus of many parties and people tended to call them a golden couple. It wasn't long before they were surrounded by a chattering noisy throng. Anna was by nature a shy person and not very confident on a personal level but she managed to leave that person behind at these functions and didn't come over as being like that.

There were several Americans at the party who had been invited by the hosts, neither Karl nor Anna had met them before. It wasn't long before one of them started to flirt with Anna in a very suggestive way. He had had a skin full Anna thought before they got to the party. She was very uncomfortable as Karl would be very jealous if he cottoned on what was happening, and anyway she didn't like the American. He told her his name was Marty and he came from Texas and where he lived and that he was an art dealer over to find paintings to take back. "I am told you know a bit about paintings. Maybe we can get together and you can show me what I should be looking for," he said.

"I am going away in a day or so sorry," said Anna, "My husband Karl will be very happy to help you though," she smiled at him.

"Don't tell me you are married. I saw the ring on your finger but I thought maybe it was just that you like wearing jewellery. There is no reason that I can't meet you for a coffee or a drink. A beautiful girl like you shouldn't belong to one man. He should share you with his friends at least, in fact a threesome or foursome would be huge fun I reckon, what do you say?"

Anna was horrified and backing away from him looked round wildly for Karl, he was across the room talking to a couple that Anna knew vaguely, muttering an excuse me she wove her way across the room and stood by Karl's elbow interrupting she said "Hello, how are you both?" She had temporarily forgotten their names. Karl looked annoyed but Anna ploughed on, asking silly questions with one eye on the American who was watching her with a smirk on his face. Soon; however, he turned away and Anna lost sight of him. She started to breathe easy.

The drinks and canapés flowed and then it was New Year, and the hosts had got a huge TV ready to count down and soon everybody was cheering and hugging and wishing each other Happy New Year. Anna was grabbed from behind and Marty was there pressing a wet kiss on her cheek then before she could pull away he had his mouth over hers and was holding her tightly in an embrace she couldn't wriggle free from. All at once his grip loosened and Karl pulling him away hit him hard between the eyes. "You sleaze ball, leave my wife alone. Come near either of us again, and I will kill you."

Marty had fallen backwards and the commotion had got all the guests' attention. John, whose house it was, stepped forward and along with another man they bundled Marty out of the front door and told him to get lost.

Anna was very shaken more so because she could see Karl's fury and knew she would be blamed even though it wasn't her fault.

"We are leaving," he said curtly to Anna, then turning to their hosts he said, "My wife is very upset by what has happened, please excuse us."

"Of course, so sorry this has happened, that fellow came with someone else, I really am sorry about this Karl, Anna, I will be in touch," said John.

Neither of them spoke on the way home. Anna was feeling frightened; she knew none of it was her fault but knew Karl wouldn't see it that way whatever she said. Her heart was racing by the time the door closed behind them in their own home. Then Jenny came barrelling down the stairs saying, "Happy New Year, did you have a good time? You are home early."

Karl, frowning, muttered something neither of them could catch and disappeared into his study. Anna started to feel relief that Jenny had come down when she had. "Yes, good party but I am tired so I am off to bed. Was Charlie good tonight?"

"He nearly always is. I'll say goodnight then." Jenny turned away.

Anna followed her upstairs and then peeked in on her son who was sound asleep. Lucky boy she thought not daring to think what mood Karl will be in later when he comes to bed.

She didn't have to wait long before she heard him come into the room. She had hurried to get into bed and was pretending to be asleep in the vague hope he would leave it until the morning. She heard him undress and go to the bathroom then he came back into the bedroom and tore the bedclothes from the bed. Then he knelt astride Anna and pulling her nightdress up as high as he could he forced himself into her and raped her. While doing so he hissed obscenities at her. "I'll teach you to look at other men. You are mine and

145

mine alone, you ungrateful bitch, don't forget that. You always will be. No-one else will ever have you, do you hear me?"

He had hurt her physically and the tears started to run down her face. "I didn't encourage him Karl, I swear, he was horrid. I wouldn't do that I promise. I'm sorry, please, Karl, you are hurting me."

"Too right I am hurting you. This is nothing to what I'll do if you ever encourage another man again. I'll kill you, believe me I will."

At last he rolled off her and, almost immediately, fell asleep. Anna lay there a long time, shuddering and crying softly; she hurt all over. Finally she crept out of bed and, going into the bathroom, she examined her body. Her breasts were sore where Karl had squeezed them, her inner tights were red and bruised where Karl had forced her legs wide much wider than normal almost as if he was trying to tear her in two. He had pummelled her stomach too with his fists at one point. She ran a bath as quietly as she could. It took a long time as she didn't want to wake him but she needed to lay in the warm water and sooth her battered body. She lay there a long time not really thinking but aware that sooner or later he would kill her if she didn't escape from him. When the water was almost cold again, she hauled herself out and hardly trying to dry herself she found a new nightdress and got back into bed beside Karl being careful not to wake him.

The next morning she woke to find Karl leaning over her. "Darling, I am so sorry I was cross last night, really I am. It was just that Yank made me so jealous. I love you so much, please forgive me."

Anna lay looking at him. *We've been here many times before*, she was thinking but in the end all she said was, "I hope I never set eyes on him again Karl, you can believe that."

"I do, darling, I do. Just remember you are MY wife and I love you."

New Year's Day they were going to visit Karl's parents as they hadn't seen them since before Christmas. Anna was so stiff and sore she was having a job to function properly and was thankful Jenny was there to help her. Charlie at just over eighteen months was quite a handful now. He said several words, was walking well and into everything.

Afterwards Anna wasn't sure how she got through the day. She didn't want anyone to guess how uncomfortable she was. Sir William asked her what was wrong and she just said that she had somehow hurt her back. Jenny was in the kitchen giving Charlie his lunch thankfully, Anna thought, and Karl ignored the exchange between his father and Anna. Karl's mother always seemed in her own world anyway and more so since Clare's suicide.

The next day a bouquet of flowers arrived from their hosts of New Year's Eve with again an apology. They claimed that Marty was a gate crasher but neither Karl nor Anna believed that. Karl went off to the showroom and Anna breathed more easily and settled down to enjoy the day as much as her aches and pains would allow. She rang Ruth next door and arranged to go for a coffee later that morning.

Half an hour later Karl arrived back home, he looked livid. Anna, Jenny and Charlie were all in the kitchen. Anna looked up as Karl walked in and her blood turned to water. Before she had a chance to speak Karl said, "Jenny, take Charlie to the park. Mrs Von Herbert and I have some business to attend to."

Jenny took in Karl's expression then said, "Excuse me sir, but it's very cold to be out for Master Charles."

"Just GO," was all Karl said.

"Karl, surely they don't need to leave the house, we can talk here." Anna was shaking but managed to keep her voice steady.

"I said OUT," was all he said.

Jenny glanced anxiously at Anna who to tried to smile reassuringly and gathering Charlie up she fled the room. Anna found it impossible to speak; her mouth was dry. Karl just stood staring at her, and a couple of minutes later they heard Jenny and Charlie leave. Anna found a voice and whispered, "What is wrong, Karl? What has upset you?"

Karl stepped back into the hall then returned with a huge bouquet of flowers. "These arrived at the showroom for you from lover boy, and you said you didn't encourage him."

Anna stood shaking her head. "I didn't, Karl, please believe me, I didn't. Why would I when I have you, I love you," she said desperately.

Karl's fist flashed out so fast she didn't see it coming and a second later she was on the floor with her head spinning. Karl picked her up and mounted the stairs flinging open the bedroom door her threw her onto the floor and kicked her hard in the ribs. Next he stripped her naked and hit her hard again. Anna lost consciousness. When she came round, she found she was tied by her wrists to the corner of the bed head. She was vaguely aware that Karl had raped her again, but at the moment he was nowhere to be seen. She was in a lot of pain from the beating and also from being tied as she was. Her mouth was dry and she found her vision was blurry. She closed her eyes. A few minutes later she could hear Charlie's voice through the door, he was saying mummy. Tears ran out of Anna's eyes and dripped onto the pillow. She wanted so much to call out to him. Did Karl mean to kill her like he threatened, would she ever see her little boy again? She could hear Karl talking to Jenny but not what was said.

It was several minutes before Karl returned. "Ah, I see you are awake now but I am afraid you will have to stay there until I feel I can trust you to behave and not go round flirting with strange men."

Licking her dry lips Anna said, "Karl, please, at least untie me. I am so uncomfortable."

Karl sat himself down in a chair near the bed. "I think you look rather good like that, so no, not yet."

"Please, please Karl, let me at least go to the bathroom, please."

He sat considering then said, "OK, as you asked nicely, but I may tie you up again later."

When he had untied her, Anna struggled to her feet and going to the bathroom she felt very dizzy and then was very, very sick. She lay on the bathroom floor for a while. She felt so bad that she couldn't have cared at that moment whether she lived or died. Eventually Karl put his head around the door and seeing the state she was in picked her up and carried her back and laid her gently on the bed. "Anna, my Anna why do you make me behave so towards you? You know I love you but you have to obey me and I get cross when you don't, but I never mean to hurt you, just don't make me angry that's all then things like this won't happen." As he was saying this, he was stroking her hair very tenderly. Anna felt repulsed by his touch but made herself lay still and she shut her eyes. Sometime later, she woke up and was very surprised she had gone to sleep. The room was in darkness and she found she had been tucked into the bed rather like a child. As she fuzzily came out of sleep, memories came flooding back and she sat up quickly. Immediately a pain shot across her forehead and she felt sick again. Sitting still a moment she waited for the feeling to pass.

Just as she was feeling better, the door opened and Karl came in. Anna instinctively pulled the sheet up to her chin. She started to shake with fear. Karl switched on the light and on seeing her shivering said "Are you cold? I expect it's something to do with being sick a little while ago, some virus or another I think. I have told Jenny you are not well so she won't be going away for her break yet; she will go once you are better."

Anna looked at him but saw he wasn't trying to be funny or facetious but was in complete denial of what had gone on and the role he had played in it.

"I need to wash," she muttered and throwing back the covers made for the bathroom. Moments later as she waited for the shower water to warm up Karl appeared in the nude and stepped into the shower with her.

"I will warm you up," he said and, getting a generous amount of shower gel in his hand, he started to rub it across her shoulders and down her arms. Anna felt trapped, and she was repulsed by his touch but she somehow found a strength she didn't know she possessed and standing still, let him wash her. Strangely he was very gentle where he had hurt her and made a face when he saw her bruises which were becoming clearer as the warm water brought them out. Neither of them said anything and when Karl had finished, he wrapped her up in a fluffy towel and picking her up carried her back to bed. Anna's heart was racing; she was afraid he would want her again but he laid her down and fumbled in the drawer for her night dress. Once she was settled once more in bed he said he would be back soon and having got dressed, he disappeared downstairs.

Anna lay thinking about all that had gone on. She knew she no longer loved him and now wasn't so sure she ever had. She had been lonely when she met him, a successful business she may have had, but a dismal personal life and so she was more susceptible to his attentions than maybe she would have been. If she met him now, she reflected she would be far more resistant to his advances; she had changed. But then so had Karl. He was now showing his true colours, but what a mixture he was. When angry, he completely lost it then didn't believe he had done any of the cruel things that he had done and was more like he was when they met. But that had been contrived and looking back Anna realised that Karl had always sought to control her from the moment they met. She shivered then turned her mind to the present and what she should do now. She would have to escape or sooner or later or he would kill her. That was clear.

One thing she was glad she had done was that the money she had out of her business she had put away and Karl had always given her a generous allowance far more than she needed so again she had put the money aside. So financially she would be fine for the time being at least. Canada, she would go to her brother in Canada; she needed to get as far away as she could, because Karl would be incandescent with anger when he found she was gone. With Charlie of course, lucky he was on her passport at least that was in order. How was she going to achieve all this she didn't know, she just knew she must somehow.

Just as she was trying to come up with a solution, Karl returned carrying a tray with a steaming bowl of soup and toast and a cup of tea. He pulled out a small table from the side of the room and placed the tray down. "Supper is served," he said with a flourish, giving a slight bow.

Anna got out of bed and gingerly sat down; she was still very shaky and uncomfortable. Karl had also brought a bowl of soup for himself. Anna tried to eat and she managed some but she was too wound up to eat it all. Karl assured her that Charlie was fine and Jenny was looking after him. Soon Anna climbed back into bed and pretended to sleep. She felt Karl climb into bed beside her and thankfully he was soon asleep. Sleep wouldn't come to Anna though; she found her ribs very sore and thought one at least was broken, her head and jaw hurt where Karl had hit her and though technically maybe it wasn't rape but to Anna it was, she certainly hadn't consented anyway!

Chapter 21

The next day after a sleepless night, Anna dragged herself out of bed early and, looking at herself in the bathroom mirror, was surprised to see she didn't look anywhere near as bad as she felt.

She decided to get dressed but found she couldn't wear her bra as she was too sore. Her jaw was swollen too and purple bruises were showing themselves on her arms and upper body. Finally she found a very loose blouse and a baggy jumper and some old jeans that she had worn when expecting Charlie before she got very big. Sitting down slowly in front of the mirror she tried to brush her hair which was very tangled but found lifting her arms up was very painful because of her ribs and all the bruising around her upper body. Then she realised Karl was awake. She saw him in the mirror watching her. His face was inscrutable; she couldn't read his mood.

"I feel much better this morning," she tried to sound brighter than she felt. "I thought I could get Charlie's breakfast, what can I get for you?"

Karl got out of bed. "I am not sure about this Anna."

"Please, Karl."

He looked at her thoughtfully and finally said "OK. But you are not to leave the house or see anyone apart from Charles and Jenny."

Anna knew that the reason for that was because of her injuries that were obvious to anyone that knew her at least. She didn't want to see anyone in any case so it was easy to agree.

Charlie was very pleased to see his mother, so was Jenny, but Anna noticed the tightening of her lips when she saw Anna. She said nothing, though, as Anna knew she wouldn't.

Karl announced he was going to be at home all day, again Anna wasn't surprised. Jenny helped Anna as much with everything that needed doing as she could and the day passed peacefully though with underlying tension. That night in bed Karl made overtures to Anna but when he realised how sore she was he desisted and left her alone.

The following morning Karl had a sale at Sotheby's to go to. Anna could see he was reluctant to leave in case she disobeyed him and he made her promise all over again to stay indoors. When he finally left, Anna breathed a huge sigh of relief. No sooner had he gone than there was a knock on the front door. Jenny jumped up and said she would go. The two young women hadn't had a chance to speak to each other yet and Anna felt frustrated that someone had come to disrupt her time with Jenny. However, Jenny came back followed by Ruth who without a word went straight up to Anna and put her arms around her. It was enough for Anna; she burst into tears and cried as if her heart would break. Jenny had picked up Charlie to take him away from his mother's distress but he evaded her and pulling at Anna's trouser leg said, "Mumma mumma, cry, cry." His little face was full of concern. Anna bent down and gathered him up as Ruth stood back.

"Jenny came to me the other day when Karl had told her to get out with Charlie, but we didn't know what we could do and certainly didn't want to make anything worse for you. It needs reporting, Anna. You can't live like this, love, you really can't."

"I know," Anna took a deep breath, "I am going to leave him, not just leave him but disappear, because if I don't, he will come after me. Jenny, I don't want you involved because it could backfire and you have a reputation to consider, so I will speak to Ruth in private, do you mind? What you don't know, can't hurt you. The only thing I ask is that you pack a small bag for Charlie and hide it in the bottom of his wardrobe."

Jenny looked distressed but, nodding her head, she went out of the room, and they heard her go upstairs. "Anna, are you sure it wouldn't be better just to go to the police, Malcom thinks you should."

Anna shook her head, "They won't want to be involved, besides, Sir William is some sort of civil servant, I am sure he would pull strings if he had to. No, I just want to get right away and make a fresh start, so here is what I have worked out but I'll need lots of help from you, do you mind?"

"My dear girl, of course not. Are you going to your friend in the West Country that used to work for Karl?"

Anna gave a small watery smile, "No, a lot further than that. I am planning on going to Canada and staying with my brother, at least to start with."

"What about tickets and flights and things and Charlie's passport?"

"This is where you come in Ruth. Please, can you ring home and tell them what is going to happen and ask Silas to be ready to come and pick me up in two days' time. That is when Jenny goes on holiday and Karl will still be going with this big sale. Also, get him to book the flights to Montreal for me and let Matthew know I am coming. Can I also ask a big favour of you and ask you to drive my car to Harwich and leave it there. I will give you the money for the train fare back."

Ruth looked at Anna with admiration. "Gosh Anna you really have thought this through, haven't you? I guess the car bit is to throw Karl off where you have really gone."

"Yes, I have, and now, somehow, I have to get through the next two days as if nothing has happened, don't know how yet, also Ruth, can we say our goodbyes here and now, in the long run it will be easier for both of us."

Ruth's eyes filled with tears. "I wasn't expecting this, Anna, but you are right. Give me your car keys now."

Anna gave a small smile and getting up went to a small ornament on the mantelpiece and unending it a set of keys fell out.

"A few months ago Karl took my keys away when he was in one of his moods; however, I had a spare set so I hid them and here they are."

Ruth and Anna found it very hard saying goodbye as they had become very close, and Ruth loved little Charlie to bits too.

"Dear Anna, please take care of yourself, I shall miss you so much, and I am so worried about you and little Charlie. Please let me know how you are and what is happening. I do hope I will see you again one day, please stay in touch."

"I shall miss you too," Anna was sobbing again now. "How am I ever going to thank you for all your love and support,

Malcom too. I will be in touch. I won't lose contact, I promise. Maybe one day we can see each other again, you are like the big sister I never had."

They clung to each other for several minutes more until Ruth gently extracted herself and without looking back left hurriedly. She had things to organise in a hurry.

Jenny and Anna spent the rest of the day quietly. Anna, of course, was still recovering and in pain when she moved awkwardly or quickly. Both of them were a bundle of nerves too knowing what was planned. Jenny didn't know details of course but knew Anna was plotting her escape. Not before time in Jenny's opinion though as it was Karl who had employed her she said little. She was worried that Karl wouldn't give her a reference afterwards.

The next day was even worse and at breakfast Karl asked Jenny what was up with her; she seemed edgy. She told him she was just excited about going to see her family but was worried about leaving Anna and Charlie.

"Well, I could be home for part of the day if you think it necessary. Is Anna still not very well, she seemed fine to me, just a bit quieter than usual."

Jenny was horrified at this but covered it up by saying she knew she was making a fuss and there was absolutely no reason at all for her to worry or for Karl to be home. Karl was relieved as he wanted to spend the day at the Auction but knew deep down that he was responsible for Anna's situation. Jenny was leaving early and Karl offered her a lift to the station which she gratefully accepted. Anna had told her if she went first it would help exonerate her from knowing anything about Anna's disappearance. They managed to make their goodbyes very brief as Karl was watching on and soon they were gone.

Anna then got into top gear as much as her aches and pains would allow. She knew exactly what she wanted to take with her so it didn't take long she had actually put all the clothes in the same part of the walk in wardrobe and as for cosmetics and wash things she was leaving most behind. Part of the reason being the less she took the less likely Karl would think it was long term. Charlie's things were all-ready anyway and half an hour after Karl had left Anna was ready, though throughout it all she couldn't stop shaking. She tried to write a short note but she couldn't hold the pen properly she was so nervous and what she scribbled wasn't legible.

She then went down to the garage which was underneath the house and opened the garage door. With a small cry of relief she saw Ruth waiting outside and a few moments later Silas drove into the garage too. There was no time to say goodbye to Ruth they were all wound up and nervous. Karl would somehow appear around the corner. Silas had brought an old car seat for Charlie who had so far thought it all a wonderful new game. They wanted to do this in the garage so no-one from the street would see anything odd. Anna crouched down as they drove out again into the street and Ruth had out a headscarf on as she drove Anna's car out. They couldn't do much about Charlie but just hoped for the best.

Neither she nor Silas said a word until they were well away from the area; they were too tense. Anna was shaking uncontrollably and teary too. Silas looked across at her "OK little sis, you are doing great. Now the thing is we couldn't get you a flight to Canada until next week but don't worry I am taking you to Kate and Vernon's to stay not home as that will be the first place Karl will look."

"But won't he look there too?" Anna was fighting tears.

"I expect he will, but not immediately and they will both be there and have assured us they will look after you, we will have to hope for the best. Everyone else is a no-no, we thought, even your friend Muriel. Karl doesn't really know them and it may not occur to him to look there yet. The other thing is that you said to get you on a flight to Montreal but Ottawa is much nearer Sally and Matthew, so that is where you will be flying to."

"OK, but the reason I said that was to put Karl off if he looked at flights, he may not think of Montreal."

Silas patted her knee. "Anna don't you think you are over reacting a little, surely, once Karl realises that you have left him, and especially if you've fled the country, he will give up. This all seems rather over the top to me. I love you dearly and I know he is bad news but surely you are not in this much danger!"

Anna sighed. She was too tired and distressed to argue, so all she said was, "We'll see, won't we?" She leant her head back against the back of the seat and tried to relax. Meanwhile, Charlie had given in to sleep as well so the rest of the journey was very quiet.

Kate and Vernon were delighted to see her and Charlie, whom they had not met, so he was made a great fuss of. Later that day, her mother came over and many tears flowed. Marie was completely horrified when Anna finally told her and Kate all that had gone on. They found it really hard to believe and also felt guilty and sad. Guilty in Marie's part anyway because she hadn't read the signs, and they both felt terrible that Anna had gone through so much without telling anyone.

"I have just found it all so hard Mum, to speak of it and admit what was happening. Karl was always so sorry afterwards and vowed he loved me and it wouldn't happen again. I didn't want to admit it also because somehow it seemed to be partly my fault. Maybe it is maybe I am not good enough or attentive enough to him. One thing I do know though is that my life and maybe Charlie's are in danger. That is why I must get away."

"I understand that, Anna, and hopefully when things have calmed down a little you can come home and we can pick up the pieces and start afresh."

"I hope so Mum, I do hope so."

The next few days were a nightmare for the whole family and Anna spent the whole time sick with nerves. She was too scared to go outside even into the garden, though as it was deep winter that didn't really matter. Karl had indeed turned up at the farm ranting and raving, then he tried John's place. Then all was quiet for a day or so then they had a phone call from Muriel to say he had been there. Then all was quiet until he tried Peter who not liking Karl punched him on the jaw and told him to get lost. Next thing the police arrived but having talked to Peter let him off with a warning. Karl must have got the police involved though because the next day it was on the news with Anna and Charlie's photographs and the fact that Anna's car was found abandoned at Harwich.

Chapter 22

The next day it was finally time for Anna to leave for Canada. It wasn't easy but they had all got to the stage when they realised it couldn't happen soon enough. Charlie, of course, was blissfully unaware of all the upset and as he was the sort of child to take most things in his stride just sailed along happily. Vernon was driving Anna to the airport. She wore a woolly hat pulled right down so it was hard to see her face. Charlie had a woolly hat too but he wouldn't keep it on.

Thankfully Anna got through passport control with Charlie who was on her passport without any trouble. It seemed there was no-one looking there. Anna concluded that was because Karl assumed she had left for the continent. The flight to Ottawa was uneventful too and Anna was just beginning to feel more relaxed as they landed in Canada. Again all her paperwork was in order so she and Charlie sailed through without a problem. However, when they got through into the arrivals hall Anna couldn't see her brother anyway and finally sat down on a seat with Charlie on her lap and started to cry. Part of her was saying she was being pathetic but she had been through so much she was completely wrung out.

"Hey, little sis, sorry I am late, but we had a heap more snow last night and it took a while to get here." Anna jumped to her feet holding onto Charlie and went into Matthew's warm embrace with great relief.

It took some time to get out of Ottawa as it was still snowing but they made it back to Matthew and Sally's home without incident and for the first time in many months Anna felt safe. Charlie was fascinated by all the snow and the completely white landscape.

It took several weeks for Anna's injuries to heal but she was happier than she had been for a long time. Sally and

Matthew had four children who, being older, all took it in turns to look after Charlie. Anna helped Sally as much as she could and over the weeks and months that followed they became very close.

Spring came and Anna got involved with helping in the orchards. She hadn't thought about missing the outdoor life so much before but now she did and was surprised how much she had missed it.

Once the apple trees started to bloom, they looked so spectacular, Anna couldn't get enough of being outside among them. Then one day a very odd looking man called at the house and was asking Sally who was home about who lived there and all sorts of odd questions. Sally wasn't about to give him any information but he was seen later in the day hanging around the entrance to the farm. She gave Matthew the news when he came in and in turn, they told Anna.

"Karl," said Anna immediately. "It has to be, he will have hired someone."

Sally and Matthew exchanged looks. "We had wondered if this may happen Anna, and so Sally wrote to a distant cousin she has in Australia. I hope you don't mind, but he will help you if you want. It will mean getting a working visa and it would only be for two years but it is an option, that is, if you don't want to return to England just now."

Anna sat looking from one to the other. What should she do? Australia seemed so far away from friends and family, not that she made friends easily anyway she thought to herself, and it would take her family out of the equation maybe that would be good and Karl wouldn't even begin to guess where she was.

"Well, I guess I can pay for the airfares and maybe get a job while I am there. Karl won't think of looking there and it's a big place and, as you say, maybe after a couple of years, it will be safe to return to England."

It was good that they didn't live far from Canada's capitol as Anna was able to go to the Australian Embassy and arrange her visa quickly. Even that was stressful as both she and Sally who went with her were afraid they were being watched or maybe followed. However nothing untoward happened. She would be sad to leave her brother and his family and she had fallen in love with the Canadian countryside too.

Her last day and the man they had seen before was again hanging around at the front gate. Anna was by now very nervous, and Matthew and Sally were worried too that their plans would go wrong, though as Matthew said what could Karl do if he turned up. Late afternoon that is exactly what happened. Matthew was at home when there was a hammering on the front door, when he opened it there was Karl looking very angry. "I have come for my wife and son, and I don't want you to get in my way and stop me." As he said this, he barged past Matthew who didn't try to stop him.

Karl marched through the house shouting for Anna but unknown to him and the private detective that he had hired Sally had taken Anna and Charlie to the airport. They had left the farm though a little used back entrance. Anna was again shaking with fright, they had only just made it and she worried for her brother and the family. However she needn't have worried. Karl was very angry when it was obvious that neither Anna nor Charlie were there. In fact, as far as he could see, they hadn't been there. Everything was neat and tidy and there was no evidence that they had ever been there. The Private Detective however was adamant that they were there a couple of days ago as he had been watching the place. However, he had to go and meet with Karl and make arrangements for him. Somewhere to stay and car hire, so hadn't been able to watch all the time. Karl, however, wasn't that easily placated and was furious with him and giving him the money he owed him told him to get lost. The man thought Anna had a point but, of course, said nothing he just left Karl without a backward glance. Karl assumed that if she had left Canada Anna would have gone to America after all they had been there on business many times.

Meanwhile Anna and Charlie were en-route to Australia. Sitting on the plane with a very tired little boy beside her Anna wondered if all this was really necessary, was she making things worse by running away. Perhaps she should have just stood up to Karl and hoped for the best. But deep in her heart she felt that flight was at present the only answer. His family were wealthy and his father held an important post in the Civil service, Anna had never found out what, she knew he would do anything to keep his grandchild safely nearby and Anna couldn't go on being treated as she was. Flight was her best option.

Her flight was to Sydney and after an overnight stay she had a domestic flight to far north Queensland. When she found out how long the flight was, she was flabbergasted; she had no idea that Australia was so big and as for Queensland it was enormous. They arrived late at night and Anna was too tired to take in any sights on the way to a cheap hotel they were staying in overnight. It was much the same the next morning as the flight was very early. Anna started to think they would have been better off staying at the airport, just going from International Terminal to Domestic. It had all been arranged in such a rush though and before she knew it they were air borne again.

Charlie was being very good but was getting restless with all the travelling. Anna worried about the fact she hadn't really bought any toys with her, in fact they were travelling light as they wouldn't be needing winter clothes where they were going. Anna leant against the window and saw huge country below her with as far as she could see no dwellings. Charlie was in the middle seat and a rather large lady sat the other side.

"Your first trip out here, love?" the lady said.

Anna conjured up a smile, though she didn't feel like it. "Yes, it is." Charlie looked up at the lady and gave her a cheeky grin.

"You'se a smart little fella, what's your name?"

"Charlie." He had just learnt to say his name and he was very proud of it.

"I'm Trish." She smiled across at Anna who reluctantly gave her name. Trish then gave Anna lots of information about Cairns where they were going and about living life in general in the tropics. Anna listened attentively as she had no idea what to expect. It had all been such a rush, she had travelled without that many bags as she knew enough to know it would be warm especially as she had been to Thailand twice and that was tropical. She would have to stock up hers and Charlie's wardrobe when she got settled. Thank goodness she still had a sizable amount of her nest egg in the bank.

Trish asked her if she was staying in Cairns and was surprised when Anna said no she was being met and was going further north still but wasn't really sure of where.

"Mossman, is it?" asked Trish

"Yes, near there." Anna was deliberately vague as she was getting used to being evasive about herself and Charlie. She felt the less people knew the better. Again she asked herself, was she being paranoid?

Trish returned to telling Anna about all the touristy things that were available. Anna had no idea it was such a tourist destination and that worried her but she decided she would have to put up with it for now.

When she got into the arrivals hall at Cairns, the first thing she saw was a huge banner saying: 'Welcome Anna and Charlie' being held up by a big man with a cowboy hat on. Anna would soon learn that it was called an *akubra* and was standard wear for farmers and others across Australia. The other end of the banner was held by a young girl of about ten who had a huge smile on her face when she saw Anna and Charlie coming towards them.

"You must be Anna, and this must be Charlie. I'm Hugh," said the man, enveloping Anna's hand in his huge one. He had a very firm handshake and a very kind and not bad looking face. Anna took to him at once. "This is daughter Jess," he said. Jess had already made friends with Charlie and she smiled shyly at Anna. She was a pretty child who looked like her father in many ways.

Luggage collected they went outside and Anna almost gasped at the heat and the moist air. Although it was late autumn it was still hot to Anna even more so after Canada. Having loaded the luggage into the back of a big four wheel drive car they set off. Jess sat in the back with Charlie for whom they had bought with them an old child seat.

The airport was the north side of Cairns so they drove straight out into the countryside. Anna was immediately struck with the beauty of it all. Tree covered mountains to their left and flat lands towards the sea to their right. Further on the hills swept right down to the beach and a road had been carved from the hillside. It was very winding and Anna clutched onto the side of her seat on several occasions. Hugh smiled at her,

"Don't worry, I haven't rolled into the sea once yet!" He had been very busy explaining the surrounding countryside and where they were going. He told her that he had four children of which Jess was second youngest. They lived in the main house but just nearby was a cottage which had been the original house on the farm. They had had a busy few days making it presentable for Anna. Next week he told her they would start cutting the cane as he was a sugarcane farmer.

"Oh yes, Sally did tell me that but it went over my head, it's all been—" Anna didn't know what else to say and her eyes filled with unexpected tears. Hugh put his huge hand out and patted her arm.

"Don't worry, we will watch out for you. Trish, my wife, will like having you next door, I reckon, and the kids will love little Charlie there."

The road twisted and turned and suddenly they had flat land to the right of again the hills receding away to the left. They went by a turning that said Port Douglas with tall palm trees along the roadside. "That town there is undergoing massive construction, they are turning it into a tourist town, that's for sure," Hugh said. Not long after this, Hugh turned right towards the sea, which was now further away, and they bumped down a gravel road. Then they turned into a yard dominated by a largish house on stilts. Anna found out later at the style of house was called a Queenslander and the reason it was high off the ground was because sometimes the place flooded. Next door was a dear little cottage again a Queenslander but not up so high and small in comparison. This was to be Anna's.

Before they had alighted from the car a fresh faced woman came bustling out of the house followed by three children of various sizes, all very excited with the prospect of meeting Anna and Charlie. Morning tea was served, scones with jam and cream with tea or coffee. Anna was overwhelmed with the family's kindness and generosity towards her. Charlie disappeared with the children and soon Anna could hear squeals of delight coming from the back of the house.

The cottage was tiny but well-appointed with a bedroom, another tiny bedroom, bathroom and a family room and kitchen. There was a large veranda at the back on which there was a washing machine and dryer. The veranda ran right around the house but wasn't as wide elsewhere as at the back. Anna loved it straight away.

Trish had tried to think of everything Anna might need but insisted that Anna and Charlie had their first evening meal with them all. As it happened, Anna could hardly keep her eyes open but Charlie, who was the main attraction, was wide awake. Anna was pleased to go to bed though she found it rather hot and put the ceiling fan going. It was very quiet though and she slept soundly feeling safe at least for the time being.

Chapter 23

Eight weeks later and it was Charlie's second birthday. Anna couldn't really believe how quickly she had fitted in. She had arrived at the worst possible time for Hugh and Trish but they had been so kind and welcoming that she hadn't felt awkward or in the way. She had helped with the children where she could and with the cooking and cleaning at the main house. Hugh was very busy with the cane being cut then put in a small railway line that took it directly to the cane factory a few kilometres away at Mossman. The air was thick with dust and the slightly cloying sweet smell from the cane. She didn't like the cane toads however and soon learnt to be constantly on the lookout for snakes. Many lived in the cane fields and weren't too impressed to have their home disturbed.

Trish arranged for Charlie to have a birthday tea and asked some other small children that she knew to come which meant, of course, their Mums came too. Anna had met some of them and found them so friendly that she didn't feel as shy or out of place as she usually did when meeting strangers. Charlie had a wonderful time and when Anna carried him back home to bed she had the sudden thought that she was more relaxed than she had been at any time since she left Karl. She had spoken to Matthew in Canada and her mother briefly as using her host's phone wasn't something she was comfortable with. She had written too but wasn't feeling home sick or any of the emotions she thought she should have had.

She had one worry though; her carefully saved money wouldn't last for ever and she needed to work. Trish suggested that she tried to find work in Port Douglas as with her background she felt she should get work there quite easily, the town was growing fast. Then there was the issue of Charlie and transport. Trish and Hugh's youngest was only eighteen months older than Charlie, and there was a small child care centre opened in Mossman that the boys could go to two mornings a week. Hugh took Anna to see a neighbour who had an old ute for sale and, though battered, it was roadworthy and so Anna was all set.

Having found they were still looking for all levels of staff in the recently-opened Mirage Resort just behind Four Mile Beach, Anna put herself forward for any job they had going. She wasn't fussy. However, once they had interviewed her and learning of her credentials they offered her a receptionist job.

The first day Anna felt nervous, the guests staying at the Mirage were all wealthy and she knew she mustn't make any slip up as she would be on trial for a month. However, they were exactly the sort of people she was used to dealing with when she had her own business and when she helped Karl, so she fitted in well. The management were so pleased with her they told her after a week that she was no longer on trial.

She loved the hustle and bustle of the small town which was indeed growing fast. A marina had gone in the far end of town and big plans were afoot for much more holiday accommodation. The place was buzzing. The beach aptly named Four Mile Beach was beautiful, though you couldn't swim in the sea in the summer months as there were box jellyfish around then and a sting from one of them led to certain death. The resort was well appointed with swimming pools a golf course, lots of things for all to do. Anna hadn't been this happy in a very long time. She enjoyed meeting the guests too and without realising it had change herself quite a lot in recent times. She was more confident and outgoing why she didn't know, she just felt different about so many things. In the end, she decided it was all she had been through and the fact she had resolved not to be a victim anymore. She was a lot stronger woman than she had realised and with that knowledge she had grown into the person she was now. That didn't mean she wasn't worried about Karl and what might happen in the future, but she was enjoying the here and now, she would cross her bridges when she had to.

Many of the guests staying at the resort were Americans with quite a few English and Germans. They all picked up on her English accent and would ask her lots of questions which she soon learnt to parry. Sometimes the men would chat her up but again she was very good a giving them a polite brush off. Australian business men would stay too and if it was a conference there would be men alone but Anna again was very focused on the brush off. The other girls were envious partly because she was so beautiful and got more offers than them and partly because she had the knack of saying no without offending anyone.

One day, though, a tall man with a sad expression checked in. He had his two daughters with him. Anna went through all the usual blurb about what the resort had to offer and the village too. The elder daughter, whose name was Sophie, asked Anna questions about going out to the reef and shopping in the village while the younger one just stood looking into space and saying nothing, Anna thought she was rather disconnected from her father and sister. Because they seemed rather a sad group Anna went out of her way to welcome them and even took them to their accommodation herself not something she normally did. The girls were sharing a room and Anna had by this time guessed that there was some rift maybe because their mother wasn't with them.

"If there is anything either of you girls want that I can help you with, please feel free to tell me. If I am on duty, I will help if I can, OK?"

Sophie said, "Thank you." And smiled at Anna, then nudged her sister. "Jackie, thank Anna."

Jackie looked at Anna with big brown eyes. "Thank you," she whispered.

Anna smiled and walked away. She hadn't got far when she heard steps behind her; it was the girl's father. "I just wanted to explain that Jackie and Sophie aren't normally like that, a year ago I lost my wife to breast cancer then just as we were coming to terms with it. Jackie's horse that had helped her through losing her mother died unexpectedly. Jackie is rather a mess right now. This holiday was planned before that happened and I'm not so sure it was a good idea now, but thank you for what you said."

Anna looked at him properly and saw a tall man with sad brown eyes like his daughter. He had dark curly hair that was greying at the temples. He had a pleasant face, she decided, a kind face.

"No worries, you know where to find me if you need anything," and she walked away conscious of the fact he was watching her go.

A few mornings later Anna was walking the beach. Two mornings a week she went in early so she could have a good walk on the beach. It was one of her favourite things early in the morning with the sun coming up over the sea. Very often calm and beautiful, sometimes wild and windy but always spectacular. No sooner had she set off than she heard her name called from behind her and turning round saw the girl's father Michael walking towards her. "May I join you?" he asked politely. Anna could hardly say no so they fell into step together and soon she relaxed and enjoyed his company. He did the talking and seemed to need to talk for he hardly stopped. So Anna learnt that his wife had had a double mastectomy and as he was a surgeon. He had overseen the operation. He seemed to be blaming himself for the fact she still died but it turned out to be a long time later. She had fought the cancer hard but had lost her battle. The girls were young to have lost their mum but had been a great comfort to their father. Then Jackie's horse that she always said was her best friend had died and Jackie seemed to have gone backwards in her grief.

Michael suddenly stopped talking and stood looking at Anna. "Hell, I'm sorry. I don't usually talk that much, especially to strangers, whatever must you think of me?"

"It's OK, you needed to get it all off your chest, I guess. Don't worry about it," said Anna.

"I feel really bad, I don't know what came over me, please can I shout you a coffee or something as an apology later this morning?"

"Not necessary, really," said Anna, though she felt she could listen to him forever; he had a beautiful voice, she thought, and was attractive too.

What am I thinking? I never want to be involved with any man ever again, but he is nice.

"Please, the girls would like it too. They think you are very kind."

Anna found herself relenting, and later that morning the four of them had coffee together. Then Anna found herself promising to take the girls down to the marina where a few shops were springing up. It was her day off the next day so having arranged with Trish to look after Charlie for a couple of hours drove to the Mirage and picked up Michael's girls. They looked rather startled at her old ute but didn't make a comment and the three of them drove off leaving Michael to play a round of golf. Anna didn't really know what she was doing with two teenage girls but sensed that they needed some girl time.

It was a lot more fun than Anna had hoped. They tried on lots of clothes had lots of giggles and though shopping still wasn't really Anna's thing, she enjoyed it all and Jackie came out of her shell and seemed happier. When they had exhausted themselves, Anna said they should have a milkshake or iced chocolate or ice-cream even before they went back. The girls agreed, once they had given their orders in Anna sat back looking at them both. "I'd love you both to meet Charlie, my little boy," she said.

Both girls looked surprised. "Are you married then?" Jackie asked.

Anna nodded. "But my husband isn't here, I don't live with him. You'd love Charlie." She was suddenly sorry she had said anything. But both girls didn't press her any further just asked about Charlie and then said they would love to meet him. They then almost pestered Anna so in the end she agreed for them to come out to her cottage later that afternoon and meet him. Sophie said their father had hired a car would it be ok if he brought them. Anna wasn't comfortable with that but realised she had backed herself into a corner so said yes and drew them a map on a napkin.

She dropped them off hurriedly as she didn't want to see Michael in case it made her want to retract her invitation. She didn't want to give him the wrong idea.

She drove home wondering what she should give the girls for afternoon tea and decided on scones as they were easy to make and she was good at making them. Then she realised she hadn't any cream to go with them. When she picked Charlie up, she told Trish about the girls coming and asked her what she thought she should give them for afternoon tea as she had no cream to go with scones.

"Well, that's lucky as I have some cream in the fridge that I got yesterday when I went down to Cairns, there is plenty there, help yourself."

"You sure? I feel bad about that," said Anna.

Trish looked at her with a broad grin on her face. "Anna you've been here four months now, and you have changed so much in that time, and we feel maybe we have helped. When you came, you were such a scared person, so uptight and hardly said a word to anyone. You are a different person now and this is the first time you have had any visitors, so please have some cream with my blessing to celebrate that and the new you."

Anna had tears in her eyes after this speech, *Yes,* she thought, *I have changed.* Aloud, she said "It's thanks to you and this magical place. I can't thank you enough." Trish hugged her tightly.

"I love having you here, Anna. You've been good for all of us. The kids love both you and Charlie, you can stay for ever as far as we are concerned."

A shadow passed Anna's face; she didn't want to think ahead, just the present was enough for now.

Anna swept and cleaned and baked like mad when she got indoors. Charlie decided to be as unhelpful as possible Anna thought picking up a truck he had placed under her foot so she nearly went skidding across the floor. She was so busy trying to tidy that and several other likely hazards up she didn't hear her guests arrive. She was wearing just a singlet and shorts and had intended to change so was embarrassed when she found them on the veranda. Looking through the fly screen. Michael was with them.

He looked embarrassed. "Not sure if I am invited too," he said.

Anna wasn't sure herself so she just said, "Come in, all of you. That is fine." The tiny house seemed a bit crowed to start with; however, Anna guided them out onto the larger back veranda where she had a small table and some picnic chairs. She had borrowed two more from Trish but in her wisdom Trish said take three just in case.

Charlie seemed almost fascinated by the girls and was trying to show them everything at once. Finally, Anna said, "Why don't you show them your bedroom, Charlie, and the things you have in there." So the three of them trooped back into the house. Michael smiled at Anna.

"What a lovely little boy, you must be very proud of him, how old is he?

"He was two last month, well July, we are nearly in September, I suppose. Time goes so quickly, don't you think?"

Anna was aware she was gabbling but was suddenly self-conscious and very aware of Michael's proximity.

"His father?" Michael wanted to know but sensed Anna may not want to talk about him. He watched as the emotions flitted across her face. Finally she said,

"I have run away from him, I don't know what the future holds. I just know I never want to see him again."

Michael sat quietly for a few minutes then said. "He hurt you in more ways than one didn't he, and you are frightened of him." It was a statement, not a question.

Anna felt tears prick the back of her eyes. "Yes," she whispered, just then the children appeared and no more was said. Later when they were leaving, Sophie said to her father "Go on, ask her?"

Michael turned to Anna with a rather sheepish expression on his face "The girls wondered, well, me too, if you and Charlie would come up to do a river trip on the Daintree with us on your next day off?"

Anna didn't know what to say then she looked at the children's eager faces and said yes she would, thank you. So it was arranged for three days' time.

She then worried about it during those three days and finally asked Trish what she thought. "Go for it. You need to have fun Anna, Michael knows the score you've told him and anyway you would disappoint the children so much if you don't go."

So Anna and Charlie went, and they all had a ball. They saw crocodiles and all sorts of birds. It was a beautiful day and there weren't that many other passengers on the boat. Then later they had barramundi and chips at the local café, as they drove back Anna felt sad the outing was drawing to a close. She looked across at Michael; he was concentrating on the road which was unsealed in many places. He was such a lovely gentle person, it would be very easy to fall in love with him. In spite of the age difference, the children got on well too. Sophie and Jackie loved Charlie. *Easy enough really,* Anna thought.

Michael glanced at her. "Penny for them?"

Anna blushed. "Nothing really, just what a great day it's been and thank you all so much for inviting us both."

When they got back to Anna's house, she didn't invite them in though she was tempted. There was only three days left of their holiday and, Anna thought once they got back to their home in Brisbane, they would soon forget all about her so she must play it cool. Michael got out of the car and helped her with Charlie's things then leaning towards her gave her a very brief peck on the cheek. "See you tomorrow." Then they were gone leaving Anna staring after them feeling very happy, sad and regretful all at once.

"Mummy, mummy. I want to see Tish." That was Charlie's name for Trish and he couldn't wait to tell everyone about his day.

The next morning Ana's heart skipped a beat when she saw Michael walking towards reception. She made a mental note not to feel like the silly girl she was! Michael was taking the girls up to the tablelands that day and after a few brief words that was it for the day. Anna felt as if a big hole had opened up and deny it to herself she might but she knew she had fallen for this man. It was a totally different feeling to what she had felt with Karl. Looking back she knew much of it had been sheer lust, he had pushed the right buttons and as she was very lonely and lost she had taken it for love she had wanted to feel needed and he had made her feel needed and important, but she now realised she had never loved him. Not truly loved him, and she very much doubted that what he felt for her had ever been love either. Possession yes, love no.

The next day the resort had an influx of new arrivals from America that were all booked on the same tour. There was a mix up between their tour company and the booking agent so Anna had a lot of disgruntled guests to placate and she had a very full on and busy day. She saw Michael and the girls hovering in reception early on in the morning and they waved as a few moments later they left and that was it. Anna drove home feeling very depressed and for the first time since she had arrived in Australia, lonely. However, Charlie soon cheered her up with his chatter telling her about his day and as she hugged him to her she told herself off. How could she be so silly as to think of Michael in that way, he only lost his wife just over a year ago and while she might be a holiday distraction he certainly would not even think of her when he returned home.

She was only working a half day the next day and sometimes when that was the case she took Charlie with her. He was very good playing behind reception and some of the staff loved to play with him at odd moments. She had her head down looking at some papers when a familiar voice said "Hello, how are you going?"

Anna's heart did a flip flop and as she looked up Michael caught the look in her eyes and on her face. It confirmed to him she felt the same way as he did though she quickly hid it.

"Hello, where are the girls?" Anna said the first thing that came into her head.

"Gone for a walk on the beach, what time do you finish?"

"Lunch time, but then I have to go and get some food in as Charlie and I will starve." Anna thought, *Why am I saying silly things*? Her heart was racing away and she knew she was blushing.

"I don't suppose it's the done thing for staff to have dinner with the guests, is it?"

Anna shook her head dumbly, she so wanted to spend some time with them before they left her forever.

"OK, leave it with me and I will find you back here at three o'clock or whatever time suits you. I just want to sort one or two things out. Is that OK with you?"

Anna nodded, not quite sure of this turn of events as Karl could be rather the same, telling her what time to be somewhere. Michael sensed her unease, "Tell me if that doesn't suit you, Anna, please," he said.

He isn't Karl though he is just trying to please she thought. Aloud she said, "That suits me well, I'll see you then."

At three o'clock on the dot Anna waited in reception for Michael and his daughters. Ten minutes passed, there was no sign of them. Charlie was getting bored and Anna anxious at twenty passed Anna decided to take Charlie home; he had put up with a long day. Anna felt drained too, she had got herself excited all for nothing. As she was gathering her things up, tears pricked her eyes. Just then she heard the girl's voices "Anna, Charlie," they called. They were carrying bags and parcels and had mischievous expressions on their faces. Michael appeared behind them looking somewhat worried.

"Thank goodness you are still here, I was afraid you would get fed up waiting. We had to go down to Cairns and it all took longer than I thought, I am sorry."

Anna blinked rapidly; she didn't want them to see the tears that had been threatening. "It's fine, just Charlie was getting fractious. I think he is tired."

"Well I have arranged for all five of us to have dinner, will that be OK? I booked for dead on six telling them we would have a small boy with us. Shall we let him have a little sleep now, then he will be OK."

Now Anna felt flustered again she had changed out of her work clothes into a t-shirt and shorts.

"I am hardly dressed for dinner."

Michael laid his finger along the side of his nose. "Can you put Charlie down to nap then we will sort out your attire if you are worried though you look good to me. What do you think girls?"

Both girls laughed and nudged each other. Anna feeling mystified laid Charlie down on the sofa in the staff room behind reception and a few minutes later he was asleep.

When she went back out having asked one of the girls to tell her if Charlie woke up, she found Michael and the girls waiting patiently. "Can we go across and wait by the pool?" Michael asked.

"Yes, that is fine, but do you want to take your shopping to your room first?" Anna asked, following them to the pool area. There wasn't anyone much about and so they all sat down. Jackie burst out

"I can't wait any longer." As she spoke, she thrust one of her packages at Anna. "This is for you, Anna, you and Charlie have cheered me up so much during our time here, it's just a small thank you for everything."

Anna was completely taken aback but opened the package and inside was a beautiful emerald green top, it was pure silk and shimmered in the sunshine. Anna gasped. "I hope you like it, it's your size. I had a sneak peek when we were with you the other day to find out your size. I hope you like it."

Anna couldn't stop the tears in her eyes this time. And getting up, hugged Jackie. "It's so beautiful, but you didn't need to do this, thank you so much."

"My turn now," said Sophie passing another parcel over. This time it was a silk sarong that was blues and greens and turquoise and would match the top beautifully.

Anna hugged Sophie now and the tears overflowed. Michael gave a small cough. "I am not sure I should give you this as the girls' presents have made you cry." With that he handed Anna a small parcel gift wrapped in gold paper. Anna's heart began to thump, what could it be she daren't try to guess she sat staring at it for a few moments.

"Open it, open it," the girls chorused. With trembling fingers Anna tore it open to find a little box and when she opened that she was dumbstruck with delight. Inside was a beautiful bangle, quite wide and all around it were greenstones, they looked like emeralds though Anna knew they couldn't be.

"Michael, it's so beautiful, what can I say? Thank you doesn't seem adequate." She leant across and brushed her lips across his shyly, "You are so good to me, all of you."

"Anna, the girls and I have had a horrid time, and so have you. However, you have helped us so much this holiday and so has little Charlie and we wanted to give you these things to show our appreciation. The other thing I want to say is that we don't want to lose sight of you, we want, I want, to stay friends will that be alright with you? How do you feel? Would you consider coming down for a visit to Brisbane soon, you and Charlie? Please say yes."

Anna started to really cry now, she felt overwhelmed by their kindness and Michael's words. Suddenly she found herself wrapped in three pairs of arms and they all tried to hug her. It made Anna laugh through her tears. "I can't think of anything I would like more," she said.

A little time later when Charlie woke up, there were little presents for him too. Anna again was teary with their kindness.

Then they got ready to go for an early dinner. They were going to a restaurant high up on the point overlooking the park near the church and museum and of course the sea. Anna had put on her new things and as she walked into the restaurant, she didn't realise just how many heads she turned; she looked amazing. There was a guy playing a piano softly and the sides were all open to the balmy breeze that blew in from the sea. It was magical. Michael had even arranged a special dish for Charlie as they didn't normally serve such small children. Charlie seemed to know it was a special occasion and was very good.

All too soon, the evening was over. Michael and his daughters were leaving very early in the morning so when they got back to the Mirage it was time to say goodbye. The girls hugged Charlie and Anna then drifted away while their father said goodbye to Charlie. Then he turned to Anna who was struggling not to cry again. He stood in front of her and took her hand. "I will be in touch in a few days and I will see you soon. Don't be upset." He could see the tears threatening again. "I know this has been something of a whirlwind but I think you will agree with me that all of us have made a kind of connection. The girls seem to have really taken to you both in a way I never thought would happen after their mother died. Me too, come to that. I think Sandra must be looking down with a smile; she didn't want me to be alone and she told me to find someone else. No, don't say anything," Anna had opened her mouth to speak. "Just go now and I will be in touch in a few days as I said." With that, Michael bent and kissed her briefly on the lips, and turning, walked away.

Anna stood for a moment watching him go, there was a huge lump in her throat but she swallowed it and getting in the car, drove slowly home.

As she lay in bed sleepless that night, she went over everything that had happened since she had met Michael and his daughters. In some ways, it didn't seem real but when she looked at the gifts they had given her, she knew it was real and not a dream. Could she trust a man again? Would she manage to extricate herself from Karl without too much angst? As time went on, would he be calmer or angrier? In eighteen months' time, her working visa would expire, what would happen then? When she had fled first to Canada then to Australia, all she could think of was getting as far away as possible. She hadn't thought any further than that. All she knew was that she was terrified for both herself and Charlie. Then another thought popped into her head, *Would Karl go after Michael or his girls if he ever found out about them.* Anna sat up with a jerk; she was being paranoid now, it wasn't really that bad, was it? Finally, she fell asleep without any answers to any of the questions she had asked herself.

A week later, she had heard nothing from Michael and it had been a long miserable week. Trish had been agog at the gifts and all that Anna had told her and now tried to cheer her up. "Anna, he will come good, darlin', you don't know what problems he had when he got home. He didn't strike me as a blow in blow out sort of a guy, just give it time."

Anna sadly wrapped her beautiful things in tissue paper and put them in the bottom of a drawer in her bedroom; she couldn't bear to look at them or wear them, at least not now. It was strange she had been depressed before but somehow this was different; the sadness seemed to be seeping into her very soul. She thought about ringing him as she could have got his contact details from work but something held her back. She was playing with Charlie before his bedtime when there was a frantic knocking on the door and Jess was calling her name. "Anna, come quickly. Michael, your friend, he is on the phone. I'll look after Charlie, quick, Mum said be quick."

Anna raced across the yard, heart bounding. Trish was holding the phone and handed it to Anna with a grin. "Told you so," she mouthed.

"Hello, Michael?"

"Anna, my dear, thank goodness I have got you," he said. "I rang the Mirage the other day and left a message, did you not get it?"

"No, I—"

"Doesn't matter, I am sorry it's taken so long. Truth is I must have caught some bug on the plane home and was pretty crook for a few days. I then rang and left a message for you to ring me if you could and I didn't hear from you and I thought— never mind, I got this number from the Mirage they didn't want me to have it and—"

By this time, Anna was half laughing half crying. "We sound like a couple of teenagers, Michael. It's good to hear your voice."

"Good to hear you too." They chatted for a bit then arranged a time for the next phone call and rang off. When Anna turned round from the phone, she caught sight of both Hugh and Trish sitting at the kitchen table with big grins on their faces. "All's well, then," said Hugh.

Anna grinned broadly. "Yep," she said.

Chapter 24

A few weeks later, Anna and Charlie made the journey down to Brisbane. Michael had arranged for them to stay nearby as he didn't want Anna to feel pressured in any way. She hadn't told him much about her marriage or Karl but he could tell it had been a pretty explosive marriage and he didn't want anything to upset her or put her off. For himself, his first marriage had been happy and they were a close knit unit. They had all been devastated by Sandy's death but she had made them all promise to get on with living and had told Michael many times to find someone else as soon as he could. At the time he had thought that would be impossible then Anna had come into his life and he had fallen for her in a big way. Not only was she beautiful but she was smart and kind and as they got to know her more, there was a fun loving person hidden away there, it just didn't show very often.

Charlie was very excited; he loved being with Sophie and Jackie who spoilt him rather even if Anna was watching. He loved being with Hugh and Trish's children too but Sophie and Jackie were lots of fun and they did things with him that the others didn't, like giving him piggy backs and sitting playing with his toys, when he was with the other children he had to share more. Charlie was spoilt!

When Anna saw Michael waiting for her in arrivals she didn't stop to think, she ran straight into his arms and kissed him on the lips. She then stepped back in confusion, what was she thinking throwing herself at him like that. Michael smiled at her and gently pulled her back into his arms and hugged her tight. Charlie stood by watching all this rather uncertainly. Michael then bent and picked him up. "How are you, young man? Are you going to have fun these next few days, do you think?"

Charlie nodded furiously, "Soophie, Jasie?" he enquired, looking round.

"Sorry, mate, they are at school, but if we hurry we can go and pick them up. Shall we do that?"

Charlie couldn't wait, he was off and they had to hurry to catch up with him. "Steady, young man, you are going the wrong way." Michael took Charlie's hand and picking up Anna's bag, they made their way to the car.

Michael had been in the loft and found an old car seat, so with Charlie safely strapped in the back they set off. Anna liked what she saw of Brisbane and was fascinated by some of the skyscrapers in the CBD with old buildings completely overshadowed by them. Michael and his family lived at a place called Fig Tree Pocket which was almost semi-rural and their garden which was huge, swept down to the river. There was a fence half way down through right across the garden which they had put up when the girls were small.

They picked up the girls and Michael took Anna to the accommodation he had booked for her. She was grateful in some ways but disappointed in others as she would have preferred to stay with the family. Maybe her face gave it away for Michael suddenly said, "Anna, if you and Charlie would like to stay with us we'd like it too, I just didn't want you to feel uncomfortable."

"Yes, please, can we?" Anna's eyes had filled with tears. Karl would never have been so sensitive.

"Of course. Actually, I did have beds made up just in case. I have a lovely cleaning lady who helps out, she did it for me and we have plenty of space."

Anna loved their home straight away. The jacarandas were still blooming and the garden was immaculate. It was a very pretty large house, built Queensland style with wrap around verandas which were very deep, shading the rooms and large enough to entertain on.

Sophie took over playing hostess and showed Anna to her room then took Charlie further down the long passage which ran from front to back of the house and Anna heard squeals of delight coming from her son. She went to see and found Charlie surrounded with so many soft toys and other things he didn't know what to do first. Michael came up behind Anna as she stood watching him. "The girls never let Sandy throw any of their things away, good thing too by the look of it."

Sophie and Jackie announced they were getting dinner and so with Charlie fully occupied playing, Michael got Anna and himself a cool drink and they sat out on the veranda looking out across the river. It was perfect, Anna thought and said as much to Michael.

"Thank you, we like it and having you here means I, at the moment, have everything I could possibly want. Anna, you must know by now that I love you very, very much. I don't know what the future will bring or for certain what you feel but just at the moment this is all I could ask for."

Tears pricked Anna's eyes but she blinked them back. "I love you too, Michael. I never thought I would love anyone again, but I now realise I never really loved Karl. He flattered me, swept me off my feet, didn't give me time to take stock really, it was so full on. By the time I did stand back I was too under his control to do much about it. Then I was too scared to. He didn't want children and I admit I tricked him rather having Charlie but I needed something to make my life bearable. I don't know what I am going to do either or what the future holds but somehow I have to find the strength to sort my life out and to be with you if by then you still want me."

They were sitting side by side and Michael moved his chair as close as it would go then he whispered in her ear. "My darling girl, I will want you for ever." Just then, Jackie came bouncing out to say,

"Dinner is served."

A large table was set up just outside big double glass doors that led straight out of the kitchen around the corner from where they were sitting. Anna being an excellent cook herself was very impressed with a lovely stir fry with prawns that the girls had done. They had cooked a special pasta dish for Charlie knowing it was one of his favourites.

Later, after the clearing up was done and Charlie was tucked up asleep in bed, both girls came and kissed Anna goodnight which touched her deeply. "We both have homework and we do it in our rooms as we have desks there," explained Sophie.

Michael and Anna took their wine they hadn't finished outside again and sat sipping it, not really talking. They were both very aware of the other person but neither wanted to make a move that might not be appropriate. At last, Michael said, "Anna, tell me about Karl, tell me everything. I think it will help you, and it will help me to understand."

To start with, Anna was reluctant but as she started to speak the words flowed out of her like a waterfall, she couldn't stop. Sometimes she cried a little but mostly she just talked and talked about her life with Karl, how he got rid of Muriel, how for a start he wanted her to share the business but as soon as he realised how popular she was with clients he put a stop to that. She told him even some of the very private details, a lot of the things she told him she had never told anyone and as she talked it felt as if a huge lump that was sitting inside her had lifted and was gone. She felt lighter and easier in herself than she had for very long time. "It's funny, though," she said as she finished. "I know I am not the same person that Karl seduced and married, it's like I—I have been—" she shrugged. "Somehow reborn."

She finished speaking and, for a while, they sat in silence. Michael was so horrified by what Anna had told him he felt lost for words, inadequate even; she had been through so much yet she was still a lovely, kind and funny person. *How*, he wondered, *had she managed not to be bitter and twisted or downtrodden and weak*. She was actually a strong and determined woman but vulnerable too, he realised. More so where Charlie was concerned; she had fought hard to have him in her own way.

Anna was sitting still looking up at the incredible night sky but he saw her cheeks were wet with tears. "My dear girl, I don't know what to say to you, you have been through so much, far more than I imagined. I feel unworthy of your love, but if you will let me I want to be there for you always to love you and help you and protect you if I can from this monster that you married."

Anna turned her head and looked at him. "Just go on as you are, Michael. I can't believe that I have been lucky enough to find you. Like I said, I don't know how things will pan out but we have eighteen months before my visa runs out, let's just for now enjoy what we have."

They sat talking about England where Michael had never been but his parents had immigrated just a few months before he was born. His father had been a surgeon too, his parents were both still alive and he had four siblings scattered all over Australia. His parents lived on the Gold Coast and the girls spent time with them in the holidays. Their other grandparents lived in New Zealand now; they had come over from there as a young couple and Sandy was their only child. They had gone back to New Zealand after she died. Michael and the girls hadn't seen them since but were in fairly constant contact.

Michael, who had been talking quietly and looking at the lights twinkling on the river, now looked at Anna and smiled when he saw she had fallen asleep. She hardly stirred when he lifted her gently from the chair and carried her through to the room she had been given. Laying her down she stirred slightly and smiled, muttering something and settled once more into sleep. She was barefoot anyway and just had a t-shirt and shorts on so making sure the fan was blowing gently as it was a hot night, Michael closed the door and went to his own bed. He didn't think he would sleep after Anna's disclosures but he did and was very surprised to be woken next morning by Charlie and the girls bouncing into the room. "Up you get Dad, we thought we would take Anna breakfast in bed. After all, it's Saturday!"

They had a slow start to the day but a happy one. Charlie had his first meltdown since they had known him though of course, Anna had to deal with them from time to time. They went out and about showing Anna the delights of the city and they were all tired when they got back. Anna said she would cook but Michael said they were all tired so a take away was ordered and enjoyed. They then all, except Charlie, watched a film on television and finally the girls went to bed. Again they kissed Anna as well as their father good night. "For teenagers, they are remarkable. I know I was horrid," said Anna watching them disappear.

"I think the reason for that is losing their mother at the age they were, it's made them grow up quickly. Jackie gets the sulks sometimes, but it doesn't last long."

Michael who was sitting across the room from Anna who had been sitting on the sofa with the girls got up and sat beside

Anna. He picked up her hand and looked intently at her palm. "Last night you said we had to enjoy what we have now, did you mean it?" He was very surprised when Anna laughed at him and took a mock swipe at his head with her free hand. "Michael Bishop, are you thinking of asking me to share your bed?"

Michael was covered in confusion and a little embarrassed, but before he answered her she pulled her hand away and kissed him on the lips. "What are we waiting for?" she whispered.

"Are you sure Anna, I—" Anna put her fingers gently over his lips.

"I love you completely and wholly and I want to show you how much."

Michael didn't need to hear any more and there was no more talking for the rest of the night. Anna found that it was completely different making love with Michael and she couldn't help comparing in her own mind. He was a very generous and competent lover, he made her feel so special and for her part Michael was surprised how passionate and exciting Anna was. Their lovemaking was a surprise to them both and a bonus they hadn't anticipated. In the morning, they were woken by a tap on the door, they were lying entwined and naked so Michael called out. "Just a minute," Anna was horror-struck and hissed at Michael what to do. "The girls know the score," came the laconic reply. Michael covered them both with the sheet and called out to come in. Anna was covered in embarrassment but the children had brought them cups of tea and Charlie was very excited that Sophie had given him his breakfast.

After the children had left them to drink their tea, Anna said, "Oh Michael, what will your girls think? Won't they mind? I feel terrible."

For reply, Michael gently took Anna's tea and set it down on the bedside table, he looked deep into her eyes saying "Anna, you worked your charm on Sophie and Jackie while in Port Douglas. Also Sandy told them before she died that if I found anyone I liked they were to at the very least try to be friends and like that person too. I told them before you arrived

183

that I loved you and do you know what they said?" Anna shook her head. "They told me they loved you too and little Charlie."

Anna found she had a big lump in her throat, "Are you all sure? It has happened so quickly."

"Maybe, but I have never been more sure of anything." With that Michael took her in his arms and started to kiss her fervently. The tea got cold.

When Anna got on the plane to go back, her heart was singing; they had the most wonderful three days. Charlie loved it too and kept asking when they would see them again. "Soon, soon," said Anna. They now spoke on the phone whenever they could or when Michael's work allowed him to be free. Anna worried that Trish and Hugh would mind but they were just happy for her. She seemed to have been transformed before their eyes.

Chapter 25

Christmas arrived. Michael had squared it with his parents and he and his daughters were coming up to stay with Anna. As her cottage was small, Hugh had rigged up mosquito nets outside for the girls at least to sleep on the veranda though Charlie wanted to sleep out too. Christmas dinner was going to be in the main house. Trish and Hugh had insisted that Anna, Michael and the children should join them. There ended up being 11 children, Hugh's brother and sister-in-law were also coming as were Trish's parents and Hugh's parents. That made a total of 21 to feed and prepare for. Anna came from a large family, so wasn't too fazed by it all, however, and did all she could to help Trish. She had been rostered on to work but knowing Michael had to work over the New Year period has managed to swap it.

It was, however, her first Christmas in Australia, not her first hot weather Christmas of course but her first Christmas for many years where she felt happy, warm and wanted. It was a heady feeling and she embraced it with gusto. She was quite the life and soul in the end as she cast off her natural reserve and told jokes, played silly games with the children, laughed and sang her way through food preparation; no-one could believe it was the same Anna who had arrived eight months earlier.

That night as they lay in Anna's bed with the ceiling fan going full speed Michael said, "I would never have guessed the quiet shy woman with the care of the world on her shoulders could be hiding this funny, happy, vivacious, sexy person inside them."

Anna rolled him onto his back and sitting astride him said, "It's you that have found the new me, talking through everything with you freed me in a way nothing else has, it's all

185

your fault!" With that she started to kiss him and tease him so all coherent thoughts fled.

Christmas flew by and it was the best Christmas Anna had ever had, so it was quite hard to say goodbye to Michael, Sophie and Jackie a few days later and go back to work. They managed a brief phone call on New Year's and for a couple of weeks after that Michael was very busy. However, they started to plan for Easter when Anna managed to wrangle a few days off. Michael would be working some time while she was there but they agreed it didn't matter; they would cope.

Michael came up to see Anna briefly one weekend in February and they did discuss that fact they were so far apart. Michael suggested that Anna moved to Brisbane but then child care if she wanted to work might be a problem. Anna at the stage didn't want to just live with Michael; she was enjoying her independence too much and Michael completely understood this. They decided to wait until after Easter to sort it out but just knew they wanted to be together. Anna only had a year left on her working visa anyway so that was another issue.

Anna and Charlie arrived on the Thursday evening Michael was working on the Saturday and was on call on the Friday. Anna didn't mind relaxing around the house and anyway Michael had a pool which was made much use of. Saturday Anna, Sophie, Jackie and Charlie went to a long walk by the river, and again spent the afternoon around the pool. Anna felt so happy she could burst.

That evening Michael said they would have a take away, the girls had gone to a birthday party at a friend's house. Charlie, whom Anna had fed earlier, was asleep and Anna, taking the glass of wine Michael had poured for her before he left, sat down in the lounge to see what was on television. She was half watching a quiz when the telephone rang, she didn't like to answer it in Michael's house, so left it. When the answer phone kicked in however, she heard Silas's voice and jumping up answered it.

"Hello, Silas, it's Anna here."

"Thank God, I tried Trish and she gave me this number. Anna, I have some bad news."

"What, what is wrong?" Anna's heart started to race though she was worried when she heard her brother's voice.

"It's Mum, she was knocked down in a hit and run, and she is in a bad way."

"Oh God, oh no, what happened?"

"Well, you remember Mrs Jenkins who used to help Mum with the cleaning when we were kids, she isn't well now, poor old lady, and Mum went to take her some eggs. As it was only just down in the village, she walked and coming back, a car hit her and drove off. She had multiple fractures but it's the head injury that is most concerning just now. She is in an induced coma at present but it doesn't look good. Luckily a guy was driving the other way and saw what happened so Mum at least got help straight away otherwise it would have been even worse."

For a reason she couldn't explain, Anna thought of Karl.

"Did they get a description of the car or driver?"

"No, the chap was so horror struck, all he could tell the police was it was a large black car but he was adamant it was deliberate. Who would want to hurt Mum?"

"I don't know, Silas, but I will try to get a flight home as soon as I can, in the meantime let me know if anything changes, and take care."

"I love you, sis, take care yourself." With that Silas rang off.

Anna stood there staring at the receiver in her hand. Her mind was a jumble of thoughts, that is where she was when Michael came back.

"Anna, sweetheart, whatever's the matter? You look as if you've seen a ghost." He saw the phone in her hand.

"What is it?" he said more sharply this time knowing she had some sort of bad news.

"It's Mum, she has been knocked down, hit and run." She went on to tell him all that Silas had said. "I have to go to her, I know we didn't always get on but she's my mum and I have to go."

Michael nodded, he agreed and minutes later was on the telephone for Anna to book flights. It took some time as it was of course a bank holiday and there weren't any available flight to be had just like that but eventually Michael go her on a flight leaving very late on the Monday evening.

When he finally came off the phone, the Chinese takeaway, which Anna had tried to keep hot, wasn't much good but neither of them felt very hungry anyway. "I have got you business class seats as they were more available, is that OK? I will pay for them."

Anna gave a glimmer of a smile. "No, Michael, I can afford it. I haven't really touched much of my saving as I thought I would need to, but thank you all the same."

Later when they were in bed, and Anna was lying in Michael's arms he turned and put on the bedside lamp. "Anna, I love you, and I believe you love me, please trust me."

"I do lots." Anna looked at him in surprise.

"There is something bothering you, my sweet. I can see it in your eyes. Something more than your mother's accident, something you are not telling me."

Anna opened her mouth to deny her thoughts about Karl but then had a change of mind, she did trust Michael though she never thought she would ever trust a man again, it surprised her.

"I expect I am being very silly but the truth is when Silas told me what had happened to mum I had the strangest feeling Karl might be behind it. One way to get me back to England that wouldn't fail. I expect I have an over active imagination. It's silly, I am being paranoid."

Michael looked at thoughtfully for a few minutes. "No, I don't think you are being paranoid or silly, I think you may be right. What are we going to do?"

"I don't know. I really can't get my head around the best thing to do. I guess I just have to go with it, but I have to admit to being scared."

Michael lay awake for a long time after Anna had finally fallen asleep. They had talked about all sorts of scenarios but it was difficult to see where they would lead. They knew it might be over imagination on Anna's part but both had the gut feeling it wasn't. Michael crept out of bed careful not to wake Anna and looked up Silas's number that Anna had written down earlier. She had been going to phone to tell him which flight she would be on but was waiting to get conformation from Qantas.

A woman answered the phone. It turned out to be June and after a slightly confused start Michael asked if he could speak to Silas. They had never spoken before, of course, but Silas, who had just returned from the hospital, was pleased to speak to Michael. Michael told Silas what Anna had said and how he didn't think she was being paranoid and he Michael was worried for her too.

Silas listened then said, "You could both be right. It hadn't occurred to me I must admit. Look when we are sure what plane Anna will be on I'll get either John or Peter to come with me to meet her and we will keep her close all the time till we sort something out or at least till we know more about Mum's accident. How does that sound?"

"Well it's as good as it can be I think, thank you. I guess Anna has told you a bit about me but all you really need to know is that I love her and little Charlie to bits and would do anything in my power to stop that bastard she married from hurting her anymore."

"Well said, Michael, and thank you for looking after my sister. We all love her too and hate what that cretin has done to her."

Michael tipped toed back to bed soon afterwards and managed to get into a fitful sleep.

The flight was confirmed and Anna, Charlie, Michael, Sophie and Jackie all found themselves at Brisbane International Airport saying very tearful goodbyes. Charlie didn't know what was going on really; he just thought he was going back to Cairns so was rather confused by his mother openly sobbing as she clung to Michael. Sophie and Jackie were very upset too. Sophie said "We have just found you Anna, and Jackie and I love you. Please come back to us soon, it won't be the same without you."

Michael's eyes were full of tears too. "Sophie has said it all, Anna, please come back soon. I can't be without you."

Charlie kept looking at his mum after they had said their farewells and gone through security. "Mummy, don cry," he tugged her arm. "Pease don cry."

Anna made a big effort to stop and they were soon on the plane and on their way back to England. Anna hadn't much luggage as she had only been going to Michael's for the long weekend so at least she thought she hadn't lots of suitcases to worry about. Trish said she could pack their things up and wait to hear what to do with them. The Mirage were sorry but understood and told her she could have her job back if she wanted it.

Chapter 26

It was raining when they landed, Charlie was tired and fractious. Anna was tired and nervous. As she hadn't much luggage and was in business class, she got through into the Arrivals hall very quickly and looked round nervously. "Anna!" All three of her brothers that lived in England were there. Anna was so pleased to see them. It was a huge relief she had been so scared Karl would be at the barrier waiting. None of them noticed a tall man in wearing a hat pulled down low watching from behind a pillar. Karl had seen her brothers and waited to see Anna and his son arrive, if there had only been one of them he might have made a move but decided against it when he realised they were there in force.

"Never mind," he told himself, "my turn will come."

Anna soon found herself enveloped into her family once again. The twins had grown as had John's children and Charlie was pleased to meet his cousins as of course he didn't really remember them. If it hadn't been for Marie and the worry for her and the shadow of Karl, Anna would have enjoyed seeing them all again. As there had been no change with Marie, it was decided that Anna should rest up a bit and go to see her mother the next day.

The family had certainly closed ranks around Anna though they tried not to let her see that they were actually worried. The police had evidence that Marie had been deliberately hit. The witness had been very sure that was the case as Marie had heard the car coming and when the other driver saw her she was as close into the hedge as she could get as the car was going at speed and it was a narrow lane. However, the car drove right into her the driver was absolutely sure. The police had questioned Silas mostly as Marie lived with them and he had mentioned Karl though the police seemed to rule that out as farfetched.

John and Peter left together and as it was dark and raining neither of them noticed a car parked up in a gateway further up the lane, it was well back and they drove by oblivious to it.

The next morning June said she would look after the children while Silas and Anna went to the hospital. However, Anna didn't feel comfortable with this and to her surprise Silas backed her up and said he thought Anna and Charlie should stick together, so it was the three of them went off to the hospital. The Private eye that Karl had staking out the farm rang Karl to tell him they were on their way to hospital just three of them. Karl who was staying in a hotel nearby was in his car at the hospital before they had arrived.

He wasn't quite sure what part of the car park to wait in as it was a big one, however as he was debating with himself Silas's car drove in. Just as Karl started to get out of his car another car drove up with Kate and Vernon in it and the five of them after greeting Anna and Charlie went into the hospital. Karl settled down to wait.

An hour and a half later he was getting very stiff and bored and got out of his car, no sooner had he done that than Anna came down the steps with Kate and Vernon. Charlie was walking beside her holding her hand. Karl couldn't believe his luck where was that brother of hers? As it happened as they were on their way out, Silas had been called to the nurses' station; they wanted to ask him to bring in some music to play to Marie even though she was in a coma. Sometimes it helped they said.

Anna looking round said to Silas, "Go ahead, Charlie and I will wait in the car, and Kate and Vernon are with me."

Silas had his doubts but turned back to speak with the nurses. When they got to the steps, Charlie pulled his hand free from Anna's. He wanted to show these nice people who called themselves Auntie and Uncle how well he could skip down stairs.

Leaping back into his car Karl roared across the car park jumped out of his car and scooping a bewildered child up with one arm got back in his car almost throwing Charlie across the front seats. As he slammed the door shut Anna got to the car and frantically tried to open the door to the passenger side. She was screaming, "Charlie, Charlie." Charlie was also screaming, "Mumee, Mumee," tears already running down his face. Karl floored it and the car took off wrenching Anna's hand off the door handle. Charlie's little face as they drove off was terrified and she could see he was still screaming MUMEE!

Silas came running out of the hospital. Kate had her arms round Anna who was hysterical by this time. Silas took in the situation quickly and turning ran back into the hospital and told them to ring the police there had been a child abduction. He then went to try to comfort Anna who was at the point of collapse.

The police turned up quickly and started to take down details. However, they didn't seem so worried when they found out that Karl was Charlie's father. Even more so when they found Anna had been out of the country for some time and only just returned.

"I expect he is just been missing his son, Madam," said one of the officers. "Give us his address and we will go round and have a word or you can and we will come with you."

Silas stepped in. "Karl is a dangerous man, he means to hurt my sister and taking Charlie means he can get at her."

"Well, as I say sir we can come with you or get some local chaps in as I see the address is London, I am sure we can sort this out amicably."

Anna spoke up. She had recovered herself and was drawing on the inner strength that Michael had told her she had. She now knew she had to dig deep into it if she was going to stop Karl making her a victim always. "Silas, Mum needs you. Kate and Vernon, please go back in with Silas for a little while and keep him company. I will be fine, I need to see Karl and sort this out."

Minutes later Anna sped away with the police officers. First they went to the local station and then after several phone calls during which Anna had an anxious wait she was driven to the outskirts of London where they met a young woman officer from the Met. "We have been in touch with your husband, Mrs Von Herbert, and he assures us he only wanted to see his son and he knows he acted rashly but he is sure if you will meet with him you can both come to an agreeable arrangement."

"OK, but first I promised my brother I would let him know what was going on, so may I make a phone call please?"

"That isn't a problem, of course," said the young woman "But I will have to be with you."

Anna thought, *They don't trust me, I wonder what Karl has told them.*

Silas wasn't happy when Anna told him she was going to meet Karl. She assured him she would have a police officer with her but he still wasn't at all comfortable with the whole idea.

When finally they drew up outside the house, Anna's heart was in her mouth. The young officer, whose name was Mandy, came up the steps with Anna as she rang the bell. "Would you prefer me to wait in the car, I don't mind," she said.

"No, please stay with me," Anna said. She was trembling by now but was trying to hide it. Then she could hear a child crying. It was muffled, but she knew it was Charlie.

Karl suddenly threw open the door. "My darling Anna, thank goodness you are safe, and well it's so good to see you." He made as if to kiss her. Anna sidestepped him.

"Where is Charlie? I can hear him crying," she said.

Karl stood aside. "Come in and see for yourself," he said. "I am sure this young officer won't mind waiting outside for you." He smiled engagingly at Mandy.

"No, she stays with me." Anna spoke sharply.

"I don't mind if you want some privacy," Mandy said, looking from one to the other.

"I want you to stay with me," said Anna who had already moved into the hallway, worrying about Charlie. Karl was standing to the side of her and Mandy was just outside. With a sudden swift movement, Karl slammed the door shut on Mandy's face. Anna started but then Charlie's voice grew louder and more desperate so instead, she rushed to the kitchen where the sound was coming from.

Mandy meanwhile stood uncertainly for a few moments then going back to the car radioed in and spoke to her superior officer. She had seen Anna's fear and was now worried. Normally the police didn't like getting involved with domestic disagreements but seeing how frightened Anna had been and the way Karl had slammed the door on her had set alarm bells ringing. She emphasised all this to her superior officer who after having spoken to another officer said they would send someone else out in the meantime Mandy should go back and knock on the door and make sure everything was alright with Anna.

While Mandy was busy with all this Anna had gone straight to the kitchen where she found Charlie tied to a chair. He was very frightened and confused. Anna quickly untied him while Karl stood and watched her with a cruel grin on his face.

Anna turned to him. "How could you do that to a small child, he's your son for God's sake, whatever were you thinking?"

"I was thinking of you, my sweet, and how, if I got the brat, you would come running, and you did."

"Well I'm here now, say what you want to say, then Charlie and I are leaving."

"'I don't think so," Karl drawled the words out. "Remember I told you once that I am yours for ever and you are mine for ever? Well that still holds good. You are mine and only mine, Anna, and I will not ever let you go again. As for this brat, well, the way you behaved in the past, is he really mine? What shall I do with him, do you think?"

Anna was now completely terrified, not only for herself but for Charlie too. She knew she mustn't show any weakness, though, so standing up as tall as she could, she said in as steady a voice as she could muster, "You will at least let Charlie go Karl, he has done nothing to you, he is just a little boy."

"Ah, but you love him, don't you? You used to say you loved me but you don't now, do you? I am not happy about that Anna, and I think you need to be taught a lesson."

"Why do you think hurting Charlie will make me love you? Are you mad?" Suddenly much of Anna's fear evaporated and she felt anger instead. All this time she had been holding Charlie in her arms and he had hidden his little face in her shoulder. Now he lifted his head and looked first at his father then his mother. His little face was all blotchy where he had been crying and the bindings had made his wrists and ankles sore. "Mumee," he whispered now.

Karl in his turn was incensed by Anna's words. "Well I just have to deal with both of you then, don't I?" And walking

195

round the kitchen he picked up the biggest knife in the knife block. Just then, there was a hammering at the front door and a knock at the back door which had a glass panel. Looking round, Anna could see Ruth at the door who having seen the knife in Karl's hand stood there in frozen shock.

Karl hesitated for a split second then throwing open the kitchen door pulled Ruth inside before she had a chance to run. The hammering continued at the front door, Anna guessed it was the police.

Ruth found her voice and screamed out, "Help, he has a knife." Karl grabbed her then and holding the knife to her throat dragged her into the hallway then lounge to show the police he meant business. Anna dare not leave as she knew Ruth would suffer but she could do something about Charlie so she opened the larder door and whispering to him to keep quiet moved the large red wine rack in there and gently pushed Charlie behind it. It wasn't very full and if Karl looked hard he would see him but it was the best Anna could do. Karl and Ruth shuffled back into the kitchen. The hammering on the door had stopped.

"Sit there, the two of you," Karl indicated two chairs at the table. "While I think what is best. Where's the brat?"

Anna replied trying to stop her voice from shaking. "I let him out of the back door. I don't know where he went, but at least he is away from you."

Karl swiftly crossed the kitchen and locked the door, just then he narrowed his eyes as he looked out. There were some police out there. Then the phone rang. They all started then Karl picked it up and listened for a few moments. "Unless you call your men off I will start to hurt these bitches in here," he shouted into the phone and slammed the receiver down, then pulled the socket out of the wall.

Silence after that, Karl said nothing nor did Ruth and Anna, the police were quiet too. The silence seemed to go on and on. At last Anna spoke. "Karl, you say you love me, if I agree to come back and be your wife, will you please let Ruth go? Then the police will go away too and all will be well." She dare not look at Ruth as she said this, she just looked steadily at Karl. For a minute, she saw the Karl he had seemed to be when she met him, then his eyes became those shards of ice again and she felt the fear tingle all over her body. Karl seemed to consider this, though.

"You said I was mad a little while ago, I would be if I agreed to let this interfering pile of shit go. She helped you when you left me, didn't she? She owes me big time."

Anna felt Ruth shift in her chair and put a hand on her arm she wasn't sure what Ruth intended but Anna didn't want her to do anything rash. Just then they heard a commotion outside and a loudhailer boomed out. "Mr Von Herbert, Karl, let your wife and neighbour go and your son, if you let them go now we can sort all this out amicably I am sure."

Karl sat still a minute longer then got up and going to the larder opened the door. Anna's heart was in her mouth, Karl got a bottle of red wine and slammed the door shut again. While he was doing this Ruth leant back and quietly turned the key that was still in the lock in the kitchen door. Karl looked at them as he sat down again.

"Let's have some fun while we sit here. Ruth, open that drawer over there," Ruth did as she was told, after all, Karl still had the knife and he was pointing it at Anna's throat. He told her to get the big ball of string that was in there. "I think Anna likes being tied up, maybe in the nude," he said. Just then the loudhailer boomed out again and this time it was Sir William.

"Karl, son, think what you are doing come out and bring Anna with you, it's not worth it son we can sort it all out I am sure if you come out without hurting anyone." Karl turned his head away listening to his father. Anna moved swiftly and picking up the bottle of wine brought it down with all the force she could muster. She was aiming for his head but as he realised what was happening he moved enough for the bottle to come down very hard on his shoulder. This made him drop the knife as that was the hand he was holding it in. Anna screamed at Ruth,

"Run, run." Ruth wasted no time and bolted out of the unlocked door. Anna didn't follow as she had Charlie hidden in the larder. Karl arm felt numb but he leapt to his feet and with his left hand punched Anna hard in the face. Anna staggered back and fell across the table. Karl picked up the knife and stabbed at her the knife burying itself in her upper chest. Anna was barely aware of what happened next but the police had taken their chance as Ruth bolted out the officers who were at the back surged into the kitchen and wrestled Karl to the ground, handcuffing him swiftly.

Anna was bleeding profusely and they immediately called an ambulance. She was also hardly conscious but whispered "Charlie."

"He is safe, Anna. Don't worry, just hang in there, just do it for Charlie." Ruth was back in by her side. Anna was drifting in and out of awareness but she could hear Charlie whimpering in the back ground. She stopped fighting and let herself drift away. She felt so tired, so very, very tired.

Chapter 27

Michael was worried very worried when Anna flew off and immediately got onto the hospital and told them he had a huge family emergency and would have to take some time off. They weren't impressed but he was adamant. His parents agreed to come and stay with Sophie and Jackie and two days after Anna had left he was in the air heading for England. He had Silas's number and had tried to ring before he left but only got the answer phone and didn't feel like leaving a message. As it was very last minute, he had a long flight with two longish stops on the way to England. When he landed at Heathrow, he found a pay phone and tried Silas's number again. June answered.

"Hi, this is Michael here, the guy Anna was with in Australia." Michael wasn't sure what Anna had told them and felt suddenly embarrassed.

"Hello Michael." June was now feeling uncomfortable; she didn't think anyone would have thought to ring Michael to tell him what had happened to Anna.

Michael cleared his throat, this wasn't quite as easy as he thought he had just had a gut feeling he should follow Anna. "Is Anna staying with you? Can I speak to her?"

June gasped he didn't know but then of course he was in Australia so he wouldn't, she would play in down until Silas could speak to him.

"She isn't here right now, I am afraid."

"When will she be back?"

"I will get Silas to ring you when he comes in, is that OK?"

By now Michael had picked up that June was stalling but why he couldn't think, he couldn't imagine that Anna was back with Karl but was sure something awful had happened.

Taking a deep breath he said "I am actually here at Heathrow, and I need to see her and make sure she is OK. I—I am very fond of her."

June was completely floored by this and thought the only thing she could do was to be honest however difficult it might be.

"Anna is in hospital, I am afraid, in London. She is very ill; Karl stabbed her and knocked some of her teeth out, and when she fell across the table she ruptured her spleen. She is very ill," she repeated.

"What," he sucked his breath in. "What hospital?" he barked, feeling angry and frustrated.

A few minutes later, he was in a taxi speeding as quickly as he could get the taxi driver to go towards the hospital.

He sat in the back muttering to himself "Hang in there, my darling, hang in there, I'm coming."

The taxi driver kept his eye on him, thinking he was some sort of madman.

Michael had only a small amount of English currency; however, it was just enough to pay the taxi off and Michael didn't wait for the change, grabbing his small case he ran into the hospital and a few minutes later was again very frustrated as they would not let him see Anna. He wasn't a relative and in his anxious state had seemed brusque and rude. He demanded to see whoever was in charge and dragging his passport out of his pocket tried to tell them he was a surgeon no less, it made no difference. Then as his frustration was ready to boil over Silas appeared to tell the nurses he was just going to make a call to the hospital near home to see how his mother was. He had hardly slept since Anna had been brought in and had dozed in a chair by her bed. They had removed her spleen and stitched her up but she had lost a lot of blood and her face was a mess. Silas didn't look much better though Michael recognised him from a photo that Anna had shown him.

"Silas?"

Silas looked at the tall distinguished looking man who was arguing with the staff as he had come up, "Yea, who wants to know?"

Michael held out his hand. "I'm Michael, how is Anna?"

200

Silas gaped at him. "I thought you lived in Australia." He shook Michael's hand distractedly.

"I do, but I happen to love your sister very much and I had a bad feeling when she left so I came over as quickly as I could seemingly not soon enough. How bad is she? What are her injuries? Can I see her?"

Silas blinked at this tall Australian who must love his sister to drop everything and come to her just like that. He gave a small smile. "She is very heavily sedated but I am sure it would be OK for you to see her."

The staff had overheard Michael's declaration of love and he was allowed in. He was used to seeing people looking their worst but it shook him to see his beautiful Anna lying there looking like a ghost. Her face was swollen and she was deathly pale she had a drip going into her arm. He could see the top part of her torso was heavily bandaged.

He approached the bed and gently picked up her hand which was lying limply on the cover. "Anna, dear Anna, it's me, Michael."

Anna was very sleepy and in her fizzy brain thought she was hearing things. "Michael," she murmured. Her eyes flickered open and then she focused blearily on Michael's face and as much joy as was possible on her swollen face registered.

"I am here, darling, and I am not going anywhere until you are better."

"That's good," Anna tried to smile but drifted off to sleep again.

Michael left the room abruptly with Silas staring after him, what was going on now! But Michael was wanting to speak to the doctors about Anna and what they had done for her and what the prognosis was and all medical matters relating.

Once he had spoken to the medical staff he returned to Anna's room. "Silas, I am sorry, but I am a surgeon, and I needed to find out what the score is with Anna, by the way, where is little Charlie?"

"At home with my wife, June, and my kids. He seems OK but he has had a bad time too, poor little mite."

"Tell me all that has happened please. I know you've only just met me and don't know me but believe me I love your sister and little Charlie very much and I just need to know what has happened."

So the two men sat and talked and talked. After a while, they looked round and realised that Anna was awake and listening. "My two favourite men," she mumbled. She held out her hand. "Michael, please stay, don't leave me." Her eyes suddenly brimmed with tears.

"I haven't any intention of leaving, don't worry sweetheart." He tenderly stroked her hair back from her forehead.

"I was so scared, so very scared," she whispered.

"You were very brave, it seems, and Charlie is safe, so don't worry."

Michael made arrangements for him to stay instead of Silas partly to give Silas a break and partly because Silas needed to get home and go and see his mother who was still critical. Anna had been very shocked when she had seen her mother all wired up and small in the hospital bed. Her head was bandaged and one arm and one leg were in plaster. She had had internal injuries too but so far was holding her own. Anna had taken Charlie with her but knew it wasn't the right place for him when she got in there. It was one reason she left as soon as she did.

The next day Anna was much better and managed some soup which Michael fed her. She found this somewhat amusing and Michael caught a glimpse of the fun loving Anna he had got to know in Australia. Later that afternoon the police arrived having been told Anna was much better by the hospital. They went over the whole ghastly business with her piece by piece, they insisted Michael leave the room and when eventually he was allowed to return he found Anna ashen faced, shaking and in tears again.

"They say it's attempted murder but it's likely that Karl will get bail, his father is already pulling strings for that to happen."

Michael was angry when he heard this but as he wasn't sure of British law made no comment other than to say. "It will be fine, I am sure it will be OK." He felt like Anna though, it was far from satisfactory.

Then more bad news. Marie was brain dead it seemed and it was only the machines keeping her alive. Her condition had deteriorated during the last few days but everyone thought it was best kept from Anna. It was decided to wait until she was strong enough to tell her. Then the next day the police arrived again but this time they let Michael stay. "We have found the car that ran your mother down," the older of the two officers who had come said. "There is no doubt it's the right car as we have done tests on the paintwork and even found some blood on it that is your mother's blood group. It belongs to your husband at least it is registered in his name and we don't doubt he was driving it. We found it hidden on Sir William's estate. We don't believe he had anything to do with it; however, it was in an old barn some distance from the house."

"I thought when I heard Mum had been knocked down, it was Karl. It's the sort of thing he would do to get me back to England. Thank goodness you have found it proves I wasn't imagining things."

Chapter 28

A week later Anna, who had confounded doctors with her recovery, left hospital and went immediately with Michael to see her mother. It was very depressing, the family all met then and it was decided to turn Marie's life support off. They all agreed Marie would not want to be kept alive like that and so it was done.

Anna cried on Michael's shoulder that she hadn't got to say goodbye. June butted in and told her the last time Marie had spoken to Anna on the phone she had said she thought Anna sounded as happy as she had ever heard her. "Keep that thought in your heart Anna. Your mum said she thought you had found what you were looking for and she was very glad."

So Anna did and it helped through the next few weeks. She found Marie's funeral in some ways more difficult than Tim's, partly because she blamed herself; if she hadn't married Karl, if she hadn't fled, the thoughts went round and round. Everybody was very supportive. Michael stayed with the family but then got restless, so Silas taught him to drive a tractor and he helped out a bit but was really chaffing at the bit to get back to what he knew. The girls were wanting him home and finally after Marie's funeral he broached the subject with Anna.

Karl, of course, had been charged with murder as well as attempted murder but the trial wouldn't be for many months yet.

Anna knew that it was coming and had steeled herself but still found it hard to hide her tears. She was still very vulnerable and was having nightmares as was Charlie.

"I want to marry you, Anna, and as soon as possible, but I must go back to the girls and my position at the hospital, you do see that, don't you?"

"Michael, dear Michael, I understand completely and I am going to see a lawyer about divorce as soon as possible. I want to marry you more than I can say, you have been so wonderful through all this. I will never be able to make it up to you."

"Just marry me. That will do."

Anna was bereft after Michael had gone. Then she had news that made her blood run cold. Karl had reapplied for bail which this time had been granted, there was a proviso that he didn't make contact or go near Anna and her family but they were all aware that Karl took no notice of rules. The day after this Anna's solicitor rang her to tell her Sir William had applied for custody of Charlie. "He isn't very likely to succeed but he is very wealthy, and money talks," said Jeremy, her solicitor. "There will be a preliminary hearing in ten days' time in Judges Rooms in London City of Westminster. I know it's expensive but you will need to have a barrister. I will instruct James Lamb, should I? He is very good, and family matters are his speciality."

Anna thought of Vernon, but he had recently retired. She gulped and stood feeling shell shocked for a few moments, she was so quiet that Jeremy thought she wasn't there. "Anna?"

"I'm here." She cleared her throat. This was going to be expensive but as far as Charlie was concerned what choice did she have?

Ten days later Anna found herself in the rooms in Westminster City offices. She felt sad suddenly, it was here in this building that she and Karl had got married. Not that many years ago why had it all gone wrong? Because Karl was a control freak, jealous and possessive a little voice told her.

Anna had been shocked when she walked into the room; Sir William had aged ten years since she had last seen him. He seemed diminished and uncertain of himself. Then the penny dropped with Anna; it was Karl who was driving this one way of getting his revenge. There was much chance he would serve some time in prison but if the murder charge for Marie didn't stick, he wouldn't be in jail that long. Anna shuddered, would she ever be free of this monster she had married?

In the event, the proceedings didn't take that long. Sir William's barrister made submissions about Charlie being heir to the estate and learning about it early in life. That they were getting on in years but could hire a nanny and Charlie would have everything he could possibly want as money was no object.

Anna's barrister soon pointed out that Charlie wouldn't have his mother's love and care all the time as he had now, a nanny was no substitute for a loving mother and he in time would be subjected to his father coming back to him and for Charlie's sake that was not a good idea. The judge said that the recent children's act which was now law put the best interests of the child first and in this case at least for now he thought it was Anna. Though he said if circumstances changed, he would look at the case again.

Afterwards Anna thanked Jeremy and James for their help but they both told her to be cautious in her praise as the judge had rather left the door open

That evening back at the farm Silas and June asked Anna if she could mind looking after the children for a couple of hours as they had a parents meeting to go too. Harvest was to start soon and the long summer holidays so knowing how hard they would be working Anna told them to have a meal out afterwards because life would be very hectic soon. "Are you sure you will be alright?" said Silas.

Anna wasn't really but she decided it would be very strange if Karl knew what was happening at the farm and anyway she didn't think even he would want to risk breaking his bail conditions.

After they had gone, Anna busied herself putting the children to bed, reading them a story and then tidied up the kitchen. Bessie, the very old black Labrador, was lying by the range and Anna felt comforted by this as Bessie's hearing was still very good though she was somewhat stiff these days. The phone rang, Anna thought it may be Michael then realised it was very early morning there, she thought he might ring soon though. It was Silas checking up on her.

"I am fine, stop worrying," she said. Sitting back down at the table she looked out of the window towards the barns and thought she saw a movement in the periphery of her vision. At that moment Bessie growled. She had her hackles up all down her back. Anna jumped up and locked the kitchen door then carefully peeped out of the window again. Her heart was racing and she could feel sweat on her forehead. She started to tremble violently. The sun was lower in the sky as it was getting towards evening and whoever was out there didn't think of their shadow that was showing to Anna across the garden right by the house. That person was standing just around the corner from the back door. Anna felt she couldn't breathe she was so frightened, and she was shaking so much she could hardly stand. She groped her way back to the phone which was in the hallway. She shut the kitchen door behind her so she couldn't be seen through the window. As she lifted the receiver, she heard the back door handle which always squeaked a bit. Shaking uncontrollably she tried to ring the number Silas had written down for her of the restaurant they were going to be at. The phone was dead!

Anna knew all the doors were secure as she had made sure of that before Silas left leaving only the back door which she had now, of course, locked. She knew if it was Karl though it wouldn't be long before he got in. Anna slowly, trying to move quietly walked backwards up the stairs. When she got to her room where Charlie was sleeping, she lifted him with difficultly as she was still shaking violently. She carried him into the twins' room as quietly as she could. The twins weren't asleep but had been pretending as at nine they had been rather peeved to be going to bed early especially in summer. Seeing their Aunt acting so strangely and with her face as white as a sheet they were soon asking what was wrong in stage whispers.

Anna whispered back, "I thought we would play a game." Just then there was an almighty crash from downstairs; Karl had broken in.

All pretence gone and Charlie waking up Anna slammed the door shut and getting the twins to help her they dragged the chest of drawers across the doorway. Luckily it stood just to the right of the door so they didn't have to move it far. Charlie started to cry, he had picked up the fear which now permeated the room. The boys helped Anna and they dragged the beds and another chest across the barricade the door. By this time Karl was trying to get in.

"I know you are in there, and you have my son, you whore, let me in."

Anna and the children huddled in the corner as Karl continued to attack the door. The children were all crying with fright by now and Anna was desperately trying to come up with a solution to their predicament. For some strange reason she felt somehow calmer than she had before. Maybe it was because of the children. Anna was silently kicking herself for panicking, when she went to telephone, why she had shut the kitchen door so if Karl had looked in the window he wouldn't see her? But shutting the door meant she had shut Bessie in the kitchen. Bessie was a softy really but Anna didn't doubt she would have done her best to guard her family.

The door started to splinter, then there was another noise of footsteps running up the back stairs and the attack on the door stopped and there were more footsteps running along the passage way and down the other stairs and shouting. The children stopped crying and listened as did Anna then bangs and thumps and someone running on the gravel driveway. Anna stood up and though the curtains were drawn she pulled them back and looked out. Of course it was still light and she could see two figures running. The first one looked like Karl and the second looked like her brother Peter. They disappeared round the corner of the gate into the lane. Anna could see Peter's Land Rover pulled up across the yard now. He must have come a short while ago and because of the noise Karl was making they didn't hear him.

Shakily Anna and the children pulled the furniture back more or less where it was. Charlie was still crying a little but the others being much older were treating it as an adventure. However, Anna could see they were putting on an act for her sake.

They crept downstairs feeling very wary again. Anna looked in the sitting room to a chaotic mess as Karl had smashed his way in by the French windows that led out into the garden. There was glass everywhere and splintered wood. Anna took the children into the kitchen she had heard Peter's Land Rover start up and charge off and guessed he had lost Karl so was racing after him. She wondered if Karl would double back and the fear returned. The back door was still locked so Peter must have entered the house the same way as Karl. She pushed the table against the door into the hall just in case. Bessie was very stirred up and bounced around the children which distracted them a little for which Anna was grateful.

"Now who would like some hot chocolate?" It was all she could think of just then. As she got the milk heating, she heard Peter's Land Rover return and went to the door and unlocked it, then wondered if she should have. Peeping out of the window however, she saw Peter striding across towards the house. As he came into the kitchen, all the children and Anna hurled themselves at him and everyone was talking at once. Peter didn't say much but he looked very grim. "Where has Karl gone, will he come back?" Anna whispered, not wanting to frighten the children again.

Peter shook his head eyes telling Anna to wait a minute. She had just got the children seated at the table with their chocolate when they heard police sirens. Peter drew her to one side and whispering in her ear said, "Karl is gone. I went to the Jenkins house and asked them to call the police."

Anna nodded and only moments later the kitchen was filled with two burly police officers. They then organised a phone call to let Silas and June know what had happened and before long they arrived home and took charge of the children. Once that was sorted the police started to question both Peter and Anna. It seemed Peter had spoken to Silas earlier in the day and they had agreed Anna shouldn't be left entirely on her own so Peter would come along to keep her company. When he got there, he could hear the banging that Karl was making and finding the back door locked made his way round the house to the French windows. He then thought he would creep up the back stairs and get Karl but Karl sensed he was there and made a run for it. He had hidden his Porsche behind the hedge further down the lane and though he came back for the Land Rover. Peter knew he couldn't compete with a Porsche.

The police were very sympathetic with the family even when Silas really lost his temper about what had happened. They pointed out it was up to magistrates and the one that Karl had managed to persuade that he was safe to let out on bail. The power that Sir William had didn't help either. A couple of hours later they were about to leave when the police radio burst into life. They had informed the telephone service that the line had been cut and they had promised to see to it first thing in the morning. The older officer came back to Anna with a strange expression on his face. "Mrs Von Herbert." He paused. "Ma'am I have some news of your husband. It seems as if he was driving very fast and lost control of his car."

Anna interrupted, "He always drove fast when he was angry."

"Well, this time it has had severe consequences, I am sorry to tell you your husband was pronounced dead at the scene. He wrapped his car round a big oak tree."

Anna sat down heavily, she hadn't expected that! She didn't feel happy or sad or relived, she just felt empty. She started to shake again violently and Silas came round the table and putting his arms round her said, "It's all over now, Anna, it's all over, he can't hurt you anymore."

Three weeks later Karl was buried in the family plot at the Estate where the family lived. Anna didn't go to the service as she wasn't sure how his parents and the wider family would feel about it but she wanted to pay her respects though her family couldn't understand why. She stood well away from the graveside but approached when the mourners had left. As she stood looking down on the coffin she heard someone clearing their throat behind her. She turned round and there was Sir William, Anna opened her mouth to speak but Sir William held up his hand.

"Anna, thank you for coming, it can't have been easy for you. My son treated you very badly. I realise that now, Lady Caroline and I have spent a long time in denial and I am sorry for that. In spite of that, Lady Caroline doesn't want anything to do with you, or yours which means I won't persist in the matter of Charles staying with us at any time or living nearby which is what we had hoped for. He will still be my heir but hopefully he will be a grown man by then. Karl made a will recently and has left you a very wealthy woman. When you ran away, he made a will cutting you out but after the short spell in prison, he changed his mind. He did say that it was 'safe' to do so, I expect we can now understand that he didn't expect you to outlive him. He was a very confused person and I am sorry for that indeed for the whole sorry business."

Anna stood in bewilderment at all this. She didn't really know how she felt about anything and was even more undecided now after Sir William's speech. She held out her hand to him poor man his eyes suddenly filled with tears and without thinking, Anna hugged him, something which had never happened while Karl was alive.

He patted her back as tears gathered in her eyes too and giving her a wan smile walked away. Anna knew she would never see him again. Silas was waiting by the car when she got to the church gate. "You OK? I saw you talking to Sir William."

"Yes, I will be soon. I think I will ring Michael tonight, I have some good news for him." Anna told Silas what Sir William had said and as they drove home. Anna felt more at peace than she had ever thought possible.

Epilogue

Anna wriggled a little to get comfortable on the beach. Michael did the same beside her. It was still quite dark but the first streaks of dawn were appearing across the water. The sea was like a millpond with hardly a ripple as the sun slowly lit up the beach Anna could see hundreds doing exactly the same as herself and Michael. Then she saw the silhouette of a yacht moored off the beach. It was a magical start to the new millennium and she couldn't think of anywhere better to see the sun come up on this new dawn than Port Douglas Beach. "Charlie will be sorry he missed this," she said quietly.

"He has a busy day ahead of him giving his mother away, and he did party well last night." Michael nuzzled her ear as he spoke. Somehow it seemed wrong to speak loudly just then. A few moments later the fiery red circle of the sun appeared and someone cheered. People took up the cheering right along the beach.

Anna and Michael only stayed for a few more minutes then took themselves back to their apartment. Later that day they were getting married. The road to recovery for both Charlie and Anna had been a long one and at times she wondered if Charlie would ever stop having nightmares. She too suffered broken sleep and nightmares but Michael had been there for her and it was his kindness and strength that had helped her through. She had not wanted anything to remind her of Karl so she sold the house and the business, everything that had anything to do with her life with him. She was then in a position to build and open a purpose built refuge/hospital and recovery centre for women and children who had suffered at the hands of their partners or husbands. It had cost nearly all the money from Karl's estate but to Anna it was money well spent and also helped her in her own recovery. She remained in close contact with the centre although it was now up and running and donations meant that it was nearly self-funded. Both Michael's girls had left home, one at medical school and one at university had also been wonderful to Charlie and Anna's family had been a rock she had clung too. She knew without all the support from them she would have been a nervous wreck the rest of her life but she was much stronger than she knew. Most of her family were here but only she and Michael had made it down to the beach, she didn't mind it was good to have this new beginning with Michael only.

Just as they got to the door of the apartment Anna stopped and looking up at Michael said, "I just want you to know I have wanted to be your wife nearly ever since that first day we talked. Thank you for waiting through all the rubbish that has happened. I didn't think I could ever be this happy or even deserved it, but here we are, darling Michael, this is the start of the rest of our lives." They kissed deeply and then went inside to do just that.